A HOME WITH A LION KILLER

SNAKE AND THE DOG-MAN 3

JOHNNY GUNN

**WOLFPACK
PUBLISHING**
— EST 2013 —

A Home With a Lion Killer
Paperback Edition
Copyright © 2022 Johnny Gunn

Wolfpack Publishing
5130 S. Fort Apache Rd. 215-380
Las Vegas, NV 89148

wolfpackpublishing.com

Paperback ISBN 978-1-63977-947-5
eBook ISBN 978-1-63977-946-8
LCCN 2022937874

A HOME WITH A LION KILLER

"CAN you remember why it was so important for us to be here?" Snake was hunched down near a fresh-lit fire along the rim of a deep arroyo. The echoes of thunder could still be heard off in the south, rain was still dripping from his sombrero, and his partner was still gathering their equipment that had been blown from yonder to there.

"Going to San Diego," Dog-man yelled out. "See the Pacific Ocean. Important to remember things like that, Snake." Dog-man stopped what he was doing and turned to the north-east. "Listen!" He yelled it out. "Got a train coming our way, Snake."

Snake saw the first streams of water moving through the arroyo, heard what surely was a fast freight, and stepped back from the rim. "Lordy," he mumbled. Within seconds a thunderous flood of water, trees, and debris boiled down that gully, brown and foamy, boisterous beyond words. "We could have been in there," he said, but only he heard the words.

One might be correct in thinking, two drifters off on

a lark. Snake was a long and thin Texan while Dog-man wasn't quite as tall but carried more weight. Snake was the least good-looking of the two but women were drawn to him, trusted him, and children flocked to the man. All this attention often flustered the man and tickled Dog-man.

Their odyssey began by getting escorted from Deadwood in Dakota Territory and here they were in the vast Mojave Desert of southern California. They were several days out from Yuma, Arizona Territory.

It had been a long, exciting trail for the boys, one that included them finding a profitable mine somewhere in the Mexican desert south of New Mexico, staying out of jail in numerous towns, villages, and encampments, all the time coming to the aid of many in need. Did they have a reason to travel to San Diego?

"Why are we going to San Diego, Dog-man? Ever since we left Yuma I've not wanted to be on this trail. Ain't seen another human, got nothing but jack rabbits to eat, and it's hotter'n Texas ever was. Those stories we heard ain't about this trail."

"Well, we didn't lose nothing in that thunder-boomer that just washed through here. Sure glad I got out of there. Ain't never seen nothing like that. That gully was empty and muddy one minute and a raging tempest the next. We coulda been in there."

Dog-man sat down in the sand and mud, close to the fire, and poured a cup of coffee. "I don't much care for this trail either, Snake. Don't want to go south, though. We've seen Mexico. Don't need to see it again. I thought this trail was supposed to get better as we went west but it ain't better, it's worse. San Diego is right on the ocean but I think we're a long way off, Pard."

Often on their treks the pair had crude maps drawn

for them by helpful folks. Not this time. All they had was someone pointing west, saying something like, "Can't miss it boys."

"That old codger in Yuma talked about mountain trails, underground rivers, on that trail north of here and I scoffed at him. I don't think he was lyin' Dog. I think those fools what told us about this trail were the liars. I say we head north and find those mountains, get out of this country. We're a week west of Yuma so let's set ourselves north."

They spent the rest of the day drying out everything they owned and made plans for leaving out at first light. "They got to have animals bigger than these scrawny rabbits up north," Snake said. "I could eat a whole deer right now." He shook his shaggy head and laughed. "Make that a buffalo."

"Our pack mule is starting to look good to me," Dog-man said, trying to hold in a laugh. "We been in mountains so full of trees you couldn't tell where you were and mountains so bare you didn't want to know where you were. What are we riding into, I wonder."

"That old Mexican prospector kept talking about high, rocky hillsides and deep canyons. Hope there be trees, water, and deer. He talked mostly of plata and oro, gold and silver. I want meat."

"Keep talking about it and I'm gonna take a knife to that mule," Dog-man said. "North it is then, at first light, Partner."

THE GREAT SOUTHERN DESERT, called the Mojave, covers thousands of square miles and what water that flows is generally east to west in the southern reaches and west to east in the north, which means the boys had to spend hours every day negotiating their way in and out of deep arroyos, gulches, culverts, and stream beds, mostly dry. They were able to find puddles from time to time, left over from the last thunder storm that moved through. Enough for the animals and their canteens if you let the mud settle some and boiled it hard.

"If we ever settle in somewhere it's gonna be in the mountains, Dog. Big trees, lotsa grass, and fresh water. We kilt two snakes yesterday and I don't care what you say, it don't taste nothin' like chicken."

"I ain't got any thoughts of settlin' in anywhere. What made you say something like that?" Dog-man asked.

"Oh, just thinking of those two scalliwags back near Tucson. No, Dog, I ain't ready to tuck these boots under a bed. Just would rather travel through country that has animals we can eat."

Snake rode horses from the time he was born, he says, but if you watched him, thinking you might learn something, you wouldn't. He slouched way back in the saddle, to the point of resting his head on the horse's rump sometimes, seemed to be about ready to fall off at a moment's notice, but never did.

Snake was the kind of man who never seemed to move fast no matter the chore until you paid attention. He had the reflexes of a deer in mid-hunting season, could draw his weapon and get two shots off before you could blink, could throw either a left hook or right roundhouse so fast the other guy never saw the knuckles before he felt them.

All the time telling stories, spinning debatable truths, or singing songs to the moon. Dog-man on the other hand was the pragmatist of the partnership. "If you don't like snake meat why'd you take the biggest one? I do prefer the mountains, though and I'd rather eat a deer, too," he laughed.

They were in their fourth day going north when Snake pointed out what looked like mountains, far in the distance. Gray-blue, they danced in the heat waves and seemed shrouded in clouds. That night, the sky, far to the north, lit up from time to time. "I like to call it sheet lightning," Snake said. "Can't see the killer forks coming down, just the lit up sky. Them mountains is so far off we ain't never gonna hear the thunder."

Less than an hour out of camp the next morning, Dog-man held up his hand. He was in the lead and Snake was trailing the pack mule. "Whatcha got?" Snake asked.

"Three horses crossed in front of us, Snake. Ain't shod, neither. What kind of Indian country are we in? They had to see our fire or smelled our smoke. Might be time to tighten up some."

"Take this old mule and I'll see what I can find," Snake said, handing the lead to Dog-man. The prints were fresh, not filled back in. Even the slightest breeze will alter a horse's hoof print and Snake saw that many of the prints were still well formed. He rode off at a goodly trot sitting tall and straight in the saddle for a change. "They're just walkin' along," he mumbled. He saw where one rider started holding back and drifted off to the south and Snake looked around fast.

An arroyo off to his south was less than a hundred yards away and Snake turned to it, putting spurs to his horse. He rode hard into the deep desert ditch and jumped from his horse when he hit bottom, expecting to hear gunfire or feel an assault. The arroyo was empty.

He had his horse tied to some salt brush, pulled his rifle and moved toward where he was sure he'd find an Indian working his way toward him. A chunk of mud covered rock sat in the middle of the gully and Snake crawled behind it for cover. In less than a minute he saw two men coming toward him, staying as close to the edge of the deep arroyo as possible, their rifles held at the ready.

Strangest looking Indians I ever saw. The two white men, dressed as Mexicans, moved slowly toward Snake's rock and when they were about thirty yards out, Snake called to them.

"'Bout far enough, fellers," he called out. "Drop them guns and we can talk some." Both men fell to the muddy ground and one got off a shot as he landed. Snake drove a bullet through the top of the man's head and called out again.

"Ain't no reason to join your friend in hell, mister. Drop the gun, now." Snake watched the man turn and try to crawl away, using brush, mud lumps, and rocks for cover. "That ain't nice, mister," he mumbled. He put a bullet into the mans' back, right between the shoulders and knew he had killed him.

"That was stupid, mister," he mumbled again. He gathered up the rifles and hand guns and untied his horse. *There were three horses. I wonder if there's a third man or just a pack horse waiting for me.* He mounted his horse and rode slowly up the draw following the footsteps left by the two men. *Has to be a pack horse.*

He heard the whinny and dropped out of the saddle, rifle in hand. He tied his horse to a piece of brush and slowly moved toward the sound, almost crawling, brush to brush, rock to rock. He moved around a tight bend in the gulch and saw three horses tied off, only two of them saddled. The other had a pack saddle and ragged packs attached.

"Ain't Indians crossed our trail, Dog. These boys was

out of food, money, and good tidings." He had the dead men tied to their mounts and led the three horses up to where Dog-man had a fire started and coffee boiling. "Guess we need to get them buried before the heat gets to 'em."

"Ever see'd 'em before?" Dog-man asked, pulling one off the horse. The man's clothing was as ragged as the packs. "Don't know this one."

"Trail bums, Dog. Lookin' to take us and our poke." They got the men buried and went through their belongings, scant as they were. "Gotta burn everything, Dog. Full of bugs. Even their coffee tin was empty. We'll leave their saddles as grave markers, keep the weapons and horses, though. Best move on while we got light."

"Two men flat broke with three horses in the middle of the desert. Why?" Dog-man asked. "Runnin' from the law? From other outlaws?"

"You always ask those kinds of questions, Dog. What would you do with 'em if you got the answers?" Dog-man just looked at him and stepped into the saddle. There was just a hint of a smile hidden from Snake.

2

"Them mountains are close now, Snake, and they got trees on 'em." Dog-man was again in the lead, trailing two horses while Snake had their pack mule and one horse trailed out. "I'm thinkin' two, maybe three more days. Be good to see something green, eh?"

"Tryin' to remember what that old guy said about the trail he seemed to know about. Run from a canyon, I think."

"No, he called it a wash, Snake. A long wash that would lead us to two water basins, one of which ain't drinkable." Dog-man remembered the conversation well. "You were eatin' them roasted peppers and washin' 'em down with tequila while I was gettin' all the information we would need."

"That's why you're my pard, Dog." He pointed off north. "It's either a dust devil a few miles in front of us or we're gonna have company again. What are these people doin' out here?"

"Hope they're not looking for two friends," Dog-man said. "Ain't seen nobody for weeks and now we got people two days in a row. Think these might be the friendly type?"

The billowing dust turned out to be one man leading four well packed mules. He had two fierce looking dogs with him, too. "Howdy," he said after getting the dogs calmed down. "They'll be fine as long as you don't make a quick move to hurt me or my mules. Name's Benjamin Franklyn Cruikshank."

"Howdy yourself," Snake said. "I'm Snake and that fine feller is Dog-man. He won't hurt you if you don't try to hurt me."

Cruikshank laughed and stepped down from his tall horse. "Them horses you're leading aren't yours, are they? Bailey and Simmons musta wanted to hurt you, eh Snake? Them two been lookin' to die for a long time. Good fer ya." He gathered up some scrub brush and lit a fire, got a pot of coffee boiling, and sat down in the dirt. His attitude seemed to be, 'Well, we're all here, let's get to know each other'. "You ain't prospectors, I know that. What you doin' out here in this forsaken country?"

"Coming up from Yuma and looking for a trail that leads west. Heard of one with good water holes spaced out some," Dog-man said.

"I'm heading for Dagget," Cruikshank said. "You boys need to keep going in the direction you're headed. You'll come to the Kelso Wash in a day or two and it will take you right to the Mojave River."

"River? In this country?" Snake asked. *Well, we found the muddy Colorado and steamboats, too. Might find another river.* He sat back against a rock and lit a cigar. "You ain't foolin' with us, are you?"

"Wouldn't do that," the prospector said. "Nope, ain't that kind of man. The Mojave River don't run out in the open like. It runs underground, boys. Well, better keep movin'. Got a long road in front of me." He kicked out the fire, put away the coffee pot and grinder, and mounted up.

"Hope we run into you again, boys. Look for the yellow in the pan and keep your powder dry," he said, waving and leading his caravan off to the north west. Snake stood silent, rocking his shaggy head back and forth. Dog-man just chuckled, watching the old man ride off.

"River runs underground? Man's been in the sun too long, Dog. Let's get moving before some other lunatic shows up."

"Interesting he knew the two men you killed. Benjamin Franklyn Cruikshank. We might want to remember that name." He couldn't help remembering the old codger back in Yuma talking about underground rivers. *There might be something to what Cruikshank said, after all.*

Snake didn't like what he was thinking. "Some wild-eyed desert rat wanders into us and knows the horses we took from a couple of other desert rats. Don't feel good, Dog. This Benjamin Franklyn Cruikshank seemed glad we killed them two but we might just run into friends of theirs. This is strange country, Dog."

It was two days later when they rode up on Kelso Wash. "Looks like a big dry river bed, Dog. Only water this wash has seen comes from thunder storms. Old Benjamin said follow it north, and so we will."

The wash led in a winding course into higher country but those mountains the boys were looking at all day every day were still far off. "Eyes are playing tricks on us, Dog. Maybe those mountains we been lookin' at ain't even there."

"We seen some strange things in this desert," Dog-man said. "Remember the big spires we saw? And the lakes? They just never were there."

THEY MADE a big turn and came to a great depression that appeared to be a dry lake bed, filled with nasty salts. "That wash been dry a long time, Dog," Snake said. "This must have been the lake it drained into."

On the far north end of the dry lake they came to what appeared to be a trail heading west and in just another three miles they found a fresh water springs. "Do you suppose old Benjamin really knew what he was talking about?" Snake bent down and cupped some of the water up for a taste.

"Expected alkalie, Dog, but this is good water. Let's set up camp and give us and the animals a day or two break, eh?" There was good grass for the horses and mule, enough brush to break up for a fire, and not a shred of shade within fifty miles. "All the comforts of hell, my friend," he laughed.

Heat and no shade coupled with a lack of game changed their plans. "I'm gonna clean my gear and we're getting out of here, go someplace with trees and big game. Can't imagine a place like this, Dog. Good water, some grass and not a tree in sight."

"Ain't even a rock to crawl under," Dog-man said.

Dressed in fresh washed clothes and well-oiled leather, the boys followed the bare outlines of a trail the next morning. "That old buck just walked right into our camp going for water. Nicest gift we've got in some time, Dog. We got meat for several days now."

Bitter brush, cactus, and rocks is all that grows in the Mojave desert but many miles north of their trail were tall mountains lush with grasses, trees, and spring-fed water. But they were going west now, not north and came to a deep canyon. "Every color in the rainbow in these rocks, Snake. Never seen nothing like it."

"I ain't looking at rocks, Dog. That's a running stream. A real creek coming through that canyon." They rode over to where Snake was pointing and found where running water simply disappeared. "This ain't real, Dog-man."

"It's exactly what Benjamin Franklyn Cruikshank told us. A river that runs underground. Ain't never seen nothing like it." Going upstream, the creek led them into a deep, narrow canyon, lush with grass, even a few trees and plenty more rocks. "That old Mexican back in Yuma knew what he was talking about, too." Dog-man had another one of his special questions for Snake. "How did that old man in Yuma know about this?"

"Looks like caves over there," Snake said, ignoring the question. "Need to know more about all this." They rode right up to a cave and dismounted. "More than one soul's been camped here," Dog-man said. The cave was slightly above the high water mark, easy to get to and with plenty of room for the animals to graze.

"Them souls were Indian," Snake said. "Ain't no Texan would camp like that." Animal bones were thrown about, shreds of skin could be seen, and other remnants of those who were there last.

"Those bones mean that large animals are in the area, Snake. We might be eating good, all regular like, again." They cleaned up the cave and laid out their camp, gathered wood, and got the animals staked out.

Snake saddled his horse, made sure his rifle was loaded, and went up stream for a look-see. The stream was about a foot deep and in several places filled the width of the canyon. The walls were so steep that no horse or man could climb out. *Bad place to be if someone was chasing you,* Snake kept thinking as he rode deeper into the abyss.

When he came out the other side he saw three riders way off in the distance, turned his horse and rode fast back to camp. "Got company coming, Dog. Better fort up some. I'll get the animals all close in."

3

"THEY WERE a mile or more out so can't tell you much about them," Snake said. He and Dog-man were crouched behind large rocks near their cave camp. "We're on a well-used trail so it don't mean they are outlaws."

"Maybe does, maybe don't," Dog-man said. "Might could be Indians, Snake."

The wait for the three riders wasn't long. They came through the narrow defile in singly riding tired and all but worn out horses. "That feller in the middle ain't feeling well, Dog. He's about to fall off that horse."

Dog-man waited until the group was twenty-five yards or so out and called. "Hello the riders. We're a peaceful bunch. If you are, we got us a fire going."

The lead man jerked straight up in the saddle. "Glad to hear that. Got a wounded man here. Coming in."

Snake motioned for Dog-man to stay hidden behind his rock and stood up, rifle at the ready. "Come on in slow, boys. We're a bit jittery with strangers. Name's

Snake." He didn't say anything about Dog-man or how many there might be with him.

"Orrel Winters," the man said. "Pappy Jordan's got a arrow stuck in his side and the other one is Aaron Doffleberger. Might be some Utes coming up behind us."

The riders stopped shy of the cave and helped the wounded man off his horse. They laid him out near the fire and the one called Doffleberger tended to the horses. "Got a claim near Dagget Pass and was riding back to Prescott for supplies when we got jumped by some nasty injuns," the one called Winters said.

"Utes, eh? We been told about Mojave Indians, not Utes," Snake said.

"Paiutes roam those mountains north of here and want us to believe this is all their territory. Ugly heathens, all of 'em. Been in a couple of fights with 'em. Mojave hate them Utes, too," Winters said.

"Mojave hate everybody," Pappy Jordan said. Dog-man was working to get the wounded man's clothes off. "Easy there, young feller, that's mighty tender. Yup, them Mojave bands don't care whether you be peaceful or not. They attack their own people is what I've heard."

Dog-man saw what was left of the arrow stuck in the man's hip bone and broken off near the stone head. "You ain't gonna die, Pappy, but you're gonna wish you was when I jerk this out of your bone." Dog-man turned to the group. "Got any whiskey for this fine upstanding Indian fighter?"

"Don't be mocking my friend," Orrel Winters said, letting his hand move slightly toward a holstered revolver. "He killed one of those savages before gettin' hit."

Snake moved around so he wasn't in line with Dog's

lack of aim should it go that far. "All the man asked for was whiskey. Don't need to get all riled."

"Don't like people mocking my friend," Winters said again.

Dog-man stood up and quietly walked over to where Snake was standing. "Wasn't mocking nobody. Was fixin' to help your friend. You got a bad attitude, mister. You want him fixed, you fix him." He stood with his feet slightly apart, right hand hovering close to the handle of his Remington.

Snake chuckled slightly knowing that if Dog-man had his rifle he could hit a flying eagle in the eye, but with a pistol he never knew where the bullet might go. His face tightened up, jaw muscles could be seen working hard. "My friend here killed two men in a gun-fight recently but never hit the man he was trying to kill." He wasn't laughing or smiling.

"Now you got my partner all riled, Winters, and that ain't good for any of us." *There's something wrong here. Said they have a workings near Dagget and heading out for supplies but ain't got no pack animals. These men aren't miners or prospectors and I bet they attacked the Indians not the other way around.*

"Like my partner said, you want that man fixed you better start fixin'." Snake had his back to the cave wall with Dog-man standing next to him, both men were tensed and loaded. Dog-man caught Doffleberger coming into the cave carrying his lever action rifle at the ready.

"Now," Snake yelled as Winters made his move. Snake was far the faster putting two heavy slugs through Winters' chest. Dog-man whipped his weapon out and fired twice as well but only scared Aaron Doffleberger into dropping his rifle. When he went for his revolver, Snake shot him dead.

"You need to do some practicing, Dog. See if you can hit Pappy Jordan there. I'll back you up."

Dog-man laughed, looked at his weapon before holstering it and shook his head. He gathered the weapons from the dead men. "Well, Pappy, maybe you could start in by telling us the truth, eh? You attacked some Indians and they fought back, did they?"

The old man looked away not saying anything and Dog-man knelt down next to him. When he lifted the old man's weapon he touched the broken arrow stuck in the man's hip bone. Pappy Jordan cried out in pain, anger flushing his already ruddy face. "No, please. Yes, Winters attacked a small band of Utes and they fought back hard. We had to run for it."

"We don't have any bad whiskey, Pappy," Snake drawled out. "Only good stuff and I'm not gonna waste it on you. You boys carrying whiskey in your saddlebags?" Pappy appeared to be unconscious and Snake walked out of the cave to check the outlaw's gear. "Damn, Dog," he yelled. "We got more company. Better get out here."

He didn't elaborate, just yelled and Dog-man jumped up and ran from the cave, grabbing his rifle on the way out. "Indians?" he yelled but got no answer.

The two men were again nestled behind the rocks and watched a single rider, obviously badly injured riding out of the narrow canyon. "That's Benjamin," Snake said, walking out from behind the rock. He called out and Benjamin Franklyn Cruikshank tried to sit up in the saddle and almost fell from the horse.

The two men raced down the hill and into the stream, catching up Cruikshank's horse and leading him up the sidehill to the cave. "He's bleeding bad, Snake. Get him near the fire while I tend the horse."

Cruikshank had one bullet wound in his right leg, high up, and another in his right arm, high up. "Come on, Ben, we'll get you fixed up. Anybody trailing you?"

"No, I don't think so. They all be dead, Dog-man?" He saw the two bodies sprawled out on the cave floor and Pappy Jordan sleeping near the fire. "Looks like you had some visitors. That one there is Pappy Jordan. Meanest sumbitch you ever met. Don't give him an inch, Dog-man, he'll kill you for coffee."

"Got in a fight with some Utes, they said, then tried to take us out. Do you know everybody in this desert? How is it you know Jordan?"

"Been workin' my mine for more than ten years, Dog-man. Probably ain't two hundred of us between the Colorado River and Lane's Crossing. Most of the newcomers are thieving rats, killin' good people, raising hell with the Indians. This bunch you got here is pure filth."

Dog-man had the man's pants ripped open, got the wound cleaned out and most of the bleeding stopped. "Gonna have to probe some for that bullet, Ben. Let's take a look at that arm, first. Tell me what brought all this on."

"Went to the mine after leaving you boys, packed some high grade on the mules and lit out east for Prescott. Two men jumped me, cleaned me out and left me for dead, two days ago."

"Somebody you knew?"

"Nope. They was along the side of the trail pretending one of them was hurt when I rode up on them and they turned on me like pit vipers. Lost my mules, lost my high-grade, lost my food, too. I ain't got nothing left," the old man said. "Bastards."

Snake walked into the cave carrying two earthen jugs. "Look what I found." he said putting them down near the fire. "Full of the worst whiskey I've ever tasted. Made it from coyote piss if you ask me. At least we drank good tequila in New Mexico Territory. How you doing, Mr. Cruikshank?"

"Not very good, Snake, not very good." He winced when Dog-man eased the bullet out of his arm.

"Spent, Ben. This one must have bounced off some rocks before it hit you. Didn't even go in all the way. Give me one of those jugs, Snake." He poured straight whiskey on the open wound, ducked a round-house fist from Benjamin Franklyn Cruikshank, and wrapped the wound.

"Now my friend, you got to drink some of that 'shine so's Dog can fix up your leg. Gotta be bad hurt to drink some, though." Snake laughed, moving back from the fire. "How's old Pappy doing?"

"He's gonna have to drink a lot of it, Snake. That arrow's buried deep in a bone. Get him to drinkin' some while I get Ben fixed up."

Snake looked down on his partner for a moment. *How many times has that buzzard fixed me up? He's good at it, too. I don't mind working on horses, they just kick and bite, but workin' on a man, why them varmints shoot you.*

Snake took the second jug over to Pappy's side and nudged him awake. "Cocktail hour, Pappy. Drink to your heart's content, old man. Don't rightly know why we have to fix you up, though. Might outen to just leave you out in the sun and let the ravens have atcha. Weren't a very nice thing to do to me and old Dog-man."

Cruikshank only cried out once as Dog-man probed

for the bullet in his leg, but Pappy was a screaming fool when Dog-man dug the arrow-head from his wound. the blood ran free and it took extra effort to get the wound closed. "Gotta keep Ben alive, Snake, but I don't rightly care whether Pappy Jordan lives or not."

"That ain't like you, Dog. I got beans boiling and some venison roasting. You'll feel better after supper."

"How did all this come about, Snake? We're just passing through this country and seems half of the people are outlaws looking to do us in. We gotta drag them bodies out of this cave."

4

PAPPY JORDAN HAD A TERRIBLE NIGHT, suffering a high fever, crying out constantly, and died before morning. "Ain't much of a loss," Ben said. "Men like him come into fresh country, and give it a bad smell. How am I gonna get a stake, boys? I lost everything, got nothing."

"You still got your mine, don't you?" Dog-man asked. "Can't you dig out more gold and make another trip for supplies?"

"Could," Ben said, "but I got no food, no mules, and no way of gettin' any." He tried to get up out of his blanket and couldn't. "Cain't even get out of bed. Those two men gonna pay for this, somehow."

The boys spent several hours digging three graves and listening to Cruikshank describe the two men who robbed him clean. "The one pretending to be hurt was thin, Snake. Skinnier than you, even, but nasty mean. The other was short and heavy, drinking man, too. He's the one shot me in the leg."

Snake and Dog-man got Ben up and moved over so he was sitting in the dirt next to the fire sipping whiskey laced coffee. "I got to get a poke put together. Got no money, got no mules, got a mine I can't work without the supplies I was headin' out to get." His anger was building and he added another splash of whiskey to his coffee.

"Those men that robbed you, Ben, where would they go? They got mules and gold." Snake poured some whiskey into his coffee and took a long drink, making some ugly faces.

Ben had to chuckle even if he didn't feel like it. "They'd have to take the ore to an assay office, have it exchanged. Calico is closest, but Prescott would be safest," Cruikshank said. "Anyone seeing those mules would know they're mine. If you didn't run into them two, and this is the only trail to Prescott, then I'd say Calico."

Snake looked at Dog-man who returned the look. "We got two horses from them first outlaws and now got three more horses," Snake said. "We'll get you well enough to ride and give a look to Calico. We can sell off the stock there."

"Well, hell, if you'll take my word for it, I'll take two of those horses off your hands right now, and if you'll take even more of my word for it, we could convert one or two of the horses to grub stake me."

"Ain't really ours to sell, but on the other hand, we got 'em for sure," Snake said. "Don't see why we couldn't make that kind of deal." Dog-man shook his head slightly and gave Snake a long look as if trying to get some kind of thought his way.

"This Calico a big town, Ben?" Dog-man asked. "Bringing outlaws' horses into a town where they might be known ain't my idea of a good idea." He was thinking how quick Ben recognized the horses of the two men who were settin' up to rob them. "On the other hand, we might get your bunch of animals back."

"That's my thought," Snake said. "What about the law, though? Seems if the law spots old Dog and me they just right away think we're outlaws. They got a dumb old marshal or sheriff in this Calico of yours, Ben?"

"Ain't no law within a hunnert miles of us," Ben said. "That's why these men just run wild, stealing and killing and hurtin' good people. They is a group that wants to make someone the sheriff but nobody wants the job."

"How far from Calico is your mine, Ben? Can't you get some supplies in Calico?" Dog-man asked.

"No, it ain't a real village. Gotta go to Prescott for what I'd need. Mine's a couple of days from the junction."

Snake noticed the old prospector didn't say in which direction those couple of days would be. *He ain't never said exactly where this mine of his is. I wonder if there is a mine? Gets himself a grub stake and lives the good life until it runs out and gets another. Heard about that when we were in Deadwood.*

"When me and Dog-man were minin' down Mexico way, we pretty much fended for ourselves. Game and some few necessities like flour, coffee, and sugar. What is it you couldn't get in Calico?"

Benjamin Franklyn Cruikshank took that moment to pour more coffee and add some joy juice to it. He looked around the camp area, as if thinking. "Don't seem to remember seeing things like that for sale there," he said. "Nope, don't think I have. Explosives, too. Ain't seen none of that, either. Gotta get that stuff in Prescott."

"You be able to ride with that leg tore up?" Dog-man asked. "We need to get moving if we're gonna."

"Might hurt some, but the sooner we get to Calico,

the sooner I might get my stake back," he said. "It's a two day ride from here for someone who ain't got a tore up leg. In my condition, it'll be two days to Coyote Lake and another two days to Harper Lake, which is right near Calico."

THE GREAT MOJAVE DESERT isn't just a flat depression in the ground, it's filled with rock upthrusts, deep arroyos, rocks of every size and description. There are rises and dips and the whole thing is covered in spiny plants that seem to have a desire to hurt anything that comes close. The land rolls and surges offering low hills, sharp ridges, and sheer walls. After moving out of the canyon, Snake was the first to notice that the stream they had been riding in wasn't there.

"It's gonna take me a long time to understand how this river disappears like this."

"Indians have it pretty well marked in their minds," Ben said. "It surfaces every now and then, creating fresh water springs, even lakes in some places. Knowing how and where it flows on the surface is a matter of life or death for those living in the desert."

"Your mine near one of those places?" Dog-man asked.

"No, but there is a small spring near-by," Ben said. Snake just shook his head.

I'm gonna have to sit on his head to get a straight answer. He's willing to take horses that we took from outlaws, willing let us help him but won't come clean on this mine of his. Maybe just being safe? There's more to it, I think. He gave the old codger a long look as they rode along. He let his mind run free.

Is it possible that Benjamin Franklyn Cruikshank was a con-man? That maybe he didn't even have a mine? But if he didn't, why would someone shoot him and take his animals? The deeper into this great Mojave Desert he rode, the stranger came the questions he was supposed to answer. "I gotta spend more time at the camp fire with Dog-man and less time thinking about old Ben," Snake chuckled.

They were traveling westerly through rough and rocky terrain and toward mid-day of the third day saw off in the distance what looked like water. "That's Coyote Lake," Ben said. "Not the best water but it's drinkable."

Dog-man was leading the train made up of their mule and the outlaw's horses. Ben was leading and Snake eased back to ride alongside Dog-man. "I don't think he's lied to us, Dog, but I don't think he's tellin' us the whole story either. You think he really has a mine? He was shot, that's for sure, but by bandits or for something else?"

"I don't know, Snake. Won't talk straight about his mine but everything else is right on the button. This underground river, knowing Pappy Jordan and the outlaws. He's hiding something I'm sure."

"We get to this Calico place we better be ready for anything."

"Right now, Snake, we need to think about that water in front of us. If I was an Indian or a bandito, that's where I'd wait for my next victim."

"I'm gonna tell Ben you want to talk to him and I'm gonna ride out and see if someone's waiting for us. You're the talker, see what you can get out of the old man."

5

THE COUNTRY LOOKED like one wide, long, ancient dry lake bed Snake was riding through. *If there was standing water here it's been a long time gone. Could boil coffee just settin' a water pot on one of these flat stones.* He was less than a mile from the water and saw a plume of dust off to his right.

He dismounted and led his horse behind a ledge of rocks, brush, and cactus, snugged him to a rock, and climbed to the crest. *A dust devil? Or trouble?* Snake watched as the dust cloud seemed to move toward the lake. *Ain't a dust devil.* In less than five minutes Snake was able to discern men riding horses and in another short amount of time came to know who the men were.

Indians for sure. Five men and two of them are walking, leading their horses. When the Indians dropped from sight, probably into an arroyo that would lead then to the water, Snake got back in the saddle and raced back to tell Dog-man and Ben. "At least five, Dog. They been hunting, got two nice deer across a couple of horses."

"They'll have women at the lake waiting for them.

Get the skins cared for and the meat smoked. I'd put a guess that they're Ute," Ben said.

"You seem to know everyone we've come in contact with, Ben. Think they'd know you if we was to ride up on them? You know, all friendly like?" Snake chuckled and poured some coffee that Dog-man had brewing. "Would they have more than a few women waiting for them? Maybe the rest of the tribe?"

"The Utes live in the mountains north of us, Snake. No," Ben said, "They're a hunting party bringing meat for the women to take care of. Probably stay a few days and take the meat back to the tribe."

That ain't right. Dog-man thought, almost said right out. *If they live in the mountains, that's where the game would be. Ain't no way they would come down to this blistering playa for fresh meat.* He looked over at Snake and felt his partner had the same thoughts.

"Would they know you, Ben?" Snake growled it out. *Old fool simply won't answer a question.*

"Can't answer that, Snake. Maybe, maybe not. I've had dealings with the Ute for a long time but not all of them. Don't be gettin' all riled. They be hundreds of them. I don't know them all."

"Well, fine," Snake said. "We need water, the animals need water. Let's ride in all friendly like. Everyone we've met on this trail, ceptin' you, Ben, has tried to kill us. Maybe we'll get lucky this time."

They followed along an arroyo that led them to the water, half a mile from the Indian camp. They hadn't quite reached the water's edge when Dog-man spotted three of the tribe mount up and ride toward them. "All friendly like," he muttered.

"They're Mojave, not Ute," Ben said, reaching for his weapon.

"No," Snake said. He moved next to the old prospector and growled it out. "All friendly like. This is our call, Ben, like it or not. You're wounded and protectin' yourself, we understand that, but if something happens, they're starting it." *Five minutes ago they was a Ute hunting party, now they're Mojave killers. Startin' to dislike this old man.*

Snake watched the three riders coming on but also saw the other two mount up and ride off to the south. *Looks like they're backin' their own play. Three come to talk and two get ready to attack.* He held up his horse and Ben and Dog-man did too. "They're settin' up to attack," Snake said. He took a quick look around and knew they weren't in the best place to get in a fight but one that could be defended. "Dog, give the pack train to Ben and ride off toward those two belligerent bastards over there.

"Ben, take the pack train to those rocks and watch the three coming toward us. I'm gonna get as close as I dare, but when they make their move, Ben, I want your rifle barkin' some mean words."

Snake had the three of them well separated, which threw the Indian's plans off. The long Texan saw the three coming toward them slow way down. "Well, good," Snake muttered. He stepped down from his horse next to a stand of brush and watched the three Mojave walk their mounts ever so slow. He caught a glimpse of Dog-man moving slowly toward the two men off to the south.

"It's your play, Indian," Snake muttered. "We got you boxed 'stead of the other way around."

The three turned their horses and rode back toward their camp, joined by the two off to the south. Dog-man rode back in and joined Snake. "Nice move, Snake."

"Thankee, Dog. Let's get with Ben and ride down to

the lake. This ain't over, I'm sure. They ain't gonna like bein' messed with like that."

"Ain't never seen a Mojave back off like that," Ben said when they rode up to him.

"They ain't never met Snake," Dog-man said. "Let's get our horses some water, fill our canteens, and make tracks out of here. They ain't gonna like what just happened. We got about four hours of daylight left and need someplace we can defend. Bein' in a wide open old lake bottom ain't the right place."

"See that rocky ridge some ten miles west?" Ben pointed. "Be a good place to look."

"How far is that from Calico?" Snake asked.

"Maybe another ten miles of flat, open country." Ben shook his head. "You thinkin' of riding all the way in? Pretty hot for a hard ride like that."

"Get these horses watered, our canteens full, and we'll ride natural like toward that ridge," Snake said. "If we don't see movement from our friends over there, we might just ride right on in." Dog-man nodded and picked up the lead for the pack train.

"Them Mojave want the horses more than they want us," Ben said.

"They gotta get us to get 'em," Snake said. "Let's ride."

———

WEAVING TEN MILES THROUGH ROCKY, cactus covered desert in extreme heat leading a train of five riderless horses made for a slow journey. They used up a lot of daylight getting to the rocky ridge but found a natural hole in which to hide the horses and defend their position.

"Seen anything followin'? Snake asked. "I don't think we got enough sunlight to make it to Calico."

Dog-man had been riding drag, keeping a close eye on their trail. "No sign of 'em," he hollered out. "I think Ben's about to fall out of his saddle, Snake. Been a hard ride for the old man. This is a natural fortress. I say we spend the night here."

They were about fifty feet above the desert floor, had plenty of dry wood, and some meat left from the deer they shot. "I'm gonna circle back, Dog. You set up camp, get Ben's leg treated, and I'll find out where those boys are."

He rode well off from where they had trailed in and stayed as much in low country as he could. He went out of his way to not stir up dust and it was less than half an hour that he saw dust off in the distance. "Right on our trail, eh boys? You ain't gonna like our welcome," he snickered. He didn't worry about dust on his ride back to the ridge hideout.

"They're comin' hard, Dog. How's Ben?"

"Can't move much, but I've got him set up behind that rock over there and he can surely fire that rifle of his. I'm taking that high spot over there and you're welcome to whatever else is available."

"You're a kind man, Dog, and I appreciate it." Snake had his rifle, a box of ammunition, and a canteen and headed to a notch in the ridge to set up. *Five of them and three of us. Don't seem fair somehow. We're taking advantage of those boys. Hope they brought that fresh meat with them.*

The five Mojave knew that the men who outfoxed them were waiting for them somewhere along that rocky ridge and the lead man used arm movements to get the bunch separated. They were in a wide array, riding slowly toward the rocks.

"Let 'em come in close, boys. Don't be shootin' early. The closer they are the better," Snake yelled out. He might as well have been talking to one of the rocks. Less than five seconds later, Benjamin Franklyn Cruikshank let off three quick shots from his lever action rifle.

"Damn it," Snake said. The five Indians, all un-injured, all well more than three hundred yards out, were off their horses and on their bellies. The lead man again motioned how he wanted the attack and the men snaked their way toward the rocks, using everything available to hide behind.

"Had to make it difficult, did you, old man? Well, just fine, we'll do it the hard way," Snake muttered. He left the cleft and dropped down as low as he could, moving fast along the line of the ridge, away from Dog-man and Ben. He got fifty yards out and then changed direction so that he was headed directly for where he thought the Indians would be.

"That old bastard takes a shot at me and I'll make him hurt for a long time," Snake muttered. He stopped in a slight depression and tried to hold in his breathing as much as possible. The desert isn't always a quiet place, but the sounds usually mean something. Snake wanted to hear something other than the natural desert music.

A scraping legging, a footfall, a cough, anything that would be out of the ordinary. The Mojave lived in this desert, hunted incredibly wary game in this environ-ment, and would be as stealthy as what they lived on. Snake grew up on the plains of west Texas and was as wary as the Mojave, the difference being, he was sitting absolutely still and they were moving.

There it is. The slightest scrape and just feet away. His eyes were wide, he could smell a man, and now needed to know exactly where he was. He brought his knife out and didn't move another muscle, waiting for the next scrape. The Indian had dragged a moccasin through the sand and it scraped on a twig.

He did it again, Snake edged up from behind his rock, and came face to face with the noisy one. His knife whipped out, sliced the man's throat wide open, cutting the wind pipe, not letting the Indian make a sound. Just a few seconds and he was dead, but the thrashing alerted the rest. The man couldn't scream but he didn't die easy either.

Snake stayed low, crawled twenty feet fast, out from the dead one and heard one of his companions move up to the body. Snake was curled behind a bush with hundreds of spines and needles, and saw an Indian looking for his sign. *I'm over here, Pard. Come and get me.* He laid the rifle down, kept the knife at the ready and saw another Indian join up.

Snake put the knife down, picked the rifle back up, aimed and fired, once, twice, three times and saw two dead Indians sprawled on a third. "That's better. There's still two out there," he muttered, getting back down as low as he could. He re-loaded the rifle, put the knife back in its leather, and listened. In less than two minutes he heard horses riding off fast. "Ain't even picking up their friends," Snake said.

He stayed low, just in case and made his way back to where Dog-man and Ben were. "Don't shoot, I'm coming in," he said.

"How do we know it's you?" Dog-man laughed. "Ben's ready to shoot anything that moves. Better come in slow and easy, all friendly like."

"Better have hot coffee and some whiskey when I do," Snake yelled out. He walked into where Dog-man had a fire going. "Think those boys have more friends close by?"

"Doubt it," Ben said. "Five is about right for a hunting party. "Hard to say where the rest of their tribe might be, though." Dog-man looked at him and shook his head.

"What about the women you said would be there to take care of the game they brought in?"

"That would have been the Utes," Ben said. "These are Mojave Indians." Dog-man decided at that moment that Benjamin Franklyn Cruikshank didn't know one single thing of which he spoke.

"Hope next time I say not to shoot," Snake drawled out, "that you take it serious. Me and Dog been partners for a long time and intend to stay that way. We're trying to help you. You ain't been helping us by goin' off like that. You riding with us when we're trying to help you, then Mr. Cruikshank you do what you're told."

"Don't get yourself riled, Snake," Dog-man said. "I just had that conversation with Ben. He knows he was wrong and ain't gonna do it again. Let's eat a good meal and you two get a good sleep," Dog-man said, taking some of the pressure off. Snake wanted to glare at Ben but instead stood quietly next to the fire.

"I'll take first watch ." Snake poured a tin cup half full and added whiskey from his flask to top it off. "We'll ride into Calico tomorrow."

Supper was a quiet affair, each man sifting through his thoughts. Dog-man knew that Ben was getting Snake riled and knew that when Snake got riled, people nearby got hurt. "Anybody special we should look up when we get there, Ben?"

"Only thing I want to do is get my kit and animals back. Might need a little help with that, being wounded and all."

We been helpin' you, you old fool. Snake kept his thoughts to himself but couldn't help wondering why the old man never actually answered a question. *Find his stuff or not, we'll resupply and keep moving west. And without the benefit of Benjamin Franklyn Cruikshank's company.*

Night came on fast and Snake had a small fire going. He sat well back from the fire, resting his back on a slab of rock. *Me and old Dog have a way of meeting up with some of the strangest people,* he thought and had to snicker. *Here we are in the middle of this huge desert, people talk about this desert like it's almost alive, and we come across horse thieves, murderers, and now a gentleman who doesn't seem to know how to tell the truth.*

He tried to put it together and none of the pieces fit. He knew Cruikshank had been shot, that was obvious, but was it the way he told the story? Were there really two men who jumped him or did he get into a friendly wager, lose his mules and kit, and then try to get it all back? Snake shook his head letting the thoughts wander about in his head.

"Maybe the old fool didn't even have mules and a kit," he murmured. "Or a mine." He tried to let the thoughts go off somewhere, they wouldn't, and he got up and walked around the small cave, down off the edge, checked on the animals, and came back by the fire.

"First it was Utes from the mountains coming into the desert to hunt, then it was Mojaves who would kill just because they could, and all along, all he wants is his mules and kit back." the muttering brought him back to the fire and he settled down with his back resting on that slab of rock. "Gotta dump this old fool in Calico and move on."

6

"ABOUT AS HOT A RIDE AS I want to make," Snake said. He and Dog-man were riding side by side with Ben behind them, leading the string of horses and mule. Calico was a rough-wood frontier settlement made up of a main street and a few other buildings scattered out and about. The main street featured three saloons, a dry-goods store, one selling guns, ammunition, dynamite, and prospecting tools.

Rupert's Emporium, the sign read. Dynamite, fuse, blasting caps, and hardware for the active miner. Next door to Rupert's was the multi-story Calico Hotel, and across the street, with a big hand painted sign, Calico Eats.

So much for that story, Snake thought as they passed by. *Ben distinctly said he couldn't buy mining equipment and explosives here. What have we bought into?* He led them to a sign that read simply, Stables, and stepped down from the saddle. "Morning," he said to the man standing near the door. "Nice warm day, eh?"

"Gonna be a scorcher," the man said. "Them ain't

your horses mister."

"Are now," Snake said.

"Know who you took 'em from?"

"Do," Snake said. "And why. Making it your business or just askin'?" He tied his horse to a hitch rack and helped get the string tied off, too. Dog-man led Ben to another rack and got their horses secured.

"Name's Manuel Sinclair and I know the men who own those horses. They ain't never been much for givin' things away. More likely to take things than give. Just interested in the story. That Cruikshank with you?" Sinclair was half Mexican, half American, and half trouble for those also wanting some trouble.

"Got himself in a fight and lost his mules and stake. Found us, though. He needs a doctor if there is one. You seem to know other people's animals, Sinclair. Wouldn't happen to have seen old Ben's lately, have you?"

"Take him to that building with the green roof. Mi madre, Señora Lopez Aguilar will fix him up. Got something inside here you might want to see," Sinclair said.

"I'll get Ben over there and come right back," Dog-man said.

Snake had to hold in a chuckle knowing that Dog's only thought was to keep him out of trouble. Snake reached in his saddle bag and brought out a flask. "Join me, Mr. Sinclair?" He took a long swig, handed the flask off, and started for the barn entrance.

"Them's Cruikshank's remuda there," Sinclair pointed to mules in a small corral. "They walked in yesterday, draggin' their lead ropes and carryin' no packs. Whoever took 'em from the old man lost 'em. Sure would like to hear his story, too. Let's set a spell, eh?" He slid down a barn post and sat in the dirt.

Snake sat across from him, cross-legged, and took the

flask back. "I'll let Ben tell his own story, but as far as me and Dog-man, my partner, we run into some mean characters. Know someone called Pappy Jordan?"

"Sure do. Know his horse, tied off out there, on your string. Orrel Winters and Aaron Duffleberger, too. And their horses. But that ain't all you got out there."

"No it ain't, they're just the latest. Got to know them when they rode into our camp wantin' our kit. Wouldn't give it to 'em. Just wouldn't."

"Sounds reasonable," Sinclair said. He reached for the flask and took just enough that there was some left for Snake. Gentleman like. "You and your partner must have done a good job convincing them. How about them other horses?"

"A couple of desert rats called Bailey and Simmons made a play for our kit. Just don't understand people like that, Sinclair. If you're hungry, ask and I'll feed you. If you're hurt, tell me and I'll get you fixed up. To just walk up and try to take? Don't do it, just don't do it."

"Ain't a whole lot of people like you around this country, Snake. How'd you get tangled up with Cruikshank? Man don't have a lot of friends scattered around this desert."

"Seems to know everyone, though, but isn't eager to share some of what he knows. Talks about a mine somewhere in this playa, but feels he has to go to Prescott to buy supplies when there's a store yonder that sells what he needs. Tell him not to do something and he turns right around and does it."

"He can't buy his supplies at Rupert's. Owes Tank Rupert more than his gold mine is worth. Old Benjamin Franklyn tells some good stories, will drink your liquor dry, but won't pay his way. I wouldn't let too many people know you're tight with the man."

"He actually does have a mine?" Snake chuckled. "I was doubting him all the way. Never really comes out and says what is being asked."

"That's him, only worse. He's got the Indians worked up bad around here. Sees one, feels he has to shoot him. Don't think for half a second."

"Dog-man gives him a little more room than I do," Snake said. "We got into it with a small hunting party a day or two out. Cruikshank first called 'em Utes then Mojave. Just what is the Indian situation around these parts?"

"You killed some?" Sinclair asked, standing up. He shook off dirt and straw. "Ain't good right now to be killin' Mojave. Even the Paiutes stay away from them. Ben shot one of the head man's women a month ago and they have been gathering to take revenge. And they're tangled up with a bad man called Desert Jack."

"Five of 'em got testy with us. Now there's just two. They tried their best to be nasty."

"Those five probably belong with Desert Jack's band of rascals. Desert Jack's band numbers about fifty men and of course there are women and children added on. Been raisin' hell around here since Ben shot that woman. You killin' some of them will raise the ante, I'm afraid."

He paced around the big barn for a short time. "Bad timing, that's what it is. Bad timing. Desert Jack is sure to use this as a reason to attack a ranch or two, a mine or two, maybe even Calico itself." Sinclair stomped around some more and Snake tried to understand just what he and Dog-man had ridden into.

Seems like if we try to help somebody it turns out bad for everyone. Ain't gonna help nobody ever. To hell with 'em. Should of just let Ben die and rot away, should have chased Pappy Jordan off instead of helpin. burned down a steamship for trying to help. Ain't gonna help nobody again. He was yanked from his reverie by Sinclair.

"What brings you two into this country, anyway? You sure don't look like prospectors."

"Ain't. Sold our mine down Mexico way some time ago. We're working our way to the Pacific Ocean and Cruikshank said staying on this trail we come in on would lead us, water hole to water hole most of the way. Seems like all we've found is outlaws wantin' what we have."

Sinclair had a mean look on his face as he continued pacing. "I think you've probably stirred the dust up, Snake. You and your partner. Ben Cruikshank is good at that, too. Didn't tell you about the Indian problems we have here?"

"Not a word," Snake said. "Tell me about these problems. There's more than what you've already said? Seems like you've got a mess going before we showed up. Don't much care for being blamed for something that started before we come in."

"I understand that," Sinclair said. "Ain't blamin', Snake. Ain't. It's just that what you did, without knowin', you understand, is probably going to explode on us here in Calico. Desert Jack's been lookin' for some reason to start a fight. Mojave's are like that. they live to create problems. They'll fight among themselves if they can't start a fight with others."

"Others in town gonna blame us if trouble starts?" Snake asked.

"If you hadn't ridden in with Cruikshank, no, but he's already got the Mojave riled, and now you riding in with him after killin' three of 'em. Well, I don't know," Sinclair said.

7

"WHAT'D YOU DO WITH BEN?" Snake asked. "We got a little bit of trouble, once again. Don't you never ask me to help nobody, ever again, Dog." Snake had a lot to say and was going to try to get it all out at one time. He and Dog-man were walking down the main street in Calico, looking to find something to eat.

"Left the old fool with that woman. She's half Paiute and half Mexican, and gave Ben a sip of something that knocked him out cold. Like to get some of that for future use," Dog-man chuckled. "She's gonna get him well, though. What kind of trouble you talking about? Ain't we already had our share?"

Snake took the long way around and spent several minutes explaining what Sinclair had told him about Ben, about Mojave Indians, and about how, now, the boys were fully involved. "Like I said, Dog, ain't gonna be helpin' nobody again and that's final." He pulled up short and gave a long look up and down the dusty street. "Let's get something to eat, sell those animals to Sinclair, and pack our skinny butts out of this town."

"Best idea I've heard," Dog-man said. "Calico Eats is what the sign says. Hope they got something besides jack rabbit."

The cafe was dingy at best, dirty would be closer to the truth. Desert dust on everything including the lady who pointed at a table but didn't say anything. She was somewhere on the back side of fifty, skinny and had the saddest eyes Snake had ever seen. Pale gray eyes, deep set in high cheek bones with the skin stretched taut.

Snake saw a long thin nose, small mean looking mouth and almost no lips. *Gonna be hard to be nice to this old hag. She's angry just being alive, I think.* She never said a word, just stood there while the boys got their seats.

Snake looked around the narrow and long room with tables along one wall leaving space to walk along the other side. The kitchen was at the far end. One sign proclaimed, "Daily Special" but there was nothing written under it except the cost, $1. "Better not be rabbit," Dog-man said.

"Whatcha gonna have?" The old lady rasped out. She coughed hard, tried to catch her breath, and gave the boys a hard look. "Saw you ride in with that fool Cruikshank. You be eating in here, I want to see the money first. Any friend of his ain't no friend of mine."

"What is this special of the day?" Snake asked. He was quiet, soft spoken, but there was no smile. Dog-man's first thought was the word riled. Snake was getting riled.

"We ain't friends of old Ben," Dog-man said. "He was shot and we helped him get back to town." He pulled a couple of silver coins from his shirt pocket and laid them on the table. What's the special?"

"Shot? Well, that ain't all bad. Who shot him?" She grabbed up the coins and had another coughing fit, the kind that knocks your legs right out from under you.

The filthy old hag pulled out a chair and flopped down. "Come out here five years ago to get rid of that cough. Seems to be working," she said. "Ox tail stew," she said, got up and walked back to the kitchen, rolling a smoke on the way.

Dog-man got up, motioned to Snake, and walked out the door. "Let's get done with this place, Snake. Wouldn't eat there if I was starving. We'll get our mule, let the others go, and ride west. Open desert is cleaner than Calico Eats."

They were checking the pack on the mule when Sinclair came out of the barn. "Guess old Ben's gonna live, eh?"

"Seems like it," Snake said. "Want those animals?"

"If I took 'em, I'd sell 'em for two dollars each. Give you one dollar each. Leavin' out, are you?"

"Heading west. Dollar each will be just fine. Don't take this personal like," Snake said, "but I hope we don't run into each other again soon." He put the five dollars in his pocket, gathered the mule's lead, and stepped into the saddle. "Good luck, Mr. Sinclair."

He and Dog-man started turning their horses from the hitch rack when a voice rang out, "Stop right there you thieving bastards. Order food from me and run off without paying. I'll have you shot," the old lady from Calico Eats screamed.

"Didn't order nothing from you," Dog-man said. "Just asked what the special was. You the one that run off hacking up fur balls. You think we ordered, well, we didn't and you know as well as I that I left those coins on the table. You are a liar, Ma'am."

She stood still, coughed some from the long run up the street, put her hand in the pocket of her filthy apron and came out with the coins. "Be damned," she said, turned, and walked off. Didn't say another word.

"Can't get out of town fast enough," Snake said, putting heels to the horse's flanks. "West, Dog-man, as far west as we can get."

THEY MADE about ten miles before it started to get too dark to ride safely. They were following a dry stream bed leading toward a rocky ridge and found a ledge half way up the ridge where they could nest up for the night. "If Sinclair knows what he's talking about," Snake said, "this feller Desert Jack might be about. Let's munch on some dry biscuits and drink cold water tonight. Maybe risk a fire in the morning."

Night comes fast in the desert. Long, lingering sunsets aren't on the menu unless there's a storm bringing clouds or a wind raising dust. "Wonder if anyone's ever tried to count the stars?" Snake asked as the two sat on rocks looking out across the vast desert. "Be a lot of numbers lined out, I think." He was leaned up against his saddle and reached for his saddlebags, brought a flask out, and took a long swig. "Care for some?"

Dog-man took the offered flask and drank some. "This is the good stuff, Snake. Didn't think we had any left."

"Never know what you'll find in the bottom of a good saddlebag," he chuckled. He didn't tell about having it filled from Sinclair. "We gotta quit meeting up with strangers, Dog. Just ride west until we come to the ocean. Ain't never seen the ocean. Don't even know what it might look like. Ain't gonna look like a big river, is it?"

"Well, now," Dog-man said, "I ain't never seen it either. We got any kind of plan, Snake? I mean, a real plan? Seems we been bouncing off other people's lives."

"We had a plan, Dog. When we left that wonderful lady and her rowdy kids, we had a plan. When we left Las Cruces we had a plan. Don't know where it went." He fished in his shirt pocket and came up with a half smoked cigar and chewed on it for a short time.

"Think we need to lay it out again. We talked about California and finding some good ground and working some cattle, growing some food. Got turned around somewhere." Snake stretched out, his head on the saddle, his eyes on the stars, his heart back in Tucson. "Miss that lady and them kids, Dog."

"Knew you would, Snake. Interesting, though, I don't miss nothing we've been through except working that old mine we found. Loved working that mine, breaking them rocks, working that rocker. I still want that ranch we've talked about. I like hard work, like working cows, need a place called home."

"Maybe we've worked all the trails out of our systems," Snake chuckled. "Best not run into some pretty lady with a ranch, Dog. Either of us."

It got quiet as the night, the two men looking at the stars, remembering just what their plan was. Snake left April because he was sure his days of following whatever trail he was on weren't over. "Told her right out, Dog, that I might up and leave. Sittin' her right now wondering if I did the right thing." He tossed the well chewed cigar into the rocks. "It was the kids, Dog. I loved the kids more than her."

Dog-man grunted something and continued counting stars. "We could have stayed," he said. "But it wouldn't have been our ranch. I think after all these fools we've been dealing with that it just might be time to find that ranch of ours. Just might be."

Snake was first up, just as the sky started turning morning gray. A cold wind blew down from the ridge above them and he started making ready for a fire when he saw dust a few miles out on the desert floor. "Company coming," he said, shoving his boot into Dog-man's rump. "Best get yourself up."

He walked out on the rocky ledge and tried to see what caused the dust. *It ain't a herd of cows, that I know. Can't think of nothing but a bunch of men would make that much dust. Is that Desert Jack's band that Sinclair talked about?* "Think there's fifteen or twenty men riding horses, Dog. Come take a look. Bring my glass."

They spent several minutes watching the group, trading the spy glass back and forth. "Indians for sure, and in a hurry to get somewhere," Dog-man said. "If we lit out right now, we'd cross trails out there in an hour or so."

"That's what I was thinking, and we don't want to do that. Don't want to go back to Calico, neither. Let's just watch, Dog. Wherever they're going, they're in a hurry to get there."

The band of Indians rode north toward the long rocky ridge and turned east, as if to follow along the base of the hills. "Be comin' mighty close, Dog. think they'll spot our sign?"

"We would," Dog-man said. "You can bet if they're looking, they will. Let's get packed just in case we have to leave quick. Did you get a good count?"

"Maybe seventeen," Snake said. "That man in the lead sure would stand out, eh?" Most of the Indians were in breech clouts and that's about it, while the man in the lead was dressed in buckskins as if he lived in the mountains instead of the desert. "Those men by the lake were dressed that way, Dog. Wish we knew more about the Paiutes and the Mojave."

They had their horses saddled and the mule packed, and were ready to ride out. "Should we climb over the ridge or try to work our way along the flank?" Dog-man asked.

"Likely to be seen either way, Dog." He saw the band, still at a lope, only a mile or so out from the hillside. "Let's let 'em ride past us before we light out. They'll be riding east and we'll ride out west. Hope they don't look back and hope they miss our tracks coming up here."

They had the horses and mule well back from the ledge and were on their bellies as the band of Indians rode past some fifty feet or so below them. No one looked up and Snake made for his horse. Dog-man was right behind, grabbed the mule's lead, and they rode out, following along the flank of the ridge. they didn't look back until they were down off the hillside and on the west bound trail once again.

"You lead, Dog," Snake said. "I'll hold back just a bit and make sure we ain't being followed. Keep your eyes open for a good place to make a fight of it if we have to."

"How far to the next water, do you suppose?" Dog-man asked. "Or our next stop where there might be people?"

"Just have to keep our eyes open. All Ben said was to stay on the trail to a place called Mormon Station. Man named Huntington runs it. On the Mojave River, he said."

"Hate to have to trust what that fool told us," Dog-man said. He put his horse in a good trot, the mule not fighting the idea, and rode off.

SNAKE HELD BACK and watched his partner ride off with the mule in tow. He turned and followed his trail back and found where the Indians had joined the main trail and followed a short distance. The band had churned up the desert and following their trail was easy. He stopped after a mile and just sat his horse for fifteen minutes or so. *Don't think they spotted our tracks or they'd be coming on hard about now. Hope Calico's ready for that bunch.*

He put his horse in a strong trot and was back with Dog-man in short order. "Any idea how far this Mormon Station is? Horses are gonna need water and we could use some real food," Dog-man said.

"Said it was half way between Calico and Lane's Crossing whatever that means." Snake was laughing, thinking about it. "Old Benjamin Franklyn Cruikshank never in his life told the whole story. You know as much as I do, Dog, so lead on, ye trekker, lead on."

8

THE DESERT ISN'T AS WIDE open and flat as many expect, and it surely isn't devoid of life. The spiny bushes, odd shaped trees, and cacti are homes to many types of reptiles, which in turn eat many of the other critters that call the area home. There are rock upheavals, long ridges of rock where something extraordinary happened millions of years ago, and deep crevices and arroyos carved out by rushing waters and strong winds.

The great Mojave Desert can be as peaceful as the calmest harbor and as wild and dangerous as the strongest typhoon. It has an aroma all its own, as well. Particularly following a rare thunderstorm. Many refer to the fresh, wet aroma as desert dust.

"So, what we know is, this Mormon Station is about half way to Lane's Crossing," Dog-man said, laughing right out. "Means about as much as saying 'got no idea how far it is'." Dog-man was pointing out toward the far north horizon waving his hand about in frustration.

"Got some mighty big clouds building up to our

northwest, Snake. Last rain we saw is when you thought you heard a train coming down on us."

"That was a real show of Satan's anger, Dog. Just thinking about that flood coming down that arroyo scares me today. Let's stay out of gulches." He thought about that and chuckled. "That don't make any sense either. The damn trail is in a gulch. The damn river is under our feet. This is crazy country, Dog."

Within an hour or so they could begin to hear the rumbling of thunder way off but getting closer with each crescendo. "Clouds are bright and white, all billowy when they're far out there, and look now. Black and mean and ugly, looking to stomp on us, Dog." Snake stretched out from his slumped position in the saddle and pointed at the mass of storm rolling down on them.

"That curtain of shadowed gray is rain, Snake. Best find a piece of high rock and overhanging ledge to get under. It would be nice to find some fresh meat, too."

"Don't be asking for too much, Pard. Let's head for that jumbled up mess of rocks over there and get a fire going." He snickered. "Before the rain, this time." The mound was probably half a mile long, narrow at the north and wide at the south end. The ridge stood well over a hundred feet high and they found a trail that led to a small cavern.

"No room for the horses, Dog. At least there's some grass up here. They'll enjoy the water, though." He took care of the animals while Dog-man gathered as much wood as he could find and got it in the cavern and then moved their packs in, too.

"Good timing," Snake said as the first big drops of rain splashed on the rocks, hissing like an angry snake. They had watched the thunder and lightning march across the broad expanse of desert as they rushed to make camp. The sky lit up noon-bright and the thunder came right with the light. "Can't get any closer than that."

The cavern had been home or resting place for many over the years, some four legged, some without legs, and even a few men had found safety more than once in its rock walls. Dog-man used a previously built fire pit to get a good blaze going, with a coffee pot ready to boil, sitting on a rock in the middle.

The crashing rumble of a thunderstorm doesn't allow for much conversation nor was one able to hear anything else that might try to make a sound. It was not sound but sight that caught Snake's attention as he got wood to add to the fire.

"Look at this," he said and motioned toward the desert below the cavern. "Two Indians following our trail, Dog. They'll be here in five minutes or less. Riding some pitiful horses, too. They're dressed in buckskins like that one leading that big group. Looks like one might be injured."

"They following our tracks or just making a bee-line for these rocks? Might make a difference in how they react when they get here," Dog-man said. He moved to their packs and pulled out rifles and boxes of ammunition.

Snake was on his haunches back in the dark of the cavern, rifle at the ready, while Dog-man was closer to the opening but behind a large rock when the two men hobbled in. They moved straight to the fire, both dripping rain water from their buckskins, and one dripping warm blood as well. Dog-man stepped out from the rock, rifle held almost casually but in both hands.

"Welcome," he said. The two obviously knew there were men about, somebody lit that fire, so they didn't jump or show surprise when Dog-man spoke. The wounded man slowly let himself fall to the rock floor and looked up at Dog-man, as if to say, 'go ahead, finish me off. It can't hurt any more than it does.'

Snake stepped out of the shadows and stood behind the one left standing. "Your friend needs help. What happened?"

The startled Indian moved to the side quickly, saw that Snake had a rifle too, and let his fall to the floor. He said something in his native tongue and Snake shrugged his shoulders and held out an open hand. "No comprende, friend," He picked up the rifle and tossed it to Dog-man, found his tin cup, and filled it with coffee. "Get a couple of cups out, Dog. Let's make these two comfortable, eh?"

After a sip or two of hot coffee, the Indian moved to help his partner. Dog-man got out the medicine kit and the two got the man laid out by the fire. "Took a nasty fall, Snake. Not shot or stabbed, but busted up some. Bleeding from a gash in his side. We'll have him cleaned up shortly but he won't be in a fightin' mood, for sure."

Snake sat down and motioned the other to sit with him while Dog-man worked. He pointed at himself and said, "Snake." Then he pointed at the Indian and motioned as if asking a question.

"Good Inyan," the man said, showing about a half smile. Snake laughed and reached for the coffee pot.

He pointed at Dog-man and said, "Dog-man."

The Indian pointed at his injured partner and mumbled something that sounded very much like asshole. "Well, there we are," Snake said, "in a cavern with Good Inyan and Asshole. Couldn't be more delighted. Been hanging around a town somewhere to get those names?" He looked at Good Inyan and said, "Paiute?"

The man nodded and pointed north making a motion like riding. "Heading home, I think he's saying," Snake said. "How you comin' with, um, the other one?"

"Busted ribs and a gash in his side," Dog-man said. "Other than that just cuts and bruises. Looks like he was throwed from his horse. Don't see that much. Most of these fellers can ride about as good as you." He turned to the man. "You speak English?"

"Yup," he said. "Plenty good, too. You got coffee?"

"Now we're getting somewhere," Dog-man said. "You been trailing us?"

"Yup. Two days now. You kill bad inyan, we come follow."

"He must be talking about the fight we had near that lake," Snake said. "So you weren't with those we fought?"

"No. We follow them, find you. You kill them, we get rifles, follow you. Bad trouble now."

Snake was watching the man closely as he spoke, thinking there was more to the story than that. *They don't have any food or weapons other than the two rifles. And they took those from the men we killed. I wonder if maybe they were prisoners of those Mojave and we set 'em free. Maybe these are the ones walking alongside the horses carrying the deer?*

"You say bad trouble. Why?" Snake asked.

"You kill Mojave, they come to make trouble. You see. Need food."

"So do we, friend," Dog-man said. He got up and walked to the front of the cavern. "Rain's gonna be here for a spell, Snake. Do we share?"

"Might's well. We're social experts, Snake, besides, it's on the edge of going bad now." He chuckled moving to the packs. "Got enough of that meat for each of us to have some, got a few dried up biscuits left, and coffee. Set for a banquet, old friend."

"THOSE TWO ATE everything we offered and went right to sleep. They've been on a rough trail, Dog-man. What do we do now? I'd rather not go back to Calico and on the other hand we don't have the slightest idea how far it is to Mormon station."

"We made a mistake riding out of Calico without buying supplies," Dog-man said, "but you're right about going back. Our hurt friend here ain't going anywhere for a day or two so why don't you and Good Inyan take a ride out when the rain quits and find us some food."

"Yeah, and you can watch my back, too. If that is the real story that we heard then these two would be our friends. If they're Paiute, not Mojave, then we can trust them. Sure, Dog-man, I'll ride out with old Good Inyan here and get us some food."

Dog-man tried to hold in the chuckle and poured coffee. They sat under the rock ledge and watched the rain, in sheets, splash into the desert. "Rain like this in Colorado would be a blessing, Snake, but here it just messes up the trail."

"Well, it allows for all them varmints to live, for all them bent up trees to grow, even sprouts a blade or two of grass," Snake said. "On a mountain with dirt, not like these that are all rock, a rain like this would mean your cattle would be good for some time and water would be in the well. Some things that seem all bad and dangerous can also be good and friendly."

The downpour lasted another hour or two and the sun returned just as hot as when it left, creating a steam bath on the desert floor when Snake and his Indian friend left to find food. Snake let Good Inyan lead the way, thinking of his back, and they started to circumvent the upheaval and follow along the edge of a deep arroyo as well.

The Indian picked up some sign coming down from the rocks and pointed it out to Snake. "Yup," Snake said. "Deer and fresh, too." They dog trotted, staying as low as possible, following the well defined tracks until Good Inyan pulled up. He all but flung himself into the wet sand and mud, snake right with him.

The two squirmed under some brush and the Paiute pointed off to his right. Snake saw fear in his eyes and raised up a bit to see, ducking back immediately. Three Mojave Indians were walking slowly, following the trail Snake and Good Inyan had left. Snake nodded at the Paiute and raised his rifle.

Good Inyan rolled over twice and eased his rifle up as well. Snake let the three get within fifty yards or so, started to put pressure on his trigger when a shot from the rocks above the three Mojave rang out. One howled with pain and fell to the ground while the other two raced for some bushes to hide behind. Two more rifle shots kicked up mud around their feet but didn't hit them.

Snake couldn't see who was shooting but had to believe it was Dog-man. He reached out and touched Good Inyan, and using his hands, told him to work around to his right, that he would go more to the left, and put the other two Indians under a three-way blanket of fire. Good Inyan smiled and wormed his way through the wet brush.

Wet brush don't make noise, Snake thought, moving quickly out about fifteen yards. *There they are, trying to spot old Dog. I'll give 'em something else to look for.* He took a long sight on the smallest of the two and put a bullet through the middle of his back. The third Mojave jumped to his feet and started running toward where he thought the shot came from, firing his rifle as fast as he could work the lever.

Good Inyan killed him with a belly shot followed by a head shot. "Let's find their horses," Snake said, following their tracks along the hillside. "Can't be too far off. Must have been following you and your friend," he said. Good Inyan nodded as if he understood, and they again went into a dog-trot, and again it was Good Inyan who pulled up short, pointing off to his left.

Three horses were tied to a stunted tree and a third animal, it had horns, was nibbling sparse grass with them. "Must be our day," Snake said, kneeling down and taking a long aim at a mule deer standing side-to, offering a perfect shot. "We'll eat well this week," he murmured dropping the buck where it stood.

Dog-man joined them for a minute to make sure all was well and then left to get the bodies hidden in rocks just in case they might have friends near-by. Good Inyan and Snake had the deer gutted and were skinning it out when Dog-man returned, carrying rifles and extra ammunition from the dead. "Bet they have food on their horses, too," he said. "I'll lead them up to ours. We need to get this meat packed and get ready to pull out. Our friend won't be comfortable, but you can bet those boys have friends near-by."

"Get Asshole up to the front of the cavern, Dog. He'd be a good lookout while we get everything loaded up. Gonna be a pack train again," he laughed.

9

"WE AIN'T GONNA MAKE five miles before dark," Snake said. "Let's just stay here, have a fine meal of hot meat, sleep good, and leave out at first light. I'll take first watch, let Asshole take the second, and we'll be fine."

The moon was full giving the desert scene some brightness as the wet branches, spines, and brush all but glowed. Fox, wolves, and other predators mingled with their prey and their interactions could be heard in that cavern. Snake took in the sounds with the hint of a smile. The desert at night has its own song for those who enjoy being alone. Snake was one of those, had always been, and yet those few who have needed help come to him.

Dog-man always asks why I don't settle down when the opportunity comes, and tonight is one very good reason. Can't see nothin' like this on a chair under a roof. Can't never hear a wolf sing a song this pretty tied up in blankets under a roof. That's part of it, and another part? Yup, I'm alone but I ain't lonely.

Good Inyan and Asshole knew instinctively that

Snake was a good man. That lovely lady with two children and a dead husband knew, too. *I miss that lady and those rascals. April would be a good man's best friend, wife, and lover. Just not mine.* Snake sat at the wide open mouth of the cavern looking out across a land based sea called the Mohave Desert trying to stay awake knowing there were some out there who wanted him dead. He could hear the soft bark of fox, the mournful cry of wolf, and the yip-yapping of coyote, but it was the others he was thinking about.

Them critters singing out are hunting in the full moon light and they ain't worried about nothing. That tells me ain't no men are wandering around out there, either.

A quick bite to eat washed down with hot coffee and Snake led the pack train off the mountain. Everyone was mounted and they had their pack mule along with a pack horse added on. "We're going west, Dog. Don't want to go back to Calico even if they do have trouble from them Mojave. We got food, know where there's water, and have a clear trail to follow."

Good Inyan rode out well in front, making sure they stayed on the trail. The heavy rain created washes and the trail would vanish for great distances. They ran into puddles of water the size of small lakes where the ancient and slightly below ground Mojave River intersected with a wash-out. Good Inyan would return and tell his companion something who would then tell Dog-man.

"Seems there has been traffic moving toward Mormon Springs this morning or late last night, Snake. Good Inyan has found sign from as many as five riders so far. He says the horses are shod."

"Runnin' from Calico, maybe? Runnin' for help or just runnin'?" Snake was sprawled across the back of his horse, watching some lazy clouds move through a soft blue sky. "Might want to watch the road behind us from time-to-time, Dog."

The party moved along at a good pace and it was late in the day that Good Inyan reported smoke some miles off. Snake had the Paiutes stay with Dog-man and he rode ahead to check it out. Turning slightly north around a rock outcrop Snake saw tendrils of smoke, not from burning buildings, as he anticipated, but from someone's chimney, and rode on into the little settlement he thought was Mormon Station.

A few buildings, rough built, corrals, and few people. "Don't see a bunch of scared people," he muttered. "Howdy," Snake called out to a gentleman standing in front of what looked to be the stage stop. "This Mormon Station?"

"Sometimes called Mormon Grocery, sometimes called Fish Ponds Station. Take your pick. You runnin' from them Indians in Calico? Look a bit trail tired to me."

"Guess I do," Snake chuckled. "Got in a fight with some Mojave, saved a couple of Paiute, and lookin' for some good information on riding west. My partner and the Paiute ain't too far behind me."

"They got a big fight goin' on in Calico. I've been trying to raise a bunch to go back and chase them devils off. Desert Jack needs a good scolding." The man stood about five feet and eight inches tall and had to weigh two hundred and fifty pounds if he weighed an ounce. "Ain't got no money to offer you, but you'd be doing the right thing."

"Almost ran into that bunch after we left Calico a day or two ago," Snake said. "That feller Desert Jack dresses as a Paiute but rides with Mojave? How is that?" Snake asked.

"He's a white man come west from the Territories. Thinks he's a injun. What he is, is a sadistic killer. That's what he is. Robs and steals and kills. Abducts children and sells 'em in Mexico. Kills the men and uses the women until they ain't nothing left of 'em. Man needs killin' in the worst way."

Snake sat quiet for just a moment or two, absorbing what the man said. *Abducts children and sells them in Mexico? Fiend, that's what I'd call him. Horrible. He ain't a man. Animals are better than he is.* "Yup," Snake said. "He needs killing and soon ain't soon enough." He stepped down from his horse and thrust out his hand.

"We been jawin' up a storm here and I have left my manners out there on the trail somewhere. They call me Snake, my partner, comin' in shortly is Dog-man. What you're saying about this Desert Jack changes the picture I had of him."

"Name's Alphonso Barrington. Helped old Pete Huntington get this place operating. Friends call me Big Al. Glad to know ya. I got a jug inside and you look like you could do with a snort or two."

Big Al had shoulders too wide to go through the doorway, Snake noticed, and hands that hid the bottle when he picked it up. "How many men you got for this ride to Calico?" Snake asked.

"Everyone that's come through just kept on going. So far, it's just me gonna ride to Calico and kill Desert Jack."

The conversation ended as Dog-man and the two Indians rode up to the stage stop. "That must be your partner and the Paiutes." He stopped talking and walked up to the open door. "Hell's Bells, Snake, that's Good Inyan. I was sure he was dead. Knows his horses, that Paiute does. By God, and Asshole, too." He grabbed Good Inyan and wrapped those short, heavy, strong arms around the skinny Paiute, and lifted him right off the ground. "So, you got away from those bastards, eh? Have to tell me about that."

"Him got us away," Asshole said, pointing at Snake. "Pretty good feller, him."

"You're standing tall in my eyes, Snake. Seems you might have some kind of story to tell. Have a drink, Dog-man, and let's find out all about this."

"Where are the people?" Dog-man asked.

"West, I guess," Big Al said. "When Desert Jack started this rampage of his, the good people cleared out. Stage ain't come through for more than two weeks. Last man come through said Calico is forted up, that fires are burning. Don't know who Desert Jack thinks he is, but he's gonna go down hard when I get there."

"We have some fresh venison if you have somewhere we can build a nice fire," Snake said. "If it's only you goin' to fight that man, you need to eat."

Good Inyan didn't understand what Snake said but with everyone else laughing out, he did too, then walked out the door to stand in the street looking east. "Something caught his attention," Snake said and followed him out. Good Inyan pointed at dust coming in and walked to the horses for his rifle. Snake followed suit.

When five riders pulled up in front of the stage stop they were met by another group of five men carrying rifles. "You boys seem to be in a hurry," Big Al said.

"Desert Jack has taken over Calico. We're heading for Lane's Crossing. Had enough," one man said. None of the five dismounted and most were ready to run again.

"Take a minute and tell us what's happened," Big Al said.

One of the men, thin, scrubby beard, dirty clothing, pulled up his rifle and yelled out, "There's one of them filthy killers." When he raised the rifle, Snake leveled his and fired, levered another and fired again. Two quick shots threw the man back and to the ground, dead. No one moved as Snake stood in the middle of the dusty road, a cocked rifle slowly moving from one man to another.

"You boys seem to have found your courage. Anyone else want to get brave or did I mean to say stupid?" Snake's eyes were just slits, his jaw was shoved out half a foot, and no one saw the least tremble in his trigger finger.

"I think it's time you boys rode off." Big Al eased his rifle into more of a ready position, saw Dog-man do the same thing, and watched as Asshole moved behind the horses, his rifle also at the ready.

"You come flying into our little town here threatening to kill our friends don't make for a good introduction." Big Al looked at each man in turn. "You ain't brave enough to fight Desert Jack, that's one thing, but you want to kill a good Indian, that ain't to my liking. Set your spurs, boys, or I will."

The man who spoke when they rode in started to say something but a man behind him went for his sidearm. Two more shots echoed up and down the almost empty street and the stupid one fell to the dirt, two holes in his filthy shirt, about at the mid-chest level. Snake motioned to Dog-man, as if to say, take charge here, and started reloading.

"Five cowards rode in," Big Al said. "Right now, at least three can ride out." He walked to the man who did the talking, pushed the rifle's barrel into the man's gut and nudged it hard. "Now, mister."

The three rode out fast leaving their dead sprawled in the dirt. "See too much of that out here in the desert. Liars, card sharks, cowards, and criminals," Big Al said. "They come here to hide out and destroy what's truly beautiful." He stood like a rock in the middle of the street, shaking his head. "Asshole, you want to help me kill Desert Jack?"

"Okay," he mumbled. He said something to Good Inyan who nodded also. "Bad man, that Jack feller." Asshole looked over to Snake. "You come? Big fun. Kill Jack, drink whiskey."

"No whiskey, Asshole," Big Al laughed. "That's how you got your name, Remember?" The Paiute laughed, pretended he was drunk, then straightened right out. "We go quick or party be over."

Big Al looked with questioning eye at Snake, then Dog-man. "Sure could use you. Jack rides with fifteen or twenty men most of the time."

"There were seventeen when I saw him," Snake said. "Me and old Dog there got to talk a minute, Al. We'll join you in the stage office in a couple of minutes. Get that fire going." He and Dog-man walked over to the horses and mule, watched Big Al go in the office and saw the Paiutes drag the bodies off to be buried.

"I'd rather just ride on out, Dog, but I don't think we're gonna, are we?"

"Might be easy to step in the stirrup and go, Snake but we'd only make about fifty feet. We'd have to turn around and come right back. We'll settle those problems in Calico, then ride west, eh?" They were laughing on the short walk into the stage stop.

"By the way, I'm supposed to tell you we aren't to help people what we meet. Remember?" Dog-man kept right on walking when Snake pulled up short.

10

SNAKE TRAILED their mule and Big Al trailed the one packed for him and the Indians. Dog-man and Asshole were well out in front leading the little train, while Good Inyan protected their backs. "Ride hard and we'll be there all wore out and not ready for a good fight. Take two days to get there and we'll whip the fight right out of old Desert Jack and his nasty band." Big Al was ready for a good fight.

"What makes you so sure that the five of us are just gonna ride right in there and take out fifteen or twenty Mojave led by a white man?" Snake asked. "It seems the folk that live in Calico haven't been able to."

"We'll have a little help, but not from most of those who live there. Town's made up of those that take, not those that give, but there is one man who will join us. Name's Sinclair, owns the stables. Fine blacksmith."

"We met him," Snake said. "Seemed to be a straight talker." Snake spent the next several minutes telling Big Al how it came to be that they rode into town with Benjamin Franklyn Cruikshank.

"That man will never outright lie to you but never ever put the least trust in him. He's the kind would sell his mother if he needed a dime or two." Big Al told a couple of stories about Cruikshank and Snake told about the big fight with Pappy Jordan's gang.

"I've always had it in the back of my mind that old Ben was behind a lot of the robberies and murders on this long trail." Big Al said. "Some of those people you met may have been set up by old Ben."

Camp was made, fire lit, and venison was roasting just as the sun went down. "We're a short ride from Calico," Al said. "Maybe two hours out. Desert Jack don't have control over his gang, doesn't even try. Most likely they'll be drunk about now and worthless in the morning."

"Sounds like we need to be at the gates before sunrise, Al," Snake said. He looked at Dog-man who nodded right away. "We had a good meal. Now we can sleep for a couple of hours and ride off while it's still dark. You know your way around that little village, so you'll have to lead us in."

"I will. We'll let Good Inyan and Asshole be on their own. They'll search out the Mojave, we'll search out Desert Jack. We'll ride straight for Sinclair's stables, use that for our headquarters if it's still standing. Those boys that rode in talked about Calico burning, but I think that was coward talk."

"Is Asshole going to be able to fight? Broken ribs and bruises everywhere. Man's tough, but even so," Dog-man said.

"That man would fight a Mojave if he had two arrows in his heart and a knife in his back," Big Al laughed. "After being abducted by them and physically abused too, he's just shy of being a psychopath right now. He'll put up one hell of a fight."

Snake had everyone up well before the first graying of the sky and on the road to Calico. "You have a great hatred for this Desert Jack, Big Al. Something personal?" Snake asked.

"Might say that," he allowed. "Me and my brother and our wives come up from Mexico two years ago, run into the man trying to make the stage stop, and hired on. We built most of those buildings. Pete Huntington owns all of that. He was a Mormon, hardest working fool I ever run into.

"Well, Desert Jack was on one of his rampages and came through what Pete called Mormon Station. That's when Good Inyan got his name. He's one of the meanest fighters I've ever run into. Desert Jack's gang overran us and stole the women. I had a broken leg, brother Sammy was dead, and Desert Jack mocked us as he rode out."

Snake could see the anger building in Big Al as he told the story, wished he hadn't asked. "I shouldn'ta asked, Al. I'm sorry," he said.

"No, it needs to be told, Snake. I chased that bastard for three weeks before catching up. Me and two others rode hard into their camp shooting everything that moved. Jack and a few of his gang got away but what I found tore my heart apart. My wife and Sammy's were tied to posts and dead, their bodies mutilated. I vowed at that moment I would kill Desert Jack. Don't get in my way when we get to Calico, Snake."

Snake looked at the man with new eyes, so to speak. He had been married, obviously loved his wife, and lost her in the most horrible way. *What if I had stayed with April and the children and the Apache had abducted her? My God, what would I do?* He was glad they were riding in mostly dark and no one could see his face. The idea of losing someone precious and then discovering the mutilated body almost made the scrawny Texan sick to his stomach.

"I'll stand back to back with you, Big All. By God, I will," Snake said.

"No sign of anyone guarding the main street coming in," Dog-man said. He and Asshole were leading the group. They didn't draw a peek as he led them to Sinclair's stables, which were still standing and in good shape. "I think those boys were wrong about burning the town."

It was the quiet that had Snake coiled and ready. *Is most of the town dead? Sunrise in a little village like this is a busy time and there ain't a soul out. Don't even see smoke from the chimneys.* "Best be ready for something, Dog. Too quiet for my blood."

"They're either dead or gone, Snake. Ain't a case of sleeping in or settin' up an attack on us. They ain't anyone in those building you're lookin' at." Sinclair said as he walked from his big barn. "G'mornin' to you, Big Al. Here to whup on Desert Jack are you?"

"Morning, Manuel," Big Al said. "That's the plan. Your men run out on you? Figured."

"Most are gone, rest are drunk. Boys are moving the horses. Desert Jack is taking the place apart one building at a time. Killing anyone who resists. Town's got no fight left."

"Why you still here?" Snake asked. "Seems to me you got a lot to lose by staying."

"You boys are standing on about four hundred pounds of dynamite I've got buried in a maze of trenches all around the stables. I've been moving the animals quietly every morning over a few miles where I'm plannin' on the new community. This place is sure to burn."

"What's with the dynamite?" Snake looked down at his feet, saw the outlines of trenches in the early morning light. *Best not be stompin' my feet about now.*

"When Desert Jack and his murdering Mojaves get here, I'm gonna have the fuse lit and run like hell," Sinclair laughed.

"Where might we find this fool?" Big Al asked.

"Probably in bed with Brenda-Eve Pollock over at Calico Eats," Manuel said. "He took to her like a dog to a bone. A couple of my boys will be back shortly if you want to wait for them. They're itchin' for a fight and I've been holding them off. The Indians are scattered around town, still passed out from liquor."

"Tell your boys to catch up with us, Manny. We're going after Desert Jack right now," Al said. He motioned for Asshole and Good Inyan to go look for trouble, and checked his rifle. "Been waitin a long time for this."

"Those boys will find us," Sinclair said. "I'm with you."

11

THE CALICO EATS BUILDING, like most in Calico, was a stand alone affair with narrow spaces between it and its neighbors. Construction was simple board and batting, and the wood was desert dry. The diner and its kitchen faced Main Street and where Brenda-Eve Pollock lived faced Mojave Avenue. Both ends had covered wooden walkways.

"Best bet I think is for you and Dog-man to move in from the diner side of the building and Sinclair and I will attack from the back," Big Al said.

Snake looked to Dog-man, then to Sinclair before talking. "If they be in the house end of the building how easy is it to make their way to and through the diner? Splittin' us up like that ain't to my liking. If you and Sinclair attacked from front and Dog and I from each side, we'd concentrate our efforts on where that fool probably is."

"I like his thinking," Manuel Sinclair said.

"So do I," Big Al said.

"Well," Dog-man said, "Snake has a good plan but we

don't want to kill that old hag in the process. We got to get him separated from her some way."

The four of them paced around the barn for a couple of moments before Snake thought he had the answer. "You and Sinclair stay in the shadows across Mojave Avenue from the house and I'll stay near the south side window, and Dog will go to the café door and bang on it. Hopefully it will be the woman who answers."

"What then?" Al asked.

"Dog will grab her and we can start shooting. O'course if it's Desert Jack, well, Dog-man can take him out right then."

"Clumsy," Manny Sinclair said. "Why not just throw a torch through the diner window? Desert Jack won't give a hoot if the building burns and will just get out while Mrs. Pollock will try to save her business."

"Best plan," Snake said. "Stay wide front and back when I break a window and throw the torch in. I'll make as much noise as I can doing that, too. It's really nice when a plan comes together. Couldn't have thought of a better one myself."

There were chuckles all the way around and Dog-man just shook his head. "I think next time we would be better off just doing something. Wasted half the morning working on a plan."

It took just a few minutes to build a good torch and move into position. Big Al was across Mojave Avenue and slightly to the north and Sinclair to the south of the building. Dog-man was on the front porch of Rupert's store, across Main Street from the diner. Snake got a high sign from Dog-man and Sinclair, lit the torch and walked up onto the porch, ready to break a window and toss the torch.

Shots rang out from the second floor of Rupert's and

from the second floor of the Calico Hotel, next door to Rupert's. Snake broke the window, flung the torch inside, and dove for cover behind a horse trough along the front of the porch. *I said I wanted to make a lot of noise. Guess I did that. Damn.* Bullets were flying everywhere as if the shooters couldn't really see their target.

Snake was in a terrible position, trapped behind the trough with bullets kicking up water, splintering wood, and throwing dirt in every direction and had his back to the diner's front door where Desert Jack might come flying through at any moment.

Were these shooters part of Desert Jack's gang of Mojave or were these local townspeople finally getting enough courage to fight back? If they were gang members, Desert Jack would surely have the upper hand if he came through that door. But if they were locals, it wouldn't be right to kill them.

This is what I call a pickle, Snake chuckled. He saw fire belching from inside the diner, thought of the greasy walls and tables flaring up and had to laugh. He could hear people running inside, and got as close to the trough as he could. Rifle bullets continued pounding the water trough, it leaked enough that Snake was sprawled in a puddle. *Whoever comes through that door is gonna die. I don't care if it's that old hag or not.*

Gunfire erupted from the north alleyway followed just seconds later by gunfire from the south side. Big Al was on the north and Manny Sinclair was on the south. "Quit shooting, Rupert," Sinclair yelled out. "It's Sinclair."

His yell was answered by three quick shots in his direction. *Well, there's my answer." That's Jack's gang members in those upstairs windows.* Snake tried to squirm into a better firing position and yelled at Dog-man too. "Try to spot one of those bastards, Dog. I'm trapped."

Dog-man could see both Big Al and Manny Sinclair and got their attention, motioned for them to do some quick shooting, and when they did, he ran across the street and got behind a delivery wagon. The Mojave doing the shooting weren't aiming at anything in particular, just shooting and Dog-man waited until one stuck his head up and killed him.

"I wonder how many are up there?" Dog-man murmured. He looked over to where Snake was and saw the man bracing and turned toward the café door. Someone inside was desperately trying to get out. Whoever was bashing the door into splinters didn't have the key, and that, Snake hoped, would be Desert Jack.

"Come on you murdering bastard, come on out here. I got a whole load of hot lead waiting for you. Come on out." He was screaming, holding his rifle so hard his fingers hurt. Shots from Big Al, Manny, and Dog-man had the upstairs shooters covering themselves, and Snake stood up, dripping mud, took two steps toward the front door and opened fire. One, two, three shots, jacked in one at a time, broke whatever lock held the door, and killed or wounded whoever was on the other side.

He jerked what was left of the door open, standing slightly to the side, stepped inside and saw Mrs. Pollock's dead body sprawled across the floor. Most of the diner was fully involved from the torch, and Snake stepped back out and onto the porch, motioned for Dog-man, and ran for the alleyway. Dog-man ran down the south side, and Snake, Big Al, and Manny Sinclair ran down the north alley.

"He's got to be on the run," Snake yelled when he found the door wide open. "Where would he go?" *So that's what happens when you get to thinking about shooting something and forget the man you're after might get out an unguarded door,* Snake thought, racing onto Mojave Avenue.

Sinclair pointed back toward the main street. "The hotel has a saloon, stairs to the rooms lead out from there. Those are his men upstairs doing the shooting."

"Is there a back door? That's how he got out of here."

Sinclair nodded and Snake took off at a hard run across the street. Shots rang out and dust flew, but none of the bullets found their mark as Snake ran down an alley and into the street behind the hotel. *Gotta quit doin' things like that,* and he saw the back door still shut and took up a position across the back street where he was protected from shots coming from upstairs rooms, and the saloon doorway. *Kinda fits the rest of the day, I guess. Here I am hiding behind the outhouse.*

12

DOG-MAN WATCHED as Snake made it across safely and turned his attention to Rupert's building. There were two windows on the second floor overlooking the main street. Sinclair was closest and Dog-man yelled at him. "Would Rupert invite those Indians in or was he killed?"

"I'd guess the second, Dog-man. He ain't got a wife or kids. It's just him so they probably killed him. Got plenty of guns and ammunition," Manny chuckled.

"And dynamite," Dog-man said. "Where does he store that dynamite? Might want to toss a torch that-a-way."

Sinclair laughed right out. "Keeps it, blasting caps, and fuse in a locked room behind the counter."

Dog-man built a torch and had it lit, motioned for Manny Sinclair to give him some cover fire and ran across the street, kicked in the front door, saw the locked door to the explosives closet, and threw the torch at the door. *I better run faster than I've ever run,* he thought racing out of the building. Bullets chewed up Main Street dust as he raced across.

"Get back, get back," he yelled dodging around the

wagon he hid behind earlier and racing down the alley to get behind the inferno once called Calico Eats. It took the fire just moments to eat its way through the desert dry wooden door and when it found a keg of black powder, that in turn found the cases of dynamite, blasting caps, and burn fuse, the building exploded in every direction. A giant orange blossom at its heart sent pieces of Rupert's Mercantile to the four points of the compass and beyond.

Snake, behind the Calico Hotel, but right next door to Rupert's, was lifted bodily from his perch and thrown fifty feet to land up against a shed. The blast's concussion was such that he couldn't hear anything, had a hard time focusing, and found the hair on his face and head had been partially burned off.

"Dayam." He coughed it out and had to say it again. "Cain't hear myself talk," he said. "Hey," he yelled, digging his fingers in his ears, but not hearing a sound. *Gotta get squared around here. Damn.* Pieces of Rupert's building were still falling from the sky, most on fire, and Snake found what was left of a small shed close to the Calico Hotel and slipped inside. He could see the back door of the hotel and took up his watch again.

The blast was such that besides Rupert's building, the hotel was damaged and on fire north of Ruperts, and the building to the south was totally destroyed. The Calico Eats building, already fully engulfed in flames was leveled by the blast and Dog-man found himself flat on his face clear back on Mojave Avenue.

Big Al Barrington helped Manny Sinclair to his feet after the two were rolled down the street. Flaming debris was falling everywhere, lighting other buildings on fire, and it was Big Al who spotted half a dozen

Mojave trying to fight their way through the remains of the hotel.

"Here they come," he yelled, turning quickly to them, rifle at his shoulder. Dog-man was on his feet racing to the sound of gunfire, Sinclair was firing as fast as he could lever rounds, and five Indians lay bleeding or dead.

"Any more?" Big Al asked. He looked around at the rubble. "Snake. Where's Snake?" Manny pointed and said, "He was running behind the hotel last I saw him. Let's go." They heard screams and moans coming from what was left of the hotel as they fought their way through to the back of the building.

"Gunfire," Big Al hollered. He was leading them through burning wreckage when rifle and sidearm fire was heard. When they reached the back of the hotel they found Snake with a smoking rifle stalking toward a wounded Indian.

"Where's Desert Jack?" Big Al yelled. Snake motioned that he couldn't hear, and Big Al headed toward where the back door should have been. "Think he's still inside?" Snake just shook his head.

"If he is he'll be coming out fast. That building's about to collapse," Sinclair said. He turned quickly to the outhouse and saw it was leveled and laughed. "I thought he might be in there." He looked around. "Where's Dog-man?"

"He stayed out front in case some others tried to escape," Big Al said. "Are these your boys coming this way?" He pointed at three men walking toward them.

"Yes," Manny said and waved at them. "Probably sitting at the barn wondering where I was when the blast went off." He waved to hurry them along. "Somebody needs to be with Dog-man just in case there's a breakout."

Snake's hearing must have returned as he said, "I'm on my way." The ringing in his ears was loud, penetrating, and hurt when he yelled out Dog-man's name. As he made the turn through flaming debris toward what was the front of the hotel, he spotted Dog-man bringing his rifle to his shoulder. Snake took a quick look at where he was aiming and saw three Indians and Desert Jack racing out of the burning hulk.

Two rifles barked twice each and four of the group fell to the ground, but the white man in buckskins wasn't one of them. Desert Jack raced across the street, firing his revolver as he ran, and jumped on a horse, tethered but terrified. It was a hell of a bucking show that horse put on. Desert Jack stayed on the bronc's back, and actually got the horse running for the great open desert just a couple of blocks away.

One of Sinclair's boys, almost as big and heavy as Big Al, came around the side of the hotel at a full run and leaped right at Desert Jack, knocking the outlaw to the dirt. Jack had his knife out, whipping it at the boy's face when Big Al Barrington came up and put two pistol shots to the man's head.

Desert Jack's reign as the bad man of the Mojave Desert was over. Big Al's campaign to kill the bad man was over, and most of Calico was now on fire. Sinclair led the group back to the stables, got a pot of coffee boiling and brought out an earthen jug of whiskey. "A lot of dead people out there," he muttered. "Gonna need burying real quick."

"What we need, Papa, is to get that dynamite dug up before that fire gets over here." Wayne Sinclair, all six feet and two hundred pounds of him said.

Manny Sinclair jumped up. "Almost forget about that. Boys, heave to."

Good Inyan walked into the barn, helping the limping and hurting Asshole. "Mojave dead," Asshole said, sitting down in the dirt. "We go home now, for short time. Be back later," and Good Inyan helped him to his feet and to his horse. No waving, no shaking hands, the two simply rode off toward the mountains to the north.

"Best kinds of friends to have," Dog-man mumbled. "I think it's time for us to ride off, Snake."

"Like to do that, Dog, but Big Al needs some help with that stage stop of his and they ain't nobody around but us." *Now I've done it. We coulda just rode off, not a care in the world, but, oh no, I gotta open my yapper. Next we'll be rebuilding Calico.*

BIG AL OFFERED the boys one of the small cabins at the stage stop but they refused immediately. "Ain't slept inside a building for a long time, Al. Cain't tell north from south, up from down inside a building. We'll just make camp out by those trees yonder," Snake said. Dog-man nodded as the small group rode into the way station.

Snake looked around and thought, there's nothing more forlorn than a village left alone, empty, filled with dirt and debris. "Where's the life? This place needs people, Big Al," Snake said. "That open door there, just swinging back and forth in the breeze should be shut. Some of those who lived here just walked out, didn't they?"

"Fraid so, Snake. It's just me, now. The men who

worked the stables left first off. Fools, that's what they were."

Some people called the stop, about half way between Lane's crossing and Calico, Fish Ponds, but the builder and owner, Huntington, called it Mormon Station. Big Al needed help to clean the place up. The stage would be running again, as soon as the word spread that Desert Jack was no more a threat to traffic.

"We'll have travelers again, coaches coming on a regular schedule, and I need some help until people know it's safe to live here." Big Al was putting on a good speech. "Mr. Huntington can pay you a dollar a day and feed you too, if you'll stay for a while. I sure would like that."

"We'll stay a week, Al, but that's all. Gotta make it to the ocean. Just gotta," Snake said, looking to Dog-man to back him up.

"Yup," Dog-man said. "But just a week. Let's set up our camp."

It didn't take but a few minutes to get a lean-to set up, a fire pit dug, and wood stacked. "I shouldn't have said what I did, Dog. If you're angry with me, spit it out."

"Not angry, Snake. That's just the kind of people we are, have been, and will always be. Big Al needs our help, but just for the week. Ain't no such thing as winter around here so we aren't losing anything by staying."

Snake stood there shaking his head, a little boy's grin spread across his rugged face. *I think he's right. Just the kind of people we are. Probably why we cain't never settle down. Had a chance with that woman and those kids, but I know in my heart it wouldn't have lasted a year. He says he wants a ranch and cows, and he might even try, but it won't last. That road out yonder has what both of us need. Open air.*

He just reached out and whopped Dog-man across the shoulders, smiled at him, and started talking.

"If this is half way between Calico and Lane's Crossing, we must be close to that ocean we want to see. We'll use this week to get as much information as we can from Big Al." Snake looked around at the way station and shook his head. "One man with a bunch of renegade Indians closed this place. These desert people don't seem to have much spine, Dog."

"I think it's the hangers-on, Snake. The real desert people are the Big Al's and Sinclair's. I wonder if Benjamin Franklyn Cruikshank survived the Calico event?" He lit the fire and started to put a pot of coffee together. "Something else bothering me, Snake. If this is a way station for a stage line, where are the horses?"

"Been thinking on that since we first got here but never asked. Suppose Big Al was rustled? Not likely. We got to think about food, too. Ain't been in one spot for a week in a long time, old man."

They were racked back against a fallen log drinking coffee when Big Al walked up. "We was just talking about you," Snake said. "Pour a cup and set a spell."

"Glad to," he said. "First thing we got to do is try to find the station's horses. A stage show up and we ain't got a change for them, old Mr. Huntington will be out of business. You boys good at tracking? There's twelve horses out there somewhere. Damn fools left the gates open when they ran off, afraid of Desert Jack."

Snake was shaking his head when he looked over at Dog-man, doing the same thing. "We'll find 'em," Snake said. "Every last one of 'em."

13

"THEY KIND OF MILLED AROUND some before they wandered off," Snake said. He and Dog-man were near the corrals looking at prints that were several days old. "No rain for some time," he said looking up a small ridge off to the north.

"What are you looking at?" They had followed the small herd of horses for a few miles knowing they were not being herded, just wandering, following what grass might be available.

"Don't know," Snake said. "Thought I saw something moving up there. Yeah, there it is again. See it? What is that?"

"Ain't a horse," Dog-man said. "Let's ride up that way. Horses are probably down here on the desert floor, though. Along this underground river, following the grass."

It was several miles to the bottom of the rocky ridge and Dog-man spotted the tracks first. "It's a person, Snake, wearing moccasins. Dragging something." They followed the tracks through the open desert and up into the rocky ridge. Whatever was being dragged left a good trail to follow. "Over that way," Dog-man said. "Nestled in those rocks, see?"

"Yup. Move off to your right, Dog, and I'll come in from the left. Cover me good cuz I think I see a rifle barrel, too." He dropped from his horse and stayed still for a long time, watching Dog-man move away, hoping whoever it was up in the rocks would watch the Dog-man as well.

He dropped down as low as he could and moved slowly, bush to cactus to bush, keeping a close eye on the rocks above. *Whoever that is ain't much keeping track of us. Watching Dog all the way. Another fifty feet, maybe a little more, and I can get a good shot at 'em.* He was on his belly worming his way along a slight depression in the desert floor, almost to the rocks where the person was.

Well, damn me, that's a woman and a dog. Snake was less than thirty feet from her hiding place when the dog came to full alert. Snake stood up, his rifle cocked and aimed at the woman. "Don't move, woman. I ain't here to kill you." The big cur dog was tethered to a small travoise growling and snarling, but tied off tight.

Snake waved to Dog-man to come on in and slowly approached the woman, keeping a close eye on her hands, just in case, and the dog, just in case. "Ain't here to hurt you," he said. "You hurt?" The dog was ready to rip Snake's throat out and the woman motioned, just a slight movement of one hand, and calmed him down.

"You're just a girl," Snake said as he moved close. "What are you doing out here, alone like this?"

She was sitting with her back against the rocks and pulled the blanket aside, showing a deep gash in her thigh. "My goodness," Snake said. "We better get that fixed and soon," He saw the festering puss, bright red skin around the wound and knew she was suffering and probably had a fever besides.

She ain't more that sixteen or so, alone with a dog and an Indian travoise? Don't make much sense to me. "Want to tell me your name? They call me Snake, and that big feller coming up the rocks is my partner, Dog-man."

"Louise." She had to fight to get it out and Snake could see in her eyes that she was close to passing out. *Clean her up and she'd be mighty pretty. Right now, a rag-a-muffin for sure. She's been alone for some time, I think. Ain't just a whole bunch of young girls dressed in buckskins running around in these parts.*

"Come on in, Dog. We got a injured little girl here. Watch the dog, he's mighty protective. Get your medicine kit out and bring some water, too." Snake knelt down and laid a gnarled hand across the girl's forehead. *Whew! Burning up. Green eyes, light hair, but dressed in buckskins. She said her name was Louise.* He moved aside and let Dog-man settle down next to the girl. He had a wet kerchief laid across her head, and started cleaning up the wound.

Louise whimpered slightly as he worked and Snake almost gasped. "That has to hurt, Louise. It's all right to cry out. Ain't nobody around to hear you except us deaf boys." She looked up at him, pain and fear showing in her eyes, but still managed a slight smile. "You're a tough one," he said.

"Better get a fire going, Snake. Might be here for a while. We ain't three miles from the station. Did you see a wagon anywhere around?"

"Yeah, but no horses, remember? Better do what you can here and think about moving her later." He gathered some sticks and built a fire. "Did bring the coffee pot so I can heat some water for you."

"Get that started and go back, hitch our mule to a wagon, and we'll get her back. Surely Big Al has harness there. That dog seems to know we're friends. How do they know?" He had the wound cleaned and shook his head looking at the ragged and nasty gash. He could see bone, it was that deep. "She was hit with something horrible, Snake."

Snake rode hard back to Mormon Station, got the mule, found harness near the barn and fitted it to the animal, backed old Jack into the forks, and made the connections secure. "Hope you drive like you lead, Jack," Snake said. He had to chuckle remembering how many times he'd put on real shows hooking un-broke horses to buggies and wagons. *I've made some good kindling in my time.* He tied his horse to the back of the small wagon, climbed into the seat, and snapped the reins. "Let's see what you got," he said.

Jack stepped right out, responded to the reins and the ride back to the rocky ridge was smooth and quiet. *Can't get these questions out of my head. What's a young girl doing alone in the desert, wounded, wearing buckskins and moccasins, and saying her name is Louise? Lordy, but I'm confused.*

It was a beautiful day in the great Mojave Desert, no wind, hot as hell itself, with a sky that seemed to have no end. The horizon was as blue as the sky and all but hidden in a heated haze. He drove the wagon as close to the rocks as he could and tied the mule off. "Brought an extra couple of jugs of water, Dog. How's she doing?"

"Sleeping right now. I got brave and unharnessed the dog and let him curl up next to her. He's careful, doesn't want to be touched by me but wants to be as close to her as he can get. Look at this," Dog-man said.

He moved her small pack over by the fire. "Smoked meat, roasted corn cakes, and this," he said, holding up a flint knife. "Sharp as a razor, too. She ain't no Indian but you'd never know it from all this."

"Heard about white children being abducted and made slaves by Indians. I don't think that's the case, though. Something else here." He was looking at the two pieces of wood the girl used to make her travoise. "These been around for a while, Dog. Can't imagine the story we're gonna hear when you make her well."

Dog-man chuckled and put another pot of water on to heat. "She's about as tough a girl as I've ever seen," Dog-man said. "She only cried out once as I cleaned the wound, and actually smiled at me once."

"Watch it now, Pard. Smilin' girls are more dangerous than any bad man I know."

"You've met your share," Dog-man laughed. He brought the pot of water to where Louise lay and pulled the blanket back. "Infection is clearing up nicely," he said. He dipped the kerchief in the hot water and did more cleaning, wiping away the infected skin and meat. "She's gonna be fine. Gonna have a scar to brag about, too. Get me some clean rags from my kit, will you?"

He wrapped the wound and pulled the blanket back over her leg. Louise opened her eyes and looked at the two men. "Thank you," she said.

"Can you tell us how you come to be all tore up like this?" Snake sat down in the dirt next to her. The dog looked at him but didn't growl and she ran her hand around his ears and down his back. "That's a big dog."

"Simon was my father's lion dog." She said it slowly and Snake saw tears running down her cheeks. She tried to look away, hide her crying, but not for long. "He won't be hunting lions anymore," she said. She ran her hand back and forth, wiped her nose, sniffled, and looked at Snake.

Most sorrowful eyes I've ever seen. Gonna be a horrible story. "Tell me how you come to be here."

"Pa's a hunting man, bear, deer, lions, wolves, anything with a good coat. Simon helps him hunt and I help him with the hides. Me and Simon were following a wolf pack and Pa was several hours behind us with the wagon when he run onto a swarm of some pretty mean Indians a few days back." Tears welled in her eyes and dribbled across deeply tanned cheeks. She wiped her nose again and looked away. "It's hard," she said.

"You got all the time you want, Louise," Snake said. He reached out and took her hand, got a welcome squeeze back and smiled at her. *Even caked with dirt this little one is something to look at. I don't want to hear the rest of this story but I know I'm gonna. Those eyes are as soft as the down from a goose.*

"You got burncd," she said. He ran his hand over his face, felt where the hair had been singed, and chuckled.

"You tell me your story, Louise, and I'll tell you mine. These Indians attack you and your father?"

"Attacked Pa, killed him, stole our mule, and burned the wagon. I saw the smoke from up in the hills and got back as quick as I could. It was horrible. Hurt my leg gettin' back." Snake could see the pain of her father's death written all over her pretty face as she tried to tell the whole story just as fast as she could talk.

"Take it easy, Louise. Slow down some," he said, giving her a full face smile.

She smiled back, took a big breath, and continued her story. "Trail along a deep ravine went out from under me and I fell off the edge and into some rocks that tore me open." She looked at Dog-man. "Thank you."

She caught her breath, gave Snake another devastating smile, and continued. "I've never been here but Pa talked about a man he called Big Al at Mormon Station. That's where I've been trying to get to. This is as far as I could get, though. Me and Simon climbed up into the rocks hoping they would give us protection if the Indians were still about."

"We're stayin' with Big Al at the stage station," Snake said. *She's just a child and has done what many a grown man couldn't do. How many miles has she got under her belt with a leg tore up like that? I better quit looking at those eyes, too. Hell, I'm worse than Dog-man.*

"Need to get you and Simon moved down there, get you all healed up. I'll carry you to the wagon, yonder, if Simon will let me."

Louise giggled and motioned for Simon that it was all right. Snake was as gentle as a long scrawny Texan can be lifting her up and carrying her down the steep slope and setting her down in the wagon. Simon stayed as close as he could, actually nudging Snake's legs a time or two, saw she was in the wagon, and sat down, wagging his bushy tail.

"Most of the coon dogs I've seen are long legged, short of hair, and long thin tails that'll whip you some. This guy looks like he belongs in deep snow country," Snake said.

"Yup," she said. "Me and Pa got him from a trader up near Green River in Wyoming country just after Ma died. That was two years ago." Snake saw more tears form, course down tanned cheeks and wanted to squeeze the girl tight.

"You've had a rough time of it so far in this thing we

call life. We'll get you as fixed up as we can. Get comfortable and I'll drive this old wagon nice and slow."

Her kit was in the wagon and Snake jumped up to
drive the rig back to the station. Dog-man rode along
one side and Simon patrolled the other for the ride back.

14

"SENT you boys out to wrangle some horses back and instead you bring in a pretty little girl. Might want to keep you boys around for a spell." Big Al Barrington was laughing and held the door open to the stage stop office. Snake had the girl in his arms and she had her arms wrapped around his neck. "Put her in the back where the cot is. I got a shelf full of medicines back there too. What happened.?"

"Might not have the best news about your horses, Al. Indians jumped her father and stole their mule. Your horses were moving in that direction when we found her. Soon as we make sure she's gonna be fine, we'll get back on our round-up," Snake said.

"Can't have that," Big Al muttered. "Gotta have those horses. Be terrible if them redskins got 'em. I'll take care of her. I really need those horses, boys. Sure as I'm Big Al a stage will come thundering in."

Snake gave him a long look and Al knew what it meant. "I can doctor her, Snake. She won't be the first and I'll take excellent care." His eyes pleaded with the boys to find those horses.

"We're on our way," Dog-man said. Louise reached out and kissed Snake on the cheek, squeezed her arms tight around his neck, and gave him a big smile. He reddened some as he eased her down on the cot. She pretended she couldn't let go of his neck and he had to pry her loose.

"We'll be back, pretty lady. Let Big Al doctor you up, and stay warm." *I gotta shut my mind off or I'm gonna be in deep trouble. Too damn young, too damn good lookin', and I think I like her too damn much.*

"Ain't fair," Dog-man said climbing into the saddle. "I fix her up and you get the hand holding and smiles."

"I'll let you find the next one, Dog. Make you feel better?"

Following the small herd of horses wasn't difficult. They were just wandering along the desert floor, moving from one patch of grass to the next. "Gotta be thinking about water," Snake said. "Horses seem to smell it way before we know it's around. Look for fresh trees way out and we might get lucky."

"If there is a spring there'll be grass, too." Dog-man said. They moved through the open desert with little difficulty until they came to the burned out wagon where Louise's father was killed. His burned body was under a small pile of rocks.

"She done her best," Dog-man said. "Leg all tore up, father's body in the hot sun, and she tried her best to build him a cairn. That's one mighty tough little girl, Snake. You take good care of her."

"Let's not start that kind of talk, Dog. Our horse tracks are mixed up with tracks from those Indians.

They got 'em, Dog and we gotta get 'em back. Gotta get those horses back or Big Al's out of business." He stopped quick and frowned. *There I go again, takin' on someone else's problems. I swear it's just something me and Dog do. Gotta quit. Gotta think of our problems once in a while.*

The obvious trail led north, toward some steep mountains and the boys followed along at a steady trot-walk-trot most of the day. The herd and Indians were following along the Mojave River. Although it was underground in this area, there were puddles, sometimes ponds, where it surfaced.

"Easy riding, plenty of water, sparse grass, and those red devils will go for many miles at a time, Dog. We're moving a lot faster than they are and it's time to start watching for trouble. Did Louise say how many there were?"

"Never saw them," Dog-man said. "They were long gone when she found her father. I think there's four, though. I've been watching their trail close. The station's horses are shod and the Indian's aren't. We got to get them before they get to those mountains, Snake. Got to."

"You're right about that. They'll have friends up there." They let their horses pick the speed of their trot and continued following the herd. It was getting late in the day when they saw the small cloud of dust a few miles in front of them.

"Now we're getting somewhere," Snake said. "Let's ease off, ride at a walk, not kick up our own dust."

"You working on a plan?" Dog-man chuckled.

"As a matter fact, Dog, I am. There's only four of them. We need to get as close as we can before dark if we're gonna attack them and get the herd back."

Dog-man chuckled. "We're gonna attack four men just as it gets dark? I do enjoy riding with you, Snake."

Dog-man continued the chuckling but had his eyes sweeping the desert in front of them, just in case, you understand.

"See that little rise off to their right? I'd put money that's where they'll camp. Let's circle out north some and come in from a different angle, like we're not following their tracks. They'll have eyes on their back track." Dog-man said.

Despite what so many believe, the desert is not a flat plate. There are dips and rises, upthrusts of rock, stands of native brush, even sand hills. Staying out of sight was the order of the day as Snake and Dog-man moved toward the hillocks where they believed the band of killers might be. Ride slow, don't kick up dust, stay in depressions, behind rises, and always moving, they made their way closer as the sun made its way to the horizon.

"Darkness is our friend tonight, Dog," Snake said. "See that stand of mesquite? It's less than a half mile from what looks like standing water. Those killers will be near that water." He dismounted and the two worked their way closer to where they hoped the Indians had made camp.

Sunset on the desert is either a long and lingering delight of colors working through a cloudy sky or it comes as fast as the blink of an eye. "Got dark quick tonight," Dog-man said.

"We're lucky, though, Dog. No clouds, but no moon either." Coyotes were crying their hearts out, wolves, way off in the distance had a better song going, and the boys quietly led their horses closer in.

"Look," Snake whispered, pointing. "Glare of a fire on them rocks out there. They don't care if someone's following or not." They found some strong brush, tied their horses off, and got as low as possible, creeping toward that glare.

Dog-man spotted the small herd being kept in a rope corral and pointed, not saying a word. Snake turned toward them, almost crawling through the rocks and sand. *One man there watching 'em.* The lone Indian was looking toward the fire, probably waiting for someone to bring him some food. The camp was a good two hundred feet from where the horses were. The corral bumped up against a stand of rock on one side and some scrawny trees on the other.

"Let me take him out, Dog and you keep close watch on the others. Don't want to spook the horses, either."

He ain't goin' anywhere, Snake. I'm going back and get our horses, then you take him out. We'll need our horses to move that lot out."

"Good, Dog. Good," Snake said. "Go now." Snake watched Dog-man for a moment and started crawling closer to the lone Indian. He saw someone throw more wood on the big camp fire, blood red sparks flew into the night sky, heard some laughter from the camp and continued moving. The guard was pacing around near a tree, looking out at the camp.

Gettin' hungry are ya? Already had your last meal, you just don't know that. The horses in the rope corral were moving about, more searching for grass than anything else. All of a sudden they stopped, raised their heads, and had those ears searching for something, twitching, stiff, and pointed straight up.

The guard came alive on the instant as well and Snake pulled his big knife out. *They've heard Dog bringing our horses.* Snake saw the Indian take his cue from the horses and started moving toward what they were trying to look at. The guard was moving toward Snake.

Snake moved less than three feet, had his feet under him but was hunched as low as he could get as the Indian slowly walked toward him. *Gotta make this quick and quiet. Any sound is gonna be heard by those three down there.* As the Indian passed, just inches from him, Snake leaped up, grabbed the Indian's hair, yanked his head back, and slashed the knife across the man's throat, slicing the wind pipe, effectively stopping any chance for yelling or screaming.

Snake eased the still twitching body to the desert floor and held him tight until he bled out. Dog-man quietly walked up with the horses and Snake motioned for him to follow, moved quickly to the rope corral and cut the rope.

Snake mounted his horse and screaming like the devil was chasing him, drove the small herd right through the Indian camp. He was lashing out with his rifle, ran his horse right though their baggage, smashed one man's head in, and kept riding at breakneck speed in the pitch dark. After a hard three mile run, he and Dog-man brought the horses down to a slow trot and kept moving on the trail they came in on.

It was a solid two hours before Snake was ready to bring the herd to a stop. They were along the bank of a small pond and he let them get a belly full of water. "They won't be chasing us, Dog. We got their ponies too. I think I see a couple of mule ears in the bunch, too, so Louise will get her mule back."

Snake was fired up, Dog-man liked to call it being riled, and it was going to be some time before he could relax. "I whopped that one fool so hard I thought I broke the rifle's stock and then my horse got his feet all tangled in those blankets. Knew I was going to take a header, Dog. Just knew it."

"It's dangerous when you get riled, Snake. I'm gonna make a pot of coffee. Use some of that energy to find some dry sticks for me." He gnawed on a chuck of smoked meat while he got a fire started and water boiling. It would be hours before sun-up, the Indians were miles behind them and Mormon Station was miles in front of them.

"Did you make a count?" Dog-man asked. "Big Al said he lost twelve horses. I think we got more than that."

Snake dropped an arm load of wood near the fire and chuckled. "We got the twelve station horses, Louise's mule, and five other horses. Ain't that what's called making a profit?"

Dog-man laughed and poured some coffee. "Grab the flask out of my saddlebags, Snake. this calls for a small celebration."

They warmed some jerky in their coffee, softened a biscuit or two as well, and were back in the saddle, driving the horses to Mormon Station through the bleak of the night. "Got a good trail to follow, might as well use it," Snake said. "Think what's left of that band will follow? They'd be on foot."

"More than likely they'll head back to their tribe and make up a party to come after us. We'll be safe getting back to Mormon Station. It's what comes after that I'd think about."

"You are a thinkin' man, Dog."

15

MID-DAY FOUND Big Al in a predicament. A stage coach filled with mail and five passengers, too, standing in front of the offices, with a driver and his messenger berating him unmercifully. "I tell you, we was hit by Indians and they stole the horses. I ain't got no horses. I got two good men out chasing those red varmints now, but that don't mean they're gonna be riding in here all victorious."

Almost on cue one of the passengers pointed out a cloud of dust less than half a mile out. Big Al had the slightest smile on his face. *Sumbitch. First they hunt for my horses and bring me an injured girl, and now they bring me more horses than I lost. Gotta keep those two around.*

"Like I said, Messenger, those are the men who were hunting my horses. Soon's they get here we'll pick out the best six and make the switch. You ain't lost a minute on your schedule, so far."

Getting the animals separated, in their proper corrals, the old hitch uncoupled and the new hitch coupled took well over an hour and was quite a show for the passengers. Some of the horses were rowdy, the mule insisted on being involved in everything, and the horses belonging to the Indians refused to cooperate at all.

"Everybody on board, now," Big Al yelled out. "Let's not cause a delay." He looked up at the driver when everyone was inside. "They're all yours, Patrick. Give 'em hell."

Patrick's "Hyah," carried out across the desert and the leaders were dancing in front of the wheelers. That carriage literally leaped out from the station to the cheers of those inside, hanging on tight. "Hyah," Patrick yelled time and again, moving at a high speed toward Lane's Crossing.

"That's where we should be going," Dog-man said.

"We promised him a week, Dog. We'll get there." The three men walked into the stage office and Big Al plopped down in his swivel chair behind the desk.

"Where'd them extra horses come from?" He asked.

"Figure they belong to the Indians that held the station's horses," Snake said. "Might bring a bunch of them savages down this way to reclaim them. Four men held the horses and I know I killed two, but they had to walk back to their tribe. Ain't gonna be all friendly like if they come this way."

"No, they won't and they won't get a friendly welcome either." Big Al pulled a jug from the bottom drawer of his desk. "Let's have a drink, boys. You two are something else. Got the station horses, five extra besides, a mule, and a pretty little girl, too."

He poured generous drinks in tin cups and settled back. "Louise is feeling much better. You did a fine job cleaning up that infection, Dog-man. I've got an herb compress on the wound now. She'll be up and walking in a couple of days."

"Don't got nothing left except that cantankerous old mule out there. Lost her mother and father. Just her, that dog, and a mule." Snake was shaking his head and took a long drink of whiskey. "What's to become of her?"

"She's one tough little woman," Dog-man said. "Gonna make somebody a fine woman if he's strong enough to keep up with her."

Big Al laughed. "Ain't gonna be me and that's the truth of the matter."

Snake got up and walked toward the back room. "Gonna say hello," he said. Dog-man had a broad smile across his face watching his partner go through the door.

SNAKE AND DOG-MAN spent the next day repairing damage to a few of the buildings in the little settlement, watching for dust out on the desert all the time. Snake would take a break more often than usual and would slip in to check on Louise.

"Think those devils will attack, Snake?"

"Don't know that much about them, Dog. They didn't steal the station's animals, remember. They killed Louise's father and stole the mule, but they simply ran across the station's horses and took them in. They would think we stole them, for sure." He chuckled thinking about it. "We being the thieves in this case."

"They would have a good argument," Dog-man said. "If they come to talk about it instead of attacking, Big Al will be on the short end. Don't know how he'd handle that. Got himself a short fuse, kind of like you. The two of you get riled quick."

They put their tools away and headed for the stage

stop office. "He needs to know about this," Snake said. "I don't get riled, Dog, I just don't like to be messed with."

"Hmmm." Dog-man mumbled something else as they walked. "You and Louise must have had quite a bit to talk about, Snake. Anything I might want to know about?"

"She's about as young as I can ever remember being, Dog. I asked her if she had thought about what was to come and she just looked at me for the longest minute. She has kin somewhere in Wyoming. Her father's sister, she said."

"She planning to make that ride? Whew me, that would be a tough one."

Snake had a far-off look on his face and didn't answer the question. "Her aunt and her husband have a big ranch along the Green River. That's where she got Simon, the dog. Raise cattle and sheep."

"You holding something back? Didn't ask about a ranch," Dog-man said.

"Louise said the rolling hills are covered in grass, there be plenty of water, and they ain't had an Indian problem for some time. She said the railroad comes right along the river."

"And she wants to go back?" Dog-man asked again. He had to chuckle watching Snake do everything he could not to answer the question. "You promise her something, did you?"

"No, not a promise, Dog. No, I wouldn't do that." Snake kicked up some dust, shoved his hands in his pockets, and wagged his head back and forth, ever so slow. "Well, just, aw, what the hell, Dog. She's too young, ain't gonna have the strength after her injury and all."

"You told her we'd be glad to take her to Wyoming, did you?" Dog-man stopped, right in the middle of the street, and looked Snake in the eye. "Well?"

"Guess that's probably what I did." He got the little ten-year-old boy's grin on his face. "Yeah, I said I'd talk to you about escortin' her back to Wyoming. Told her about the ocean and us looking to maybe get a ranch, too. Said she'd never seen the ocean either. Like us, Dog."

Dog-man was well aware that there was a considerable amount that Snake wasn't telling and that it would come out, little pieces at a time. "We'll talk more about that, Snake. We need to think about what them Indians are gonna do, what Big Al might do, and how it's gonna affect us."

"He's got that saloon open. Five men rode in this morning. Came in from Calico. Wanta guess who one of 'em is?"

"Don't have to, Snake. I'm looking at Benjamin Franklyn Cruikshank as we talk." Dog-man waved to the old miner standing in front of the Stage-Stop Saloon, puffing on his pipe. "Wonder what kind of tall tales he'll have to tell?"

"Wonder who those men are with him? Got mean looks on their faces when they rode in. Old Cruikshank might be in trouble again." Snake started walking toward the office instead of the saloon. "Need to talk to Big Al before we see Ben. He might know something."

"If those Indians come to town might be a good thing to have some extra guns, though," Dog-man said. Snake nodded as he stepped up on the boardwalk in front of the office.

16

"MIGHT HAVE A LITTLE PROBLEM, BOYS," Big Al said when Snake and Dog-man walked into the office. The day was a hot one and Al had both windows and the door open hoping for a wandering breeze to blow by. "Your friend Ben Cruikshank showed up with some unsavory friends. Something about you selling horses that belonged to their friends. Do you know what they're talking about?"

"Sure do," Snake said. "Sold 'em to Manny Sinclair in Calico. He mentioned it to you, I think. Jumped by some rude men who were gonna take what we had."

"Yeah, I remember now. Well, those four with Cruikshank say you stole them horses, killed their friends, and they come to collect, they said."

"Only thing they're gonna collect from me is a forty-five slug or two," Snake said. "I ain't a horse thief. I ain't no outlaw and those boys are gonna find out that I ain't a liar either." Blood was nearing the boiling point and Dog-man could see the signs as if written out for him.

"Ben knows the truth." Dog-man said.

"Ben don't know the truth about his mine, Dog."

Snake was getting riled fast. One thing that he couldn't stand was someone thinking or saying he was an outlaw. "He can't tell the truth even if he knows it's the truth. No, he led them here to get some kind of ree-ward. You can bet on that. Sorry we ever ran into him even if he did put us on the right trail."

Dog-man needed to change the subject or Snake might just start shootin'. "Watched for them Indians all day, Al. Wondering now if they will show up. You've dealt with that band. What do you know about them?"

"Good Inyan and Asshole are from that band, boys," Big Al said. He was shaking his head as if he wanted to say more. Dog-man took a quick look at Snake and Al continued. "Fine fighters and good people. Hard to say how they'll take this. Don't expect an attack, though. Asshole's the smarter of those two and they'll arrive wanting to talk and this group with Cruikshank might get in the way."

"How do you figure that?"

"Just like Cruikshank, they hate all Indians, will probably want to shoot first and talk later over celebration drinks."

"Damn," Snake said remembering how the old miner started shooting even after he was told not to. "Same types, eh? And you say Ben brought them here to talk to us about their friend's horses? Another pickle that old fool's got us in, Dog. Well, ain't no sense chewin' on it in here, let's go have a cold beer and get it over with."

"I'll go with you," Big Al said. "Don't like the odds." Snake just chuckled some as he led the group out the door.

Benjamin Franklyn Cruikshank was still sittin' near the open door of the saloon when the three made the short walk. "Ben," Snake said. "Understand you brought us a little problem. Why?"

"Didn't know what these men wanted to talk to you about. Just said they wanted to find you. Just bein' friendly, Snake," Ben said. "Heard what you did in Calico. Did you have to kill that woman?"

Dog-man saw Snake tighten up like a diamond back rattler and said, "As a matter of fact, yes we did, Ben. Glad you were there to help put a stop to Desert Jack's rampage. Best stay out of our way, old man. I warned you about gettin' Snake riled." He looked at Snake, over to Al, and made for the open door.

"He's proddin', Dog," Snake said.

Dog-man didn't say a word just walked into the dark interior of the saloon. Windows were clouded over with years of built up tobacco smoke, dust, and dirt and no one had lit the oil lamps hung about. Big Al called it the saloon, it was where stage passengers were brought in for cool drinks while the horses were changed out. There was a bar for the men to stand near and tables for ladies.

"Yup, cold beer time, boys. Been a long day a-fixin' things around this old town." Dog-man was putting on the kind of show that was normally Snake's doing. "I'll even do the pourin' Big Al." He strode past the four strangers lined up at the bar, went behind the long plank, and got some mugs down. It was an excellent move that Snake saw instantly as he moved toward the middle of the narrow room. This placed Dog-man, Snake, and Big Al in a triangle with the four strangers in the center.

"That's mighty nice of you, Dog. Think I'll have a whiskey instead of a beer, thank you."

The quick moves by Dog-man and Snake registered with Big Al, and he tried to hold in a smile. "Beer would be fine with me, Dog-man." He looked at the four men, took a quick look at the open door and saw Ben standing there. Snake saw that too, saw that Ben had a rifle in hand, too.

"You boys here on business or just passing through?" Al asked.

"Comin' for a couple of horse thieves and I think we found 'em. You filthy scum won't be killin' and stealin' in this country." He made a move for his side-arm and died with it still in leather. Snake put the second round into the heavy man next to the dead one. The air was thick with gun-smoke as Snake's still smoking side-arm held down on the other two standing quietly at the bar.

"Ain't never stole a horse, exceptin' a couple of days ago," Snake muttered thinking of the Indian raid. "Ain't gonna listen to a dried up old desert rat calling me a thief. You two want to carry this out, make your move or get out of my sight."

Dog-man saw Ben lifting his rifle and yelled out. Snake twisted around, fell to the floor as the bullet passed over his head, raised his pistol and shot Cruikshank dead.

Dog-man found the shot-gun Big Al kept behind the bar and pulled it up. "Three dead, two to go," he howled and pulled both hammers back. Big Al had his revolver aimed at one, Snake was aiming at another, and Dog-man had the two well covered.

"What'll it be, men?" Snake was moving the barrel of his pistol around from one to another. "Easy now, drop those guns and kick 'em away, grab your dead and drag 'em out of here. We got shovels a-plenty and those boys need to be buried right away. Too hot to let them just steam away."

Slowly, one at a time, the weapons hit the floor and

were kicked away. The two men had ugly looks on their faces and Snake kept waving his revolver at them, motioning them to get the bodies out. They were slow to move, despite the prodding, probably looking for a chance to attack. Dog-man came around the end of the bar to do more prodding while Big Al gathered the weapons. "We'll be taking names after we get these fine upstanding citizens underground," he said.

There was a lot of grumblin', gruntin' and groanin', and the dead gunmen and Cruikshank were buried with a bit of dignity. Snake had the remaining strangers sitting in the dirt, catching their breath. "Don't know what old Benjamin Franklyn Cruikshank might have told you about how we got those horses we sold to Sinclair, but I'm telling you now, we did not steal them."

He reached in his shirt pocket for a cigar and got it lit. "Don't give a hoot in hell whether you believe me. I think you do believe that I'll kill you if I have to. So will my partner there. Having to is up to you. Dog-man stripped your saddles of rifles and shotguns, so walk on back to your horses and ride out of here. Or," and he smiled, "do something stupid and rude and join your friends down there." He pointed at the two graves. "Git."

"We'll be comin' back with friends," one of them said.

"You'll get the same welcome your dead friends got," Snake growled. "Those horses I sold to Mr. Sinclair belonged to outlaws who tried to kill me and my partner. I've just killed your lying, stinking, cheating friends. I'll give you to the count of three to be on your horses and riding hard for parts unknown. One …"

The two saw Snake's hand gripping the handle of that dangerous chunk of iron he carried and jumped on their horses. spurs found meat and dust rose as the two high-tailed it out of Mormon Station. Dog-man chuckled some but saw Snake glaring after the pair. "Ease it off, Snake. It's over. Let's have a beer or two."

"WHAT DO YOU THINK, Al? Will they bring friends back for more?" Snake was standing at the bar sipping on a half full glass of whiskey. Dog-man and Al were drinking beer.

"You made a good point by not killing the pair, Snake. Horse thieves would have killed them, and they know it. I think it's over."

"Hope you're right," Dog-man said. "Don't like making enemies for no good cause."

Snake drained his glass. "Something bothering me about old Cruikshank, Dog. Don't it seem strange that every time we've had an encounter with thieves, he's showed up? The first two and there was Benjamin Franklyn Cruikshank. Then in the cave, sure enough here come old Ben. And, now, he leads 'em in. He ain't got no mine. He's got a gang of thieves, killers." Snake drained the glass of hot whiskey.

"Gonna go see Louise. Probably heard all that shooting and I got to tell her that you and Dog are not hurt. She'd be worried." Dog-man and Big Al were laughing as he walked out the door.

"He was right, Big Al, now that I think about it. Ben led the road agents right to us and then came to get his part of the split only to find that we killed his men. Sumbitch."

LOUISE WAS SITTING up in bed when Snake walked into the back of the stage office. "Feeling better? Got some color in your cheeks," he said.

"What happened? I was worried." She gave him a big smile and patted the edge of the bed inviting him to sit with her. "Dog-man must have fixed me up good. I'm hungry. Me and Pa always ate our biggest meal in the middle of the day, hiding our camp smoke that way."

"Me and Dog have done that a time or two. I've been amiss, Louise. Don't even know your last name." Snake had calmed down considerably, tension in his face, particularly around his eyes, was gone, and he smiled at the girl. "Don't even know how old you are."

"Pa always said I was kind of small for my age. He and Ma was married a year when I come along and he thinks they were married for nineteen or twenty years. That would make me either eighteen or nineteen. Pick one," she laughed. "Pa weren't very good with numbers but I do know that Ma's been gone two full years."

Snake didn't care that the numbers didn't add up as he looked deep into the girl's eyes and tried to picture the life she and her father lived. *Gotta be like me and Dog. Just travelin' around enjoying the country. They had to make some money, though. That's the difference. That mine of ours pays for our way and will for a long time.*

She was looking just as intently at Snake. "Pa was a preacher when we came out here from Missouri. Thought he could teach the Indians but they taught him. Everything we owned was in that wagon, Snake."

"Burned to the ground, Louise. Moving onto a ranch with your aunt and uncle would be a big change for you. Better give it a lot of thinkin' before you make up your mind." Snake's mind was racing remembering how he felt about that woman and her children, how close he came to giving up his way of life. He smiled at the girl and took her hand in his. "I almost gave up my wandering life a short time back. Still not sure I made the right decision. I don't think I'd a made two years stuck in one place."

Dog-man stuck his head in. "Got company coming, Snake."

17

"Looks like at least ten riders coming in," Big Al said when Snake came out of the building. Dust from the riders was hanging heavy in almost still air. "Probably a mile out. Definitely Indians,"

"You know these people, Big Al," Snake said. "What's our best chance? Assume the worst and just start shooting, or what?"

"That would not be our best move," Al said. "I think it's best to just let them ride in and we'll play by their rules. That doesn't mean we shouldn't be ready for just about anything. Stand well apart and somewhere that if all hell breaks loose you have some place to dive into or behind."

The riders, single file, were coming in at a walk sitting tall and proud. Dog-man couldn't help comparing their sitting of a horse and his partner's. Snake only sat tall and straight when he was in a fight, other than that it was slouch, all the way.

Snake slipped over to stand near the horse trough in front of the saloon, Dog-man took up a place near the door of the office, and Big Al Barrington was at the corral gate when the band of Paiutes rode into Mormon Station. They were led in by Good Inyan and Asshole.

"Ho! Big Al," Asshole called out. "We come to talk. Bad things been said. Ho! Snake, you and Dog-man talk with us about taking horses. Come, we talk." He jumped off his horse along with the others. They made a large circle in the dust of the middle of the street and sat down, leaving room for the three white men.

The horses were left to mill about, creating more dust. Snake nodded to Asshole and settled in. He thought he had a good relationship with the Paiute, had saved his life, had hunted with the man, and hoped it all meant something. *I knew he was strong but didn't realize he was a headman. This is most interesting. Indians don't always think the same way that I do, but I consider Asshole a good friend. They do have a point, though, as far as those horses go.*

Good Inyan spoke first, in Paiute. He spoke for at least five minutes, walking around the circle, pointing from time to time at Snake or Dog-man but also at one or two of the Indians squatting in the dirt. It was eloquent to watch, Snake thought.

I can almost understand what he's saying through his body motions, the look on his face, and the gestures he's making. What a grand display. I'm sure he's talking about how Dog and I helped he and Asshole, but also how we killed those men and stole those horses. This is a trial and we're the accused. Good Inyan finished and motioned for another of the band to come forward.

He was short and heavy, showed scars from many fights, and there was healing burns on his arms and legs. Snake knew the man had been at the camp when they took the horses. His speech wasn't as eloquent as Good Inyan's. In fact, it scared Snake. The man gestured with his war club, shook his fist in Dog-man's face, and showed the burn marks to Big Al.

A third Indian rose from the circle, paced around the group, stopped in front of Big Al and said something, then did the same in front of Dog-man. When he came to Snake he growled some strong words at him, walked away, and sat back down.

Asshole then spoke, this time in as good of English as he could. "Bad things said, Snake. You and Dog-man are my friends, helped me and Good Inyan, saved us, even. These men say you rode into their camp and stole their horses, even killed two other men. Bad things said. They want to kill you. I have told them about you and they will listen, but not to lies."

He then said the same things to the group in their own language. Asshole gestured for Snake to stand and speak and the long thin Texan unwound to almost tower over his friend. *What the hell am I gonna tell them that they don't already know? That we rode in, killed a couple and ran off with the horses? Damn.* Snake looked into the sad eyes of Asshole and nodded to him. He walked all the way around the circle, nodded to Good Inyan, and stepped to the center. *Guess I'l just tell 'em what happened and be ready to run like hell.*

"When you captured those horses running loose in the desert you weren't aware that they belonged to the stage station here. My partner and I were chasing those horses in order to return them here." He looked Asshole right in the eye and asked him to tell the group what he just said and he did that.

There was some grumbling from around the circle and Snake continued. "What you haven't been told is this. The group that found those horses had attacked a man and his wagon earlier, killed him, burned the wagon, and stole the mule. We didn't know that either. The man had a daughter and she's inside the building there, suffering from a bad wound to her leg."

Snake didn't mention that the wound did not come from the attack on her father, left that part out. "There is much we have to talk about since there were wrongs on both sides of this issue."

Asshole hadn't heard about the attack on the wagon and the killing of Louise's father. He got in a heated discussion with two of the Indians in the circle. The argument was loud and went on for several minutes. Asshole walked to Snake, still standing in the center of the circle. "You have never lied to me or Good Inyan, Snake, and now I have heard the truth from Rushing Waters. You, Dog-man, Big Al come sit in council with us."

The council consisted of Asshole, the man he argued with, and the angry Indian who shook his fist in Snake's face. They sat in a circle in the middle of the street and Asshole spoke first. "There have been wrongs by all sitting here, and they must be answered. Two Ducks was wrong to attack the wagon, kill the man, and take the mule.

"Snake, you and Dog-man were wrong to take horses and kill our men. It is my belief that you should give us back our horses and keep the station's horses. Everyone involved could have done better. Should have done better. We are better people than that, and, Snake, I know you are a better man than what took place. For our people, I'm sorry the man had to die."

Snake sat with a long solemn look on his face, was about to say something when Dog-man did. "Wrongs such as these can not be undone," he said. "But knowing they were wrong and vowing to not do them again is a good step forward." He looked at Big Al who nodded. "We accept your offer and vow to work with your clan to make for better relations."

Asshole interpreted the little speech, almost everyone smiled, and the gathering broke up. The man who shook his fist at Snake was not pleased but was alone in his feelings and the others moved him away from the group. Within a matter of minutes the Indians were mounted, had their horses separated and pulled from the station corral, and rode out of the little village.

"I can't speak for anyone but myself," Big Al said. "I want a glass of whiskey or maybe more." There was hearty laughter as the three walked into the saloon. "That could have gone bad in an instant. Interesting that I've always had it in the back of my mind that Asshole was more than he seemed when he was around the station."

"He's a head man for sure," Snake said. "Wouldn't surprise me that he hangs around to learn how our ways will affect his people. He understands respect and honesty. He's a good man to have on your side. The angry one might still cause trouble at some point but it won't be the entire band."

"You ain't talked this much in a month, Snake. Next thing you'll be wantin' to settle down somewhere," Dog-man joshed. Snake's face clouded over and Dog-man took in a deep breath. "Didn't mean that the way it came out, Pard."

"Caught me up, you did, Dog. You two enjoy your beer. I'm gonna take a little walk." Big Al started to say something and Dog-man cut him off.

"He's fine, Al. Just his way. He's a thinking man and sometimes he needs to be alone to do it."

MORMON STATION SAT ALMOST on top of the underground Mojave River and slightly removed from where it surfaced close by. The main east-west trail followed along the river offering water holes at almost regular intervals. The country was harsh, rocky, filled with desert plants that would stick you, cut you, or poison you, and most of the wildlife, too, didn't want you around.

Snake wandered off north into a rocky hillside covered in spiny brush. He kept a sharp eye out for snakes and other dangerous critters as he moved though the underbrush. *There's just something wrong with me and I got to get it fixed somehow. This girl needs help but I wonder just how much help it is she needs. She's been hunting lions with her dog for the skins, helping her father with his hide business.*

Does she really need help? Or is it me that needs the help? He had to chuckle as he made his way to the crest of a small hill. A red tail hawk flew high overhead with a raven giving it hell as it tried to hunt in the raven's territory. Snake watched a cottontail scamper away, knew the hawk was watching as well, and sat down on a rock.

She don't need our help. We can offer it and she might even accept it, but not because she needs it. Maybe it really is me that's looking for something and I don't know what I'm looking for. Dog talks about a ranch and I like working cattle and horses but not for years on end. I like wandering around in this old world, even for years on end.

So why am I having trouble with this little situation we're in? I'm in. Hell, Dog don't even know we're in one. Snake had to snicker at his mixed up thinking. *The thing is, Mr. Snake, sir, I want a family and I could have had one. Too scared to make the effort and now I regret it. So, am I replacing that dear lady and those little scamps with Louise? And poor little busted up Louise don't know it? Well, just damn me.*

It was at least two hours later when Snake walked into the little camp that he and Dog-man had near a seeping springs. "You and Al have a good visit?" He asked Dog-man and picked up the flask near his bedroll. "Think it's time we moved on, Dog. Got Big Al's work done around here, caused enough trouble with the local Indians, and you got a little girl all patched up."

"Must have been a good talk with yourself," Dog-man chuckled. "You're right, though. It's just a few days to Lane's Crossing. Let's shoot a deer tomorrow and smoke up the meat so we have some good eating on the way."

The two men spent the rest of the evening making plans for continuing their effort to reach the Pacific Ocean. "We've swam in cold lakes, Dog. They say the ocean is salty. Don't want to get a mouthful. What do we do about Louise?"

18

"THOUGHT YOU MIGHT ENJOY a little walk around, exercise that busted up leg of yours," Snake said. He, Dog-man, and Louise were slowly walking down the main street of Mormon Station. Mid-morning heat could be seen rising in waves from rocks and buildings. Her leg was healing fast and she didn't seem to have much pain as she walked.

Amazing how strong she is, walking like nothing happened. Her leg all torn up by those rocks and here she is walking down the street like she owns it. She says her dog hunts lions, her father was a hunter. I think she's the hunter. He was driving that wagon, she and the dog were hunting. She'd wear out most men I know. Snake couldn't keep her out of his mind, couldn't keep his eyes off her, either.

"You boys are pullin' out, aren't you? I can tell," she said. She gave a little laugh. "Papa always said I knew what he was going to say before he said it." She walked over to stand near a scrawny tree that almost offered some shade.

"And, you're worried about me." She kicked some

dust around, leaned up against the trunk of the tree, and gave each of them a smile. "I got my mule and my dog. Lost my rifle, knives, and all my skinnin' gear, but I got my strength and health. You don't need to worry about me."

This little waif is nineteen and tough as any hombre I know, Snake thought. He was looking into her eyes and she was just as intent looking back. "Made some plans, have you?" He asked. "We're heading for Lanes Crossing and then on to see the ocean. You'd be welcome to come along."

"I know, Snake. I know. A big part of me says I want to." She hesitated, looked down at her feet, looked up at the tree branches, and Snake saw tears running down her cheeks. "Papa said this might happen someday. I didn't know what he was talking about. Not sure I do even now that it's happening. I'm confused," she almost blubbered.

Aw, now what? Snake did something he hadn't done since telling that beautiful lady, April Theron, that he wouldn't be staying. He reached out with both arms and gathered Louise in close, holding her tight, feeling her sobs and she grabbed him tighter than he'd been held in years.

Dog-man watched all this, turned and quietly walked off to find a cold beer. "He's got a way with these women folk, I'll surely say that," he mumbled. "They look at me and smile, look at Snake and grab hold. Gotta change my approach," he chuckled.

Snake and Louise slowly slid down the trunk of the tree and were sitting in the dust. He had an arm around her waist and she had her arms around his neck. "I guess this is what Papa was talking about," she murmured. "I don't want to let go, Snake. Ain't never felt this way. Ain't never been this close to a man, ever."

Snake knew he had to say something, anything, and had no idea what to say. "We got to figure this out and quick," he muttered. "You ride west with us and it's gonna cause trouble. I ain't ready to settle down, Louise. I just ain't and it wouldn't be fair to lie to you about it."

"I don't think I'm ready to, either, but right now I sure do want to. Big Al says I can stay here, but I don't want that, either. Without guns, knives, and skinning and curing stuff I can't go back to hunting, either. I'm a good hunter, too." She had her arms wrapped tight around his neck and their faces slowly came together.

The kiss lingered for a long time and broke off just as slowly. "Don't think we'd best do that again," Snake said. "If you come with us we both have to know it isn't for life. It'll either bust up my partnership with Dog-man or it'll bust up our partnership. It can't work, Louise."

She was crying, softly, squeezing him as close to her as she could. "I think I know that," she said. "I've been alone for a long time, Snake. Even with Papa right there. I was alone hunting, alone skinning and curing, alone when he went to sell the hides. I can't go with you and you can't come with me."

She untangled her arms and sat up straight. "I'm going to work for Big Al until I've made enough money to get good guns, knives and equipment, and I'm going to hunt my way north to find my aunt. I might not be very big but I'm strong, smart, and know how to take care of myself."

Snake stood up, helped her to her feet, and wrapped his arms around her. They stood under the tree, rocking back and forth for several minutes. "You, Simon, and the mule going north and me and Dog-man going west. I want a wife and a family, Louise, and you would be my perfect wife, and I know I'd end up runnin' off from you."

"I never gave a minute's thought to having a husband or babies until I met you, but I just ain't ready for that. Just ain't, Snake."

They walked back to the stage office and she slipped inside. Snake walked into the saloon and found Dog-man and Big All at the bar drinking cold beer. "We leave out at dawn?" Snake asked.

"I think that would be best," Dog-man said. "Al tells me that Louise lost all her hunting gear, rifles and all. He's managed to acquire everything she would need but she doesn't have anything to pay him with. What do you think?"

"Let's go talk to her. She's ready to pull out too, except for not bein' able to. You know what I mean. She's got my head going in three different directions all at the same time."

———

LOUISE ACCEPTED the boy's offer, picked out a couple of good rifles, a shotgun, and a revolver, plenty of ammunition for all and some good knives. "Where did you come up with all this stuff, Big Al?" Dog-man asked. "That's a fine Winchester there."

"People comin' through, busted broke, got no money for food, a bed, or a ride on the stage. I make fair deals, just like I'm making now for Louise. She's gonna have to build her own racks for taking care of the skins and I don't have food to sell."

Dog-man had the pouch that held cash and that little black book that allowed them to go into banks and get more if they needed it. He handed over what Al wanted for all the merchandise. "Gonna miss you, Big Al but with the stages running on time you'll have a settlement going again real soon."

Snake spent a half hour saying goodbye to Louise and wasn't in a good mood trying to get their mule packed. "Not even close to sunrise," he grumbled. "Bout noon time. Gotta do this, gotta do that. Cain't just saddle up and ride off like we should have done."

The grousing continued as Dog-man walked up. "Get it all out, Pard. Rather not hear it on the trail."

"It's about done," Snake growled. "If we see people on the trail let's run 'em off fast. Ever since we met up with Benjamin Franklyn Cruikshank we've had one problem after another." He had the mule's lead rope and mounted his horse. "I bought that Winchester from Big Al. Gonna use it on the first person who comes to us with a problem."

Dog-man led off chuckling to himself. "Al says this main road will take us right to Lane's Crossing. Takes the stage two days, so we'll be a bit slower. Ain't in any hurry are we?"

The first day's travel was over ground they knew well. They had chased horses along part of the roadway, found the burnt out wagon that belonged to Louise's father, and made camp near where they had attacked the Indians.

"Got water, grass, and about a hunnert billion stars up there, Dog. Got a big moon for the coyotes to sing to, and fresh venison to roast, too. You still thinking about getting a ranch?"

"It's always in the back of my mind, Snake. Ain't something I have to do tomorrow. You thinking about Louise?"

"Yup." Snake had the fire going good, coffee boiling, and venison steaks sizzling in a pan. "Girl's gonna be in my mind for a long time. My mind ain't willing to let go of things, Dog. For a long time now I haven't been able to say April's name. April Theron, and now, being involved with Louise, I can." Snake started laughing right out.

"What's so damn funny?" Dog-man had to chuckle watching him.

"I'm sounding like them Mormons, Dog. I want April to be mine and I want Louise too. What is wrong with me? Glad we bought that jug from Al. Gonna need it, I think."

19

"COMPANY RIDIN' in, Snake." Dog-man pointed at the dust trail from a single rider about half a mile to their north. "Ain't on the main road. Coming in cross country and making a straight line for our smoke."

The sun was fighting its way through an early morning mist, breakfast fire was going, and coffee was almost ready. Snake pulled that new Winchester out and snuck off into the brush one way. Dog-man had his rifle and found some brush opposite. "Remember what I said about people bringing us trouble, Dog. I'll shoot him sure as hell."

The rider was coming in at a lope not caring whether he kicked up a heavy dust cloud, not seeming to care about being seen or not. "That looks a lot like an Indian, Dog." Snake called out. "But Indians don't go riding off at dawn and don't ride toward someone's smoky camp. He's looking for us, special like."

The lone rider slowed considerably as he got close to the camp and when he got within hailing distance, he pulled up and dismounted. He stood next to his horse and hollered out. "Ho, Snake. Ho, Dog-man. Need more talk. Pronto."

"Come on in, Asshole. What brings a headman of the Paiute to our camp?" Snake called it out. "Sun ain't really all the way up. Coffee's hot."

Asshole tied his horse off and came right up to the fire. "Good fire. Could see smoke for many miles out. I teach you someday. Bad trouble. Your friend in big trouble. Maybe come quick."

"Maybe if you slow down and tell us all about it, we will," Snake said. He poured the Paiute a cup of coffee and refilled his and Dog-man's. "Which friend and what kind of trouble."

Dog-man took the coffee from Snake and gave him a long look, right in the eye, almost said, "Don't shoot him." Snake caught the look and set the Winchester down, suggesting that Asshole sit, too.

"Your friend, pretty girl, leave Big Al yesterday, riding north with horse and mule. Rushing Water, he who kill her father, left camp to follow. Think bad things, Snake. You help."

Snake tightened up, scowled at Asshole, then Dog-man, then the fire. "Why not you help?" Snake asked, slipping more wood on the fire. Sunrise can be down-right cold on the desert and this morning proved it. Was the air cold or was it because of the news Asshole brought that sent chills through Snake's body? "Tell me more."

"Him take two men and set out to kill or capture girl. Blames her for you knowing about him kill father." Asshole's hands were flashing as he spoke his broken English and signed as well. "Bad trouble with clan. Must get back. All mixed up because of horse problem. You hurry. Go north from Big Al. You cut trail. Goodbye."

Asshole set the empty cup down, stood up and grabbed Snake's hand and shook it vigorously, walked to his horse and rode off. "Can't shoot a friend like that, Dog. We gotta go and now."

"No question, Snake."

They broke camp fast and left out north east, hoping to cut Louise's sign by late in the day. "Take the lead, Snake and ride out. I'll follow with the mule. Remember, Asshole said Rushing Water has two men with him."

SNAKE'S MIND wouldn't let him enjoy the long lonely ride across the rolling hills of the northern Mojave Desert. Large hills rose up, steep, barren rocks climbing into a cloudless sky to his north, the flatness of the desert when looking down on it was deceiving. *I must be out of my mind. I want that girl bad, I want a place to call my own, and even more, I want a passel of kids.*

His dreams the night before included Louise, included children. There were ranch houses shaded by huge cottonwood trees, and great stretches of grass being trampled by big red cows. *I've been a fool once. not twice, Mr. Snake. I won't be a fool again.*

He told himself over and over how tough Louise was. Cussed himself for not bringing her with them. "I'm gonna find that girl and I'm not gonna let go. Ever." He couldn't get the sight of the still burning wagon and dead father out of his head, and the more his mind worked, the angrier he got.

"Can't ride up on whatever I'm gonna ride up on angry. Best way to lose a fight is to go in blood angry. Got to think, got to be ready to be surprised. Got to know who these Paiutes are that I'm gonna fight.

Shoulda took the time to talk to Asshole about them." He caught himself talking right out, chuckled some and kept right on talking.

"I know that they take what it is they want, killin' whoever has it. I know that they blame Louise for losing the horses they stole from her father and they'll kill her without a thought. I know more about them than they know about me."

Snake watched the sun make its long arc across the sky and had a general idea where Mormon Station was compared to where he thought Louise should be. "I should cut her trail at any time if she's heading more north than anything. She should be looking for water, I'd think. I am."

Some of the hills he rode into towered above him, great escarpments rose up, almost vertical, The rock faces made the mountains look like fortresses, defensive castles, and he found signs of prospecting activity from time to time. There were turrets, high solid walls, and spires all colored in shades of orange, red, yellow, brown, and even a touch of green here and there.

"There," he said, loud enough for his horse to react some. "That's a shod hoof print or I ain't Snake."

He stepped down and walked along, looking at the prints. "She bought herself a horse somehow and is leading that mule of hers. She's going at a walk, following the natural terrain, which in this case almost looks like a trail." He built a small rock pile for Dog-man to see and followed the hoof prints. "Best find a place to hold up and wait for him. Don't want to ride in to a fight."

He spotted a ledge with an overhang where he and the horse could wait in the shade, left a marker for Dog-man, and made his way up. "I will see him, too," he muttered, putting together a small fire for coffee. He was stretched out on the rocky ledge with his first cup of coffee when he heard two distinct rifle shots, maybe half a mile to his north.

"Wanted that coffee, too," he said, grabbing the Winchester. He left the horse and made his way down to Louise's trail, left the rocks to tell Dog-man where the ledge was, and dog-trotted toward those rifle shots. What bothered him was, there were only the two.

Asshole said Rushing Water took two men with him and I'm running toward three men looking to kill a young girl. The first four hundred yards or so, through broken ground following the prints left by Louise were relatively easy, but then the girl's tracks turned abruptly up into a maze of huge rocky spires, ledges, cliffs, and ridges.

"Why?" He murmured. Looking around quickly he thought he may have found the answer. Hoof prints. *She spotted Rushing Water and made for the high country. If she's up there somewhere, where are the Paiutes?*

He was walking slow, eyes trying to see everything from his far left to his far right and as high as the top ridge of the mountain he was climbing. Another rifle shot, close, stopped Snake. It wasn't aimed at him, he knew that, but it came from just yards to his right. Snake got down on his hands and knees behind a cluster of brush and rock, another round was fired, but much farther up the slope.

He saw the puff of smoke from the second shot, got a good bead on where it was, and started to move back to his feet when several shots were fired, again from just a few yards in front of where he was tucked in.

Damn. If that first shot hadn't been fired I'd a walked right into that party. He was back on his elbows and knees, that new Winchester cradled in his arms, and moved slowly around the rocks, just inches at a time. He spotted Rushing Water but couldn't see his friends, and stayed still and quiet, hoping they would show themselves.

Nothing moved for several minutes and then a rock was knocked loose, many yards up the hillside, toward where Snake thought Louise was. *That's what those last shots were for, eh? Give somebody a chance to move forward?* Snake moved back behind the rocks, eased around to the other side and spotted an Indian moving very slowly, rock to rock, up the hillside.

I gotta move back from where Rushing Water is before I shoot that bastard up there. Wonder where the third one is? Snake crept along the ground, easing his way back from the Paiute's position and got under some brush where he could see toward Rushing Water and up at the Indian moving on Louise.

My first choice is to wait for Dog-man and I don't have time to do that. I gotta take that fool out now. No, my friend you ain't gettin' another foot closer to that gal. He knew there was a chambered round and eased the hammer back on the lever action rifle, took a long slow aim and squeezed the trigger, putting a heavy chunk of lead in the Indian's back. The man lay still, stretched out on the rocks, dead, and Snake moved as quietly as he could from the brush to a stand of rocks about five yards to his left, knowing that Rushing Water would be looking toward where he had been.

Snake caught a flash of movement down the hillside from the dead man and watched an Indian sight a rifle at the stand of brush he had just left. *You surprise me, Rushing Water. You're a coward at heart, eh? Send your men up the hill instead of leading them up the hill? You ain't no kind of leader and you're gonna die because of it.*

The Indian on the hillside fired twice into the brush and waved down to Rushing Water to do the same. Snake didn't fire on the man up the hill but waited for Rushing Water to make some kind of move. *Hope Dog wasn't too far behind me and can hear this gunfire. Come on you Paiute devil, make your move.*

The slightest scrape of leather on rock, just enough for a lizard to hear, and Snake knew Rushing Water was moving. He lay absolutely still, listening. Would the angry Indian come front or side? Or would the coward come at all? Maybe that scrape was Rushing Water rushing off. No, Snake knew the Indian was coming.

Seconds seemed like minutes as Snake tried to pick up some kind of movement, either by sight or sound. There, just off to his right, another scrape, and, *yes, that's a buckskin covered arm I see under that brush.*

The Winchester was eased into position followed by a quick aim, gentle squeeze, and the scream of a wounded man echoed through the rocky mountainside. Snake turned quickly, found the man up the hill, and put two fast rounds his way, one of which found its target.

Damn, didn't kill him. He's moved behind those rocks now. Snake took that moment to race forward and dive behind another stand of rocks. He was flat on the ground, took a look around the base of the rocks and saw his prey try to scramble down the hill to a better hiding place.

"You can't run with a busted up leg, buster," Snake muttered. The Indian was dragging one leg, crawling fast through a jumble of fallen rocks. Snake could see where he was trying to get, pulled the rifle up for a killing shot and watched the Indian wrench from the strike and roll down the hillside. In just a second he heard the crack of the rifle fired from well above the Indian.

"Good girl," Snake said, right out. He stood up and waved his rifle high over his head. "Hello Louise," he hollered up at her. He saw the waving rifle and started a long climb to her ledge. It was the sound of breaking branches behind him that saved his life.

Whirling around at the sound he just had time to swing the rifle at Rushing Water, knife in hand, coming at him. He knocked the arm aside but took the rush of the Indian, rolled with the wounded body, and fell into a thorny bush, rolling again.

Rushing Water was crying out in pain, but was fighting with every muscle he had left. The knife whipped back and forth, Snake fended it off as best he could, getting slashed in the arm twice. He wrenched away from the man, rolled again, drew his sidearm and fired, point blank into rushing Water's face.

With his left arm bleeding hard Snake ripped his shirt off and wrapped the wounded arm tight. "Damn. Got me good." He heard stones rattling down the mountain, jumped toward where he dropped the rifle, and tried to find who or what made the noise.

"Snake," Louise cried out. "Where are you? Snake." Louise and that big dog, Simon were making their way down the mountainside.

Snake got slowly to his feet and saw Louise coming, a rifle in one hand and a hatchet in the other. Snake was sure it was the most beautiful sight he'd ever seen. "I'm right here, girl. My God but you're beautiful." The dog hit him first, almost knocked him to the ground, long bushy tail whirling in circles with happiness.

She ran to him and flung her arms around his neck, planting a solid kiss that lasted even longer than their first one. "Don't never leave me again. Don't never." She was crying and laughing at the same time, and trying to kiss him too.

"Your arm," she wailed. "Got to get that fixed. Come on, I've got everything up there." She took his hand and started up the hill. "They almost got me, Snake. They were waiting for me, but I saw them first and got up the hill. I've never been so glad to see someone as when I looked down that mountain and saw you. Don't you never leave me again. Don't you never." She said it over and over as they made their way slowly up the steep hillside.

"If I live through this climb I won't never leave you, Louise. I'm bleeding hard, girl. Hope you got water up there."

"Plenty, big man. I've sewed up my daddy more than once, I can sew you up, too, but you might want a sip of whiskey when I do."

"Dog-man ain't too far behind me. He's got some."

They made the ledge and Louise got him laid out. "Get a fire going, then you can work on me." He was on his side, could see over the edge of the rock shelf, and spotted Dog-man leading their mule and his horse. "Dog-man's right down below. Wave him up before he starts shooting at us."

"He's already seen us and is leading the pack train up. Let's get started on that arm, mister. You ain't supposed to fend off a knife with your arm. You remember that, now."

Snake chuckled, reached out and pulled her down to him. "Ain't fendin' you off, neither," he said, giving her a long but soft kiss. It could have gone on some but they heard horses and heavy breathing from Dog-man and broke it off. "Bad timing," Snake muttered.

20

THE LEDGE they were on was some fifty feet or so below the razor back ridge of a hill, which then continued climbing another thousand feet or so. The mountain appeared, from a distance, to be laid out in layers, stacked unevenly upward. They had a good fire going as the sun made its final plunge into the misty west. "I'd say it's pow-wow time," Dog-man said. They ate venison roasted over hot coals, drank two pots of coffee, and evaded every opportunity to talk about tomorrow.

"Yup," is all Snake said. "You start." His arm was sewed back into place, hurt like hell, and he was still under the spell of half a bottle of whiskey. "Too tired and hurt to think right now."

"Well, that might be, but the way Asshole talked, we might have company by morning. He said the clan was upset with how we worked out the horse situation. Rushing Waters is out of the picture, but what about the rest of the tribe?"

"Ain't nothing we can do about it." Snake said. His eyes were half closed, he was slowly rubbing his fingers over the bandage holding his arm in place. "Even if they get all wild eyed crazy they can't be here before sunrise. Good Inyan and Asshole will get 'em straightened out. I'm goin' to sleep now."

Louise laid her bedroll out next to Snake's and crawled in, resting an arm on his back. "I'll have coffee before sunrise, Dog-man. Goodnight." Her eyes closed but the smile on her pretty face didn't go away.

Dog-man sat next to the fire looking at the two, stretched out on the rocks, like they had been a couple for ten years or more. *I may have just lost a partner. On the other hand, I may have gained one. I'm sure she'll be riding with us all the way to the ocean, if we survive a fight with the Paiutes.*

"Interesting," he mumbled, letting his thoughts carry on. *He was more in love with April Theron's children than he was with her. He's a gonner this time, though. This little bundle of fire has him wrapped, tied, and carrying a bow.* He had to smile thinking about it and wondering if he would ever come across someone like that for himself. *Best not to contemplate things like that.*

He sat by the fire for another hour, trying to understand his partner. He and Snake became partners on the trail through the Black Hills, which led them to Deadwood. The mining claim maps ordeal, getting run out of town, pretty much cemented the relationship, and finding, working, and gaining considerable wealth from their mine anchored it.

He wrapped a wool blanket around his shoulders, threw more wood on the fire, and fell asleep thinking about a ranch filled with big horned cows, tall grass, and more horses than a man could count in a day. It was tumbling rocks on the hillside below that woke him up.

The sun was blazing and there was no sign of Snake

or Louise. Dog-man grabbed his rifle, tried to get free of his blanket and came face-to-face with Good Inyan, who also carried a rifle. It was a short lived half second of tension before Good Inyan gave out with a big smile of hello.

"Whew," Dog-man let out. "Scared me there, feller. Good to see you. You alone?" He asked but knew that Good Inyan's command of English didn't exist. Dog-man got to his feet, shook hands with the big Paiute and walked to the edge of their lair. Snake, Louise, and three Indians were climbing the hill, talking with each step.

Dog-man threw some wood on the fire, found hot coffee in the pot and poured him a cup before the group got all the way up. "Looks like I slept through most of today," he muttered. It was Asshole and two companions who reached the ledge first, followed by Snake and Louise.

"Ho, Dog-man. Came to help. Too late. We go home now," Asshole said.

"Not yet," Snake said. "You have a story to tell."

"No trouble. The people understand now. I talk good, Good Inyan talk good. They understand Rushing Water wrong thinking Paiute."

"Must have been some pretty good words, eh Snake?" Dog-man laughed. "Better than ours last night. We never reached a single conclusion."

"Well, old friend, you slept through our discussion this morning," Snake said. "Let's get another pot of coffee boiling and see what today has to offer."

The Indians stayed around for the second pot of coffee and rode off after tending to Rushing Water's and his companions' remains. "Good people," Snake muttered. "Rode most of the night in case we needed help. Can't find friends like that in too many places." He settled down next to the fire, dropped some venison jerky into the remains of his coffee, and invited Dog-man and Louise to join him.

"Got some serious plannin' to take care of. Might as well eat something while we're doin' it," he said. "Me and Louise was talkin' when Asshole showed up. Seems she's been to this Lane's Crossing. They changed the name, though. Guess Big Al don't know that. Louise says it's called Pioneer Station and the road from it leads into a fertile valley they call San Bernardino. Ain't none of those names have come up in conversation, though, have they?"

"Nope," Dog-man said. "Go on. You got something to say." Dog-man remembered the conversation he held with himself the night before. Was this to be the end of their partnership? He looked at Louise and could understand why Snake wanted to be with her. *Man couldn't ask for a better partner but spending long nights with her is sure better than sleeping on rocks on trails that don't lead nowhere.*

"Louise ain't particular interested in traveling to Colorado and finding an aunt she don't know and I ain't particular in lettin' her go anywhere without me taggin' along."

Dog-man had to chuckle. Snake was talking in Texas talk, as he called it. Wanting to say something without actually coming out and saying it. "I'm glad you got that figured out," Dog-man said.

"And you, Dog, you've said you want a ranch real bad, with lots of cows and horses, lots of grass and water. Louise says all of that is in this San Bernardino area. I think we might should go look at it. If we don't like it we can still go to the ocean."

Dog-man smiled. He's not losing a partner, he's

gaining one. "You've been to this San Bernardino Valley?" He asked Louise.

"No, but I've heard some stories. Papa wanted to go, but the hunting wasn't there, it was around here."

"Ain't got no good reason to not go look," Snake said. "We was going that way to start with. Seems like the road to the Pioneer Station continues right on through that valley."

"I think it's time for you to start thinkin' about settlin' down, Dog. We've covered a lot of country these last couple of years, met some fine folk along the way, besides."

"Met some real critters, too," Dog-man said. "You gettin' serious about picking up a ranch? I've been serious about it for some time. The way them people in Tucson talked, California is filled to the brim with people. All them gold seekers, all them trying to rip off the gold seekers, and all the Mexicans that lived there before the gold seekers makes for a lot of people."

"They need to eat good beef, old son," Snake laughed.

"Yeah, they do but I don't know if I can live with that many people. We ain't like most folk, Snake. They call us loners. How many times have we gone out of our way to make up camp as far away from people as possible? Now, you're talkin' about moving right in with 'em?"

Snake didn't say anything, just continued eating the dried venison. "Let's get saddled and get the animals packed up. Gonna be a long day and it's already hot. We can talk while we ride. We're both thinking the same thing, just kind of different like."

It was a long hour getting the mules packed, Louise's and theirs, and they led them off the mountain and back on the trail. Louise and Simon took the lead and Dog-man and Snake each led a mule. It was miserable hot, not a breeze blowing, not a bird flying.

Snake's mind drifted back to what Dog-man was trying to talk about at the fire. He and Dog-man were loners, and so was Louise. *The problem as I see it is this. He's right. Louise too. Look at her, out two hundred yards in front of us, keepin' us on track. She don't care much for people. either. Three loners off on a trek. A trek to where? The ocean was just going to be something to see and the idea of having a ranch was just something to think about.*

Snake looked across the trail at Dog-man. "We got no more idea of where we're going or why we're going there than we did when we got throwed out of Deadwood. What do you know about runnin' a ranch anyway?"

Dog-man laughed right out. "About as much as you and that ain't saying much. Puttin' a plan together, are you?"

"Only plan I got is keepin' us, all three of us, together."

They were each trailing a mule and riding side-by-side across a rocky plateau that would take them to where they had camped just a night or two ago. "Been in the high Rocky Mountains, Dog. Been in the Mexican wilds fighting trail bandits, and been all over New Mexico Territory. What we've seen of California ain't to my liking."

"This valley that Louise talked about ain't a desert, though," Dog-man said. "I'm in favor of looking it over. We got a lot of miles on us, got more to go I think, but it won't hurt to look at this valley filled with grass and cows."

"Sounds to me like you've got yourself about half sold on fortin' up."

"Maybe," Dog-man chuckled. "Maybe not."

Both men sat straight up when a rifle shot went off in front of them. "Louise," Snake said and set his spurs. He, Dog-man, and the two pack mules raced the several hundred yards over a slight rise to find Louise stepping down from her horse and walking up to a very dead buck deer.

"Fresh meat, boys." She already had her knife out and had the deer bleeding out before they were out of the saddle. "Nice and fat, too." The deer was dressed and skinned in nothing flat. Louise had the animal quartered and the men had the pieces wrapped and tied onto the mules. "Need to get a lot of this sliced, peppered, and smoked or we'll lose it," she said.

"My partner's a rancher, my woman's a hunter. Hell, I'm in heaven," Snake laughed. "Let's find that camp we were in the other night and stay long enough to take care of the meat. Pioneer Station ain't goin' nowhere that we can't find it."

21

ON THE FOURTH MORNING, with the meat sliced thin and smoked, packed away on the mules, the group set off again for Pioneer Station. "Fresh liver one night and roasted venison the next two nights. I ain't gonna eat for a week," Snake chuckled. "That woman knows how to cook, Dog."

It was a blustery day, hot winds blowing hard, dust swirling and carrying sand that stung the face, and menacing clouds building big and black to the north. "We'll be wet before mid-day, Snake. Let's make sure we can find an outcrop to hide under. Stay away from any of these low areas and the damn arroyos. We've seen enough of them."

Snake and Louise rode out leaving Dog-man with the mules, to find a likely place to weather the storm, and then wait for Dog-man to catch up. The rumbling of thunder could be heard far off. "We gotta find a hidey-hole soon," Snake said. Louise pointed at palisades off about half a mile and led them onto a small hill side just below the towering pinnacles, only twenty feet or so above the desert floor, but with overhanging rock.

"No room for the animals, but we and all the gear will be dry," she said. "There's some grass growing between the rocks," she laughed. Dog-man brought the mules up, loose wood was gathered quickly, a fire started and coffee was boiling before the first splatters of rain fell. "I love the smell of wet desert dust," she said. "Ain't nothing like it in the world."

Lightning lit the sky, thunder peeled, and rain pelted for the next couple of hours as the three sat in the comfort of their rock overhang, a fire crackling and a coffee pot boiling. "Not sure I want to trade this for a ranch," Snake said. "We'd be sittin' in wood chairs, at a table filled with hot biscuits and fresh churned butter, enjoying the heat from a big old stove." He let the words linger in the ozone ladened air.

"And here we are, sittin' on rocks, eating freshly smoked venison, hard biscuits, and drinking fresh coffee that was heated over an open fire. By gosh, Dog, I'm just not sure."

Dog-man and Louise were both laughing at Snake's way of talking and neither one said a word. Simon stirred from his position nearest the fire and growled softly. Louise saw a figure working its way up the side of the hill. "Man comin'," she said, pointing. "Two, actually." She motioned for Simon to be quiet.

Snake and Dog-man were on their feet instantly, rifles in hand. Louise moved back deeper under the overhang and held her rifle, cocked and ready, too. "Hold up, there, strangers," Dog-man yelled out.

"Wantin' out of the rain," a voice yelled back. "Didn't know there was someone up here."

You bet, Snake thought. *No way you could miss those*

tracks we left. Five animals working their way up this hillside and you didn't think anyone was around? Snake eased back from the fire and made sure neither Dog-man nor Louise would be in his field of fire.

"Come on up, nice and friendly like," Dog-man said. "Ain't room for your horses. Which way you be headin'?"

"Toward Mormon Station if it's still standin'. Heard there was some Indian trouble. Thought Big Al might need some help." The thin man, sopping wet tied his horse to some rocks below the ledge and climbed the last several feet up. "Name's Morgan, Skinny Dave Morgan. My partner there's Rocky Lawrence."

The two men carried rifles, wore their sidearms low on their hips, and both men showed scars on their faces that were sure to have been made by sharp knives. Rocky Lawrence was about Dog-man's height but outweighed him by fifty pounds while Skinny Dave was shorter than Snake. The men's eyes were quick to find Louise back in the shadows and seemed to take in the small camp's accessories just as fast.

Simon's growls were a constant as the men moved under the overhang. His thick fur stood straight up from his shoulders to his tail. Louise let her hand rest gently on his head.

Snake moved a step or two to his side putting the two men in a cross fire if something happened and Louise was back and pinned the middle stake in their triangle of fire. Skinny Dave saw the move and nodded to Lawrence who in turn tried to make a step to the side.

"Tell you what," Dog-man said, easing the rifle into a better position. "Why don't you boys drop those rifles and un-hook those gun belts. Let them fall to the floor before we have a problem of some kind. Nice and slow, now. We can talk some after. You want to be first, Skinny Dave?"

Rocky Lawrence growled loud as he lunged for Snake, swinging the rifle like a club. Snake dropped to one knee but didn't fire that new Winchester of his. Louise did, though, and that girl nailed Rocky Lawrence with a piece of lead through his middle. He fell to the rocky floor in agony.

"Nice shootin', Lion Killer," Snake said. Rocky Lawrence had one more move in him and rolled, pulling his pistol to take a wild shot at Louise. Simon yipped, and rolled over, crying out in pain. Snake shot Lawrence while Louise raced to her dog's side. He died as she gathered him close.

Skinny Dave Morgan didn't move a muscle, watched his partner fall to the rocks, dead, and let his rifle fall to the ground. "Now the gun belt, Skinny Dave. Nice and slow," Dog-man said. He saw three rifles aimed at his middle and with one hand only pulled his belt undone, letting the rig clatter to the rocks.

"Good boy," Dog-man said. "Want some coffee while you tell us your story?"

Snake chuckled while he picked up the two rifles, grabbed Skinny's gun belt and lifted the revolver from Rocky's belt. "They was leavin' out to kill some of our Paiute friends, Dog. Not sure I want to give this fool any of our coffee." He looked over at Louise. "Thank you, dear girl. Saved my skinny butt again, did you? Damn, that's a real loss."

Her smile was tempered some when she looked down at Simon's body, still bleeding out. "That man was gonna kill you, Snake. I had to shoot him but I didn't kill him. Simon," she said more than once.

"Snake called you Lion Killer. I like that," Dog-man

said. He motioned Skinny Dave to stand by the fire. "Got to get this body out of here, Skinny. Then you gotta high-tail it, too. Got a bad smell about you. Nasty." He poured a cup for himself, found the flask and poured some whiskey in it. "Well. Get to moving. Get that body out of here and keep right on going."

Skinny Dave Morgan had a hell of a fight getting Rocky Lawrence's heavy body dragged off the ledge and into the continuing downpour. Lightning had been flashing, accompanied by blasting thunder the whole time and it seemed it would continue for another several hours. "I ever see you again, Skinny Dave, I'll shoot you on sight. Don't make me regret letting you ride off." Dog-man waved the rifle at the man standing in the rain almost begging to be let under the ledge.

Morgan grabbed the reins from Lawrence's horse, mounted his, and moved on down the small hillside. The rain was so heavy that he was out of sight in just yards. "How do they find us, Dog? Do we have flashing signs that say, they're right here? Come and get 'em? Damn." He spilled some whiskey in his coffee and kicked a rock just because he could. "We got to do right by Simon."

"Said they came from Pioneer Crossing," Dog-man said. "If Morgan's going back that way, we might still have some trouble. It's like Benjamin Franklyn Cruikshank all over again." He caught a quick glance at Louise, saw tears running down her cheeks and motioned to Snake who moved to her side in an instant.

She grabbed hold of his neck and hung on like she was about to fall off a cliff. "Ain't never shot a man before, Snake. It feels horrible. Don't know anything about him. What if he had a wife? Or kids? I feel sick."

Snake eased her down by the fire, wrapped a wool blanket around her shoulders, and sat down next to her.

They sat by the fire for a long time, not talking, just knowing the other was right there, hanging on tight. *It's best,* he thought, *that she feels this way. As much hunting and killing animals as she's done, shooting a man could have come easy. I'm glad it didn't.*

As the rain began to let up and the wild winds, loud thunder, and brilliant lightning passed on south, Dog-man started gathering their kits to get the packs ready. He looked at Snake and Louise huddled by the fire and changed his mind. "Guess we might just as well spend the night here and move on in the morning, eh?"

"I was thinking along those lines myself," Snake said. "It's dry, we've got plenty of wood for a fire, and besides that, I'm whupped tired. This thing of being protected by Lion Killer wears a man out."

The tinkles of laughter coming from under the wool blanket made Dog-man chuckle as well. "Couldn't have said it better, Snake. I'll check on the horses and mules. Still have some of those wild onions to go with the venison." Dog-man took it on his own to carry Simon's bloody body out of the cavern and build a rock cairn for the remains.

"You must think I'm just a silly little girl, carrying on like I did." Louise pulled the blanket back but didn't let go of Snake's arm. "I feel terrible about shooting that man but I would have to die if I'd just let him beat on you. You saved me and now I've saved you. That part feels really good."

Snake tightened his grip on her but didn't say anything. *I wonder if other men get these kinds of feelings. Ain't never felt like this toward someone before. Scared. That's what I am right now. Scared. And stupid happy. Cain't live like this though. We both know that. Can't live on the trail, wild as a wolf. Gonna have to settle down somewhere comfortable.*

Snake's mind never slowed down and he thought about what he was just thinking. *Well, now. Why? Why can't we live like this?* He shook his head, chuckled just a bit, and patted Louise's shoulder. *We'll just answer that question in its own time. I'm warm, dry, have food, and now a woman who I think really good thoughts about.*

Dog-man moved the animals around trying to find patches of grass and it was some time before he came back into their little cave. Snake was slumped back against the rock wall, sound asleep and Louise had her head in his lap, actually snoring. *Ain't nothing like being comfortable. Gonna be looking at some ranch property when we find this San Bernardino Valley, big enough for two homes.*

22

PIONEER CROSSING WAS A NICELY LAID out little community with the main road from the Mojave Desert acting as the main street. The Mojave River had its beginnings in the surrounding mountains, there were generous forests on the hillsides, and the vast valley spread out to the west. The town was like a spoked wheel with roads leading out to the north, west, south, and east.

"A lot of grass on those hillsides, Dog. What I ain't seein' is a lot cattle spread out on those hillsides."

"I'd bet all your money that when we ride down the other side of this pass we'll see cattle, sheep, and pigs by the hundreds," Dog-man said. "I'll bet the rest of your money the grass is knee high."

"I ain't one to fritter my money away, Dog," Snake chuckled.

A stage stop with corrals filled with horses dominated the eastern entrance to the village, and commercial buildings, some two stories tall, dotted both sides of the main street, with offerings of clothing, farm and ranch supplies, mining equipment, and most importantly, a few welcoming saloons. There were two hotels, one a towering three stories tall.

"Think we should find a hotel or make up a camp?" Dog-man said. He was leading one pack mule, Louise had the other in tow, and Snake was leading the procession. "I'm thinkin' camp, myself."

"Yup," Snake said. "I don't cotton to spending a lot of time in town, not if we're looking for some rich cattle land."

Dog-man had to smile at the comment. Ever since that afternoon in the cave, after Louise shot Lawrence, Snake's whole attitude had changed. "Maybe a mile or so up in those tree filled hills."

The ride through town was slow, the three taking in the sights and sounds. The few people out and about didn't pay much attention, after all, this was a main road from the east and into the riches of California and travelers with pack animals were not uncommon. Dog-man took notice of one man giving them a rather long look, and caught Snake's attention, nodding at the man.

"I do believe that's Skinny Dave Morgan, Dog. Wonder what kind of stories he has spread among the citizens of Pioneer Crossing."

"He ain't gonna give us no trouble, Snake. Lion Killer put the fear of eternal fire in his heart." All three laughed and Morgan slipped into the shadows. "If we're gonna make camp, let's do it now," Dog-man said.

Big Al Barrington told them that after leaving town, the main road wound its way into high mountains before dropping into a long and fertile valley. "After we get out of town, look for a good camp site," Dog-man yelled out. The hillsides were covered in heavy timber so finding a place to settle in wouldn't be difficult. Louise was leading them along when a man stepped off the boardwalk and flagged the little train down.

She held up and let Snake and Dog-man ride up alongside. "Help you with something?" Dog-man asked. The man was not very tall but carried some weight that didn't appear to be fat. He had a full beard, mostly black but tinted here and there with the lighter shades of age. He wore denim pants, wool shirt, and light-weight jacket. There was no weapon visible on the man.

"Heard some nasty stories about you people. Need to talk some," the man said. He had a scratchy voice, coughed a time or two, but glared at Snake.

"I'm sure there are nasty stories about a lot of people," Snake said. "Why would ours be any of your concern?"

The man continued glaring and opened his light jacket to show a shiny tin badge. "Mostly because I'm the sheriff of this county. My office is right over there," and he pointed across the street. "Why don't you tie off your animals and come in for a visit."

"Is this a request or a command, Sheriff?" Dog-man asked.

"For the time being, it's a request," he said.

* * *

THE OFFICE WAS spare at best with an oak desk and cane-back chair for the sheriff, a pot belly stove, rifle rack, filled, and two chairs near the desk. Louise had a vice grip hold on Snake's arm as they stood around the desk.

"My name's Mallory, Tom Mallory and I'm the sheriff of this county. People been riding into our fair little town for more than a week talking about you two. One story is you helped take Desert Jack to his final resting place. Another story has you helping Big Al Barrington rebuild the Mormon Station."

Snake nodded his head at the comments since they seemed to be directed squarely at him. The sheriff never took his eyes off of him, never glanced at Dog-man or saw the pretty face belonging to Louise.

"There's another story, though, that I want to talk about," Sheriff Mallory said.

"The Skinny Dave Morgan story?" Dog-man asked.

"I haven't heard that one," Mallory said. "Tell me about it."

"Not much of a story, really, What was yours?" Dog-man said.

"Something about the Paiutes getting upset and you two being able to calm them down. I'd like to hear more about that. We've had problems with other tribes around these parts, but not from the Paiutes. What happened?"

Snake was looking around the office thinking that this was only the second time that he and Dog-man were brought into a sheriff's office and not been called outlaws. *Kind of feels good. Hope it don't change. Might want to ask him about land availability.*

Dog-man took just a few minutes to tell about the killing of Louise's father, the mix up with all the horses, and the peaceful ending to the events. "Pretty much sums it up, Sheriff. Asshole and Good Inyan have their people in fine order. We're here to possibly see if this is as good ranching country as we've heard. Any ideas on that?"

"Might have but you've got to tell me about your encounter with Skinny Dave Morgan. That slimy little outlaw is a killer and the man he rides with, called Rocky Lawrence is worse. They prey on travelers but they're quick to kill their prey so I don't get the stories with witnesses. Would love to see that man hanged."

"Might just be your day, Sheriff," Snake chuckled. "Just might be. We was hiding from a thunderstorm in a little rock cavern when Skinny Dave and Rocky showed up. Made a play to take our gear and Louise stopped 'em cold. You won't be seeing Rocky Lawrence around these parts."

"You take their guns?"

"Guns and knives, Sheriff, and made Skinny Dave take care of the body while it was still raining."

Mallory wagged his head at the thought, took a long look at Louise, and then at the two men. "Seems I've heard stories about you, too, young lady. Your father was called Preacher Raven's Hawk?" Louise smiled and nodded, looked over at Snake and smiled even more. "I'm sorry to hear of his death. Hawk was a good man."

"Thank you," Louise mumbled. Snake watched the tears well up and put his arm around her. "There was no call to kill him," she said. "Snake saw to it that his killer paid for it."

"What are your plans?" Mallory asked.

"Gonna set up camp in the mountains on the other side of the ridge and look for a nice piece of ranch land, if there is any," Dog-man said. "Ain't had a chance to look around none, so far, Got any ideas?"

"Find a man named Tony Mendoza. He knows that valley out there better than any man alive. I won't say he won't steer you wrong." There was just the slightest change in his attitude, like he was remembering something unpleasant. "I married his daughter. He's from an old family that dates back to the days of Spanish Conquistadores. San Bernardino Valley was a Spanish land-grant."

Mallory stood up quickly, like he had gone too far in his talk with these strangers. "Thanks for your time. Liked the stories."

They filed out of the office, got the train put back together and rode off toward the mountains to the north. "Don't think that man smiled one time, Dog, but he's the nicest lawman I can remember."

"Good to know what he said about Skinny Dave Morgan, too. Morgan might still give us trouble but it won't come with a badge attached." Dog-man looked over at Louise and smiled. "All right, Lion Killer, find us a home."

The rolling hills were covered in places by heavy timber and in other places great meadows of grass waving in the light breezes wafting up the long valley. It was well past mid-day and the higher they climbed the cooler the air became. "Might just find this most invigorating," Snake said.

"Good grass, fresh water, and soft ground to sleep on. Think I like this place, Dog." Snake was setting up two lean-tos separated by many yards. Dog-man had built a fine fire pit and Louise and her rifle were out scouting for fresh meat. "We can look for this Mendoza fellow tomorrow. Feels like I've been in the saddle for a hundred and forty years."

A rifle's muted report brought the two men to full alert. "I'd best go help her with that," Snake said. "She took one of the mules at least." He was in the saddle riding northwest in seconds. The timber was thick and he couldn't ride in any kind of straight line. After ten minutes and no other shots being fired, He yelled her name out and waited for an answer.

"I know I'm going in the general direction of that shot we heard." He hollered her name twice more but got no answer. Snake kept moving in what he thought was the direction the shot came from, stopping every few minutes to listen. It was the third stop that he heard a woman's scream from some distance off.

Snake stepped off the horse and got it tied off, grabbed his Winchester and started moving toward the continued screaming. As he got closer he could also hear some thrashing about and a man's voice telling her to shut up or he'd kill her. *Oh, no you won't.*

Snake moved as cautious as any Indian through trees and brush finally spotting movement a few yards in front of him. *Damn it all, if that ain't Skinny Dave Morgan. Must have followed us out and then followed Louise. Bastard's about to die.*

Snake saw Morgan and Louise separated by a few feet, but Louise was bleeding from a gash on the side of her face. Morgan had a knife in one hand but when Snake looked, the man's holster was empty. It was then he saw blood coming from Morgan's side.

She didn't shoot us a deer, she shot us an outlaw. Snake had a hard time holding in the chuckle as he stepped out from behind a tree and leveled the rifle at Morgan. "Bout enough dancing, Skinny Dave. Time to pay the piper," he said. "Get behind me, Louise, and Dave, drop the knife and you might live."

Blood was running at a good stream from the bullet wound to Morgan's side and the man wasn't able to move well at all. "Come on, you piece of pig shit, drop the knife." Instead, Skinny

Dave Morgan whipped the knife in an arc directly at

Louise who was striding toward Snake. The knife looked like it drove into Louise's back.

Snake screamed her name, fired the Winchester four times, that fast, killing Morgan with the first bullet. Snake dropped the rifle and grabbed Louise as she fell toward him, easing her to the ground. The greasy knife was stuck solidly in the middle of her back.

"Easy sweet lady, easy now." Her eyes were huge, looking up at Snake as he got her gently down. She was on her side and he could see the knife, but no blood was flowing.

"That really hurts, Snake. Is he dead? Bastard came at me from nowhere." She dipped her head and Snake could see her blushing. "I ain't never said that word," she whispered. "I shot him but he grabbed the rifle away from me. I bashed his head with a rock and he dropped his gun and mine, but had that knife. It hurts, Snake."

He had a hard time getting her long buckskin shirt pulled up so he could see the wound. "I ain't moving that knife until I know what it's stuck into," he muttered, then started laughing.

"What are you laughing at. It hurts, Snake."

"Those aren't suspenders you got hooked to your pants. That's harness leather. Crossed in the back. No knife was going through that leather. Hold still, now." He grasped the knife handle, put his other hand on her back and pulled, getting a squeal from Louise.

"I'll be damned," Snake said. "The tip of the knife made it all the way through and you have a little scratch on your back. Got a nasty slice in that nice buckskin shirt, though. Damn, girl, you are one lucky lady." He gathered her up in his arms and held her tight, letting her shirt drop back down.

I'm so glad I met you, Snake. You're mine. Forever, Snake, you're mine."

"Let's see what we can do about that cut on your face, You put a real scare in me, girl. Ain't good for a man's heart to get scared like that."

"Are we a real couple now, Snake? I mean, a real couple? Like making babies couple?"

"You got something in mind?" Snake's smile would have been seen in Pioneer Crossing if it weren't for all the trees.

23

"WHERE THE HELL have you two been? Where's the deer? What the hell's going on? Is that Skinny Dave stretched out on that mule?" Dog-man was on his feet in an instant when Snake and Louise reached the new camp. "Been gone hours."

"Had things to do," Snake muttered. He saw Louise blush, and walked to the mule where Morgan's body was tied off. She followed right along. "Gotta take this piece of shit into town. Want to come along?"

Louise kept her eyes away from Dog-man but kept giving sly looks at Snake. *I am the luckiest woman in the world. Gonna give that man as many babies as he wants.* She let her mind play out their two hours of love making the entire ride back to Pioneer crossing.

Many a frontier woman would be thinking scenes of a safe building to live in, warm fireplace and wood stove to keep out winter's winds, and barrels of salted meats. Louise wasn't what might be called a typical frontier woman,. She was a hunter, a producer, and as long as she had Snake close by, she would live in a cave, eat raw meat, and kill anything that threatened them.

She reached out and took the long Texan's hand and squeezed it tight. *This is gonna be the ride Pa said I might learn about some day. I ain't been this dizzy since the first time I got bucked off a mule.* Snake, too, couldn't get the grin off his face.

"THAT'S THE WHOLE STORY, SHERIFF." Snake said. Louise pulled the shirt back down after showing him the slice through the buckskin, and where the knife had stuck in two layers of harness leather. Even the nick where the tip of the blade made it all the way through.

"You got yourself a tough one, Snake. Any woman who'd wear harness leather braces is tougher than most men I know." Sheriff Tom Mallory said. Louise just smiled and Snake nodded in agreement. "Don't think I'd let that one get away if I was you."

The sheriff had one of his deputies take Morgan's body to the undertaker and asked the three to join him for coffee and sweet rolls at the café next door to the jail. "Morgan liked to terrorize those he killed, Louise. That's what he was trying on you. He wasn't looking to dance with a mountain lion killer."

She chuckled and blushed some at the same time. "I was as scared as I ever want to be. I shot him and he just knocked that rifle right out of my hands." She squeezed Snake's hand hard and looked the sheriff right in the eyes. "This man saved me again."

The sign on the building was simple, Hot Coffee, is all it said and the aroma of freshly roasted coffee beans filled the air. It mingled freely with that of fresh baked breads and rolls. "Didn't know I was hungry until I smelled all this good stuff," Snake said.

The coffee was hot and strong and the sweet rolls were warmed, covered in a rich, sugary glaze, and the sun coming through a clean window warmed the entire room. A beautiful Mexican woman came out from the kitchen and flopped down in Mallory's lap. "My wife, gentlemen. I, too, am one lucky man, Snake. Say hello to Maria-Elena."

She pulled a chair up to the table and it was a lively conversation for about half an hour. "You do as I say," Maria-Elena said as the three were ready to leave. "Papi's office is on the second floor, above the apothecary. I just happen to know about some land that is coming available. Go see him right away before someone else does."

As they walked from the café Snake asked where they would find the justice of the peace. "In the courthouse, right across the street," Mallory said. "You two gonna make everything legal, are you? Need a witness, do you?"

Hiram Betterman, Justice of the Peace of San Bernardino County was more than pleased to do the honors, Mallory stood for Snake and Betterman's wife stood for Louise, and the entire process was over and done with inside of fifteen minutes. It was a slow and quiet ride back to the ranch.

———

"WE LIVE AN INTERESTING LIFE, DOG." Snake was standing at the bottom of the stairs leading to Mendoza's offices. "If we do this, if we actually get some land and raise us some cow-critters, it'll be the second time we've settled down."

"I have to say our time at the mine was pleasurable,

Snake. It was a good mine and we did well. We can't just stand down here at the bottom of the stairs, though. Lead us up, Snake."

Louise took the first step up and the men followed right along. Inside the landing was a narrow corridor and two doors leading into offices on each side. Snake found the one that said Antonio Mendoza, Broker. "Here we go," he said and opened the door that led into a lovely southwestern decorated office.

Racks of deer antlers were mounted on three walls and the fourth was almost sagging from the weight of a Texas Longhorn rack. A tall, heavy man was standing, looking out across the main street. He had broad shoulders and narrow hips, long, mostly black hair hung in waves and curls and when he turned to the visitors, his deep brown eyes sparkled.

"I just saw you talking with my daughter," he said, "so this must be a friendly visit. Please, sit and tell me all about it."

He stepped behind his desk. "I am Señor Antonio Mendoza at your service." Dog-man looked at the man carefully wondering why he would say something like, 'This must be a friendly visit.' He saw what appeared to be a well-heeled Spanish gentleman not a rowdy man of questionable morals. *Strange,* he thought.

"Glad to meet you, Señor," Snake said. "I'm Snake, he's my partner, Dog-man, and this charming lady is my wife, Louise."

If she had twisted her head any quicker she might have injured her neck. *Wife? My God, he said wife. I'm his wife? Oh, my.* She felt her knees go weak and Snake had hold of her elbow, keeping her upright. It was the first time she heard the words and the weight of what they had done finally struck home.

"Here you go, girl," Snake said as he helped her into a hand carved chair next to Mendoza's desk. "Need to talk about some land that might be available. We just had coffee with your daughter and the sheriff. Nice country around here."

Mendoza eased himself into a large, ornate, and hand carved chair behind the desk. The wood shined from years of use, featured scenes of forest creatures, meadows, and intricately carved maybe a hundred years ago.

Mendoza looked the part of a Spanish Grandee, an Alcalde. as he opened a tin and offered cigars to the men before saying anything. "You must be the men we've been hearing about these last few days. I believe you, young lady are Raven Hawk's daughter, eh?"

Louise nodded, dropping her eyes some. She murmured yes but went no further. She appeared overwhelmed by the man, intimidated by the office, and how everything was happening so fast. "Always enjoyed talking with that man," Mendoza said. "Bought some beautiful packages of skins from him, too. Is he with you?"

Louise couldn't hold the tears back and Snake jumped into the conversation. "Got himself killed by some angry Paiutes, Señor. It's all taken care of now, though." He took Louise's hand and gave it a squeeze. "About that land?"

"Yes, yes. Of course. My sincere condolences, dear lady." Mendoza opened his desk drawer and pulled a sheaf of papers out. "My old friend Juan Saucedo worked his place hard but never hired the right people and died almost as a peon. There are twelve hundred acres of rolling hillside about ten miles west of here. On the other side of the pass where the grass grows year around."

Mendoza got a small smile across his dark face. "Juanito was a strange man. Didn't like most people, had a small cabin, no wife, and only ugly, mean men to work for him. Meet me here in the morning and we'll ride out. There's deep grass, good water, and timber from which to build."

"Were these men he hired robbing him?" Dog-man asked. "Is there cattle on the land?"

"Maybe fifty heifers left. Dog-man. Juanito lost most of the herd, including his bulls. Yes, the men he hired were outlaws. He owed me three thousand dollars when he passed on. I would want a small profit for my efforts, say another thousand? We'll talk in the morning."

———

"BLUNT AND TO THE POINT, Dog, but I like the man." Snake and Dog-man were riding side-by-side being led out of town by Louise. "That's a lot of money."

"It's a lot more than I was thinking." Dog-man was good with numbers and had them rattling around his head. "Twelve hundred acres is good, only fifty heifers isn't. No bulls is worse. We don't want to jump into this without talking long and hard, Snake."

It was a quick ride out to their camp site, fires were lit, coffee boiled, and supper was served on plates. "Need to do some serious money talk, Snake. Twelve hundred acres is good, grass and timber is good, but four thousand dollars is a lot of money."

Snake was sprawled out in the dirt next to the fire, his head in Louise's lap. His coffee cup held more whiskey than it did coffee, and his thoughts were locked on a ranch. "Got fifty or so heifers and no bulls. Hard to start a herd that way, Dog. Got one small cabin and no hands. Well, there are three of us. Think we can bring him down some?"

"Papa mentioned Tony Mendoza more than once," Louise said. "Called him a good trader, one who knew the value of the product and his money."

"He'll drive a hard bargain," Dog-man said.

"We're gonna need two bulls at least," Snake said. "Let's use that as part of the deal."

"The land, cattle, and two bulls for four thousand? Might work," Dog-man said. "Didn't ask the breed of cattle on the land. Rather not have long-horns. Going for meat, not hides."

"That's another thing we got to figure out. Don't know nothing about even where we are, more or less where we would be sellin' our beef. Back in Texas they had to drive their beef a thousand miles to sell it. 'Course that was before the railroads come in."

"California's full of people is what we've been told," Dog-man said. "They got to eat."

———

Snake managed to get to his feet and brought Louise to hers. "Got lots to talk about, girl. See you in the morning, Dog." He led Louise off to their lean-to, tucked in a copse of tall pines. "You and me got to put it all together before me and Dog buys that land. Got to make sure you're taken care of, girl." Snake was speaking right out, not going in circles with his Texas talk, as he calls it.

"What do you mean git it all put together?" Louise let him see the slightest smile when she asked. She was also hoping the answer would be the one he gave at the land broker's office.

"Well, you know," he stammered. "You're my wife and

all, and if sumpin' happened to me, I want you well taken care of." He stirred the small fire they had going in front of the lean-to. "You want to be my wife, don't you?"

"You never asked, Snake," she murmured, pulling him down to her. "Ask real pretty and I'll be anything you want me to be." She stopped, pushed him aside, and sat straight up. "I didn't even know your real name." She blurted it out and cocked her head, letting him know he'd best not be funnin' with her.

Snake eased her back down in the robes and held her tight. "I told you and the judge, but you got to promise not to tell anybody. Even Dog don't know my real name any more'n I know his." She looked him straight on and smiled.

"I'm good at keeping secrets. We're married so it's my name, too."

"You gotta tell me your name, then." He was chuckling at their whole conversation. "Your pa is Raven Hawk, is Hawk your last name?"

"Hawkins," she said. "He came up with the Raven Hawk thing. Everyone calls him that. So, big man, what's yours? I know you told the judge, I know it's on the papers I haven't seen."

Snake hadn't spoken or used his name since that day, he was just ten-years-old when he left home for his first cattle drive as cook's helper, and it took him a second or two to get it squared around in his mind. They called him Snake from day one on that first drive. Said he was long and skinny and could wrap around himself like an old rattler.

"My name is Alonzo Cornelius Peabody. Don't never tell nobody."

She couldn't hold the laugh in and Snake glared at

her. "I mean it, girl. Nobody." She wrapped her arms around his neck and squeezed hard.

"I'll stick to being known as Snake's wife or Lion Killer, if you don't mind," she laughed. "When did you pick up the handle of Snake?"

"That first drive north. I was skinny and fast."

"Still are," she said. "That's what I like."

24

THE STREETS in Pioneer Crossing were busy as the three rode into town for their meeting with Mendoza. A small caravan wound its way down the main street, four wagons, a few loose cows, three outriders, and some scruffy kids romping loudly with their dogs. Large wagons driven by four-up hitches belonging to some of the local ranchers who were in town for supplies, and the general chaos of a busy frontier town waking up to a new day added to the frenzy.

"Looks like the Mojave is open and safe, Dog. I think that bunch might even scare Asshole."

They found Mendoza waiting for them at the bottom of the stairway. "Right on time, Snake. I like that in a man." He mounted a tall athletic looking stallion, black. with four white stockings, a thin blaze, and flashy mane and tail. "Shall we?" he asked, moving off down the road west.

"You said your friend seemed to always hire outlaws instead of good cow men. Why would that be?" Dog-man asked riding alongside the Spanish Grandee.

"I'm not sure, but Juan was a weak man. He may have been intimidated, forced, to hire outlaws. This is wild country, señor."

"And these men, some of them, are still around? Or did they take Saucedo's herd off to market? We've already run into two Pioneer Crossing outlaws." Dog-man wanted as many answers about how things were before getting down to the serious business of money.

"There is an outlaw element in this area. Tom Mallory is a good man, a decent sheriff, but he doesn't have any help. Gold and silver is what most say they're looking for, they just don't care whether it comes from the ground or your purse," Mendoza laughed.

Dog-man wanted names and he wasn't getting them. The road they were on split from the main highway not too far from the ridge crest that formed the eastern boundary of a vast valley that slowly worked its way almost down to sea-level. "When we ride over this next little hill," Mendoza said, "we'll be on what was Juan Saucedo's land. Notice the good grass, the great stands of virgin timber, and the dark areas where springs come to the surface."

Dog-man wanted to say that he also saw a lot of rock outcroppings, and areas where smart steers could hide from riders for years. He had to admit, though, this was fine land for raising cattle and sheep. The thoughts of a man going out of his way to hire outlaws whose only thoughts were robbing the boss wouldn't go away.

The land broker was a natural salesman, only talked about what he wanted to talk about and Dog-man knew he had a chore in front of him. "I'd really like to know more about this criminal element, Señor Mendoza. If Saucedo was intimidated to the point of losing all this land and his herd, we have to know what we might be facing."

"Juan's cabin is half a mile in front of us, Dog-man. When we get there we can sit by a fire and I'll answer all your questions. Right now, think about running a herd on these beautiful hillsides." The smile was generous and Dog-man and Snake both took in the sights. Louise was following a set of prints left by a lone horseman.

"See these?" She asked Snake and pointed at the prints. "Not very old, either."

"Gonna keep you around for a long time, girl," Snake said. "A lone rider on a shod horse. I wonder if Mendoza has seen them? Or already knows they are there?" *As a land broker he knows an awfully lot about the people he deals with. He calls Juan Saucedo his old friend but doesn't indicate that he tried to come to his friend's aid, just foreclosed on his land.*

Snake casually rode up on Dog-man, and using his eyes, pointed out the prints. Dog-man smiled, gave Snake the slightest nod, and kept right on talking to the land broker.

JUAN SAUCEDO'S cabin was considerably larger than described by Mendoza and featured a grand main room, kitchen and eating area, and two bedrooms. There was a small barn, large enough to bring nursing cows and calves in, corrals for horses, and a few sheep grazing close by. Snake looked for but couldn't find hog pens or a kitchen garden plot.

Señor Saucedo wasn't really prepared to be a rancher is what I'm seeing. Seems he only knew the basics, a sound home, strong barn and corrals, but nothing to sustain his way of life.

No meat barrels, no means of growing vegetables. Saucedo needed a señora. Snake almost chuckled at his thoughts as he stepped down from his horse. "I can see what led to a few of your friend's problems," he said to Mendoza.

They walked into a dusty kitchen and Louise went right to work getting a fire built in the big cast-iron stove, pumping some water for coffee and cleaning, and the men took those few minutes to walk through the old home.

"Coffee's ready, gentlemen. Let's talk," Louise said. Mendoza almost frowned which brought a grand smile to Snake's face. Dog-man grabbed a chair and sat down, ready to get some answers.

Seems as though our Spanish gentleman doesn't much care for independent women. Gonna enjoy this little ride I'm on. Snake's eyes were dancing as he watched Louise bring the coffee pot to the table. "Talk it is," he said. "How did this criminal element get its hands on your friend's life, Mendoza? Did anyone try to help him?"

"He was one of those people who had a hard time taking advice on the one hand but also one who almost refused to ask for help," Mendoza said. "I, the sheriff, and others tried to help the man but he wouldn't listen until it was too late."

Snake watched Louise slip out the main room's door, rifle in hand, and asked who these outlaws were. He nodded to Dog-man who also saw her slip out. "There are two men who believe they can do what it is they want to do without repercussions," Mendoza said. "There is a group of men led by Freddie Barton and Pete Sanchez who most likely stole Juan's cattle. They live off the land, terrorize local ranchers and farmers, and only come to town to drink."

Mendoza was going to say more but a loud thump on

the main room's door stopped him. Snake was there first and found Louise holding a cocked rifle aimed at a man who was bleeding heavy from a gash on the side of his head. "Found him near the horses, Snake. Wouldn't do as I said when I told him to come into the house. He's ready now, though."

Snake took the rifle and pistol Louise had taken from the man and checked him over for other weapons. "Nice knife," he said, pulling one from the man's boot. "Did you find his horse?"

"It's tied off behind the barn. You'll have to check but I'm almost sure it's the one Rocky Lawrence was riding when he and Skinny Dave Morgan tried to attack us." Snake looked at her and smiled.

This lovely creature all dressed in buckskins takes on criminals, knows her horses, and hunts lions. Snake, old man, don't you even think of letting this one get away. He couldn't contain the smile forcing the man into the house.

Mendoza took in a deep breath when Snake dragged the groggy man into the kitchen and dumped him onto a chair. Dirty, as much from being knocked to the ground as he was from his life style. Long stringy dark hair, heavy beard, and close knit, almost pig-eyes He sat on the chair and glared at Louise.

"He speaks fluent, if blasphemous, English, Snake," Louise said. "He might be dressed as a Mexican peon but he ain't one."

Dog-man looked at Mendoza, still staring at the intruder. "Seems like you know this fool, Mendoza. Tell us about him. Is he the one who left the tracks we followed in? Is he connected to

Saucedo losing his herd?"

Antonio Mendoza stood up and strode to the outlaw's side, slapped him hard across the side of the head, and was about to smash him again when Snake stopped him. "This is Lefty Greene. I don't know if he's one of the men who rides with Barton, but he was working for Saucedo when the herd was driven off."

Snake looked at Greene and then at Mendoza. "Lefty Greene, eh? Why did you ride out here this morning? Did you know we were coming?" Greene didn't say anything, just continued glaring, first at Mendoza, then at Louise. "Want a go at him, Lion Killer?" Snake asked.

"No," Louise murmured. "He's all yours. His skin ain't worth a nickel."

"Tell you what we're gonna do, Mr. Greene. It's important for us to have a nice long chat with Señor Mendoza and you're being here is gonna mess that up. We're gonna relieve you of your pants, shirt, and boots, tie you to the saddle of your horse, and turn you loose. So's we can finish up our business, you understand?"

Dog-man chuckled, Louise laughed right out, and Mendoza let a good smile slip through as Snake ushered the man out of the house. Louise was right with him. "While they're gone, Tell me about Lefty Greene, Mendoza," Dog-man said.

"The sheriff thought he was involved in the loss of Saucedo's herd. I've heard about other situations where he robbed land owners through intimidation and threat, but the sheriff said he never had enough evidence to arrest him. Why is Snake just letting him go?"

Dog-man was sure that Snake would gather some answers before sending the man off but for some reason didn't want Mendoza to hear the questions or the answers. "Well, sir, Mr. Greene didn't actually commit a crime here, now, did he. You say he's tied up with the Freddie Barton gang?"

"No, I said I don't know if he is. It wouldn't surprise me, though. Let's talk about this ranch, eh?"

"Snake won't be long but I do have a few questions," Dog-man said. "About what's left of the herd, for one. What breed was Saucedo raising, and are you sure there are no bulls? Hard to build a herd without bulls."

"Saucedo brought some good Mexican cattle up and they thrived on these mountainsides. When the herd was driven off, the outlaws also took the bulls. Probably took five hundred head or more. Only a few heifers remain. Good breeding stock, though."

"You said Saucedo owed you three thousand dollars when he died. How much did you charge him for the property to begin with? That seems a large sum to me."

"The property was sold a year ago for eighteen hundred dollars, but Juan borrowed more to get the place up and running. Mexican stock, bulls, and some cash."

"Let me get this straight then. Your price to us includes the price of the land and an outstanding debt by Juan Saucedo. Is that right?" Dog-man was doing some quick calculations and didn't like what he was seeing.

"As I said, Saucedo owed me three thousand when he died, and I'd like a small profit when I sell the place." Mendoza wasn't about to make any other offer, it appeared, and Dog-man sat back in his chair, looking up toward the ceiling.

Calculations were not adding up in Dog-man's mind. *Saucedo must have borrowed almost as much as the property itself cost. But what about his personal belongings, his other stock, and equipment. there's cut and stacked grass in the barn but no equipment to cut or stack, and there are no horses or mules in the corrals or barn. Señor Mendoza is working me and I don't much care for that.*

"I'm going out on a limb here, Mendoza but I don't think you're telling me the whole story. I'm not the kind of man who flings charges about without thinking them through first, but you're trying to fleece me and Snake and I don't much care for that."

Antonio Mendoza started to argue but before he could refute what was said, Dog-man continued. "Saucedo used your loan to purchase good Mexican stock and that appears to have been stolen. I believe that Saucedo also used that loan to purchase hay cutting and stacking equipment that seems also to be gone. Did you take that back and resell it? If so, you have recovered quite a bit of that loan."

Dog-man wasn't through and wouldn't let the Spanish Grandee get a word in. "Besides all that, there aren't any horses or mules on the property. I believe you've sold them as well, Mendoza. I think that Sauce-do's balance would be far below that three thousand dollars you are claiming."

Dog-man got up from the table and walked to the stove for more coffee. "Take all the time you want to re-calculate your figures, Mendoza because Snake and I are still interested in this property. It's good land, has good water, and I think we can make it work, but not at the high cost you're asking."

Antonio Mendoza sat at the table, quiet, smoking his cigar. He took a sip of some-what cool coffee and smiled. "You're a good trader, Dog-man, and you're right. I completely forgot all about the equipment and working stock. It just slipped this old man's mind. Let me take a few minutes to work all this out."

"You'll have it figured out by the time Snake and Louise are back, I hope. Neither one of us want to be around if we get Snake all riled up after having so much fun with Lefty Greene." Mendoza just nodded his head but had the slightest smile on his face. Was it an ironic smile, getting caught like that, or was he plotting something else?

25

"GET our outlaw friend sent off for Pioneer Crossing?" Dog-man asked when Snake and Louise walked in. "Glad you're back. Señor Mendoza and I have had a fine discussion and I think he's going to revise his offer to us."

"Splendid," Snake said. "Mr. Greene is an unusual man, Dog. He doesn't have much use for the Barton gang, works with one other person of your acquaintance, Rocky Lawrence. Louise was right, that was Rocky's horse he came in on."

Dog-man cut Snake off. "Good to hear. We'll get into all that a little later. Right now, I want to hear what Señor Mendoza has come up with for us." Snake wanted to tell all about Lefty Greene, but Dog-man shushed him twice. "I think we'll like what our fine friend has to say." Snake finally realized that what Mendoza had to say was far more important than what he wanted to say.

Dog-man motioned for Snake and Louise to sit down and nodded to the land broker. "We've been talking about farm and ranch equipment as well as animals. Isn't that right, Señor?"

"Well, you were absolutely right, Dog-man. How could I have forgotten something as important as that equipment." The broker accepted another cup of coffee from Louise, offered cigars all around and continued. "Juanito bought some fine machinery to cut grass and more to get it stacked in the barn. Best the market had to offer, I believe, and I did repossess that when my old friend died."

He smiled and looked at the two men before continuing. "If my numbers are correct, I think sale of that machinery more that paid off Juan's loan. The horses and mules brought what I would say would be my fair profit in the matter. So, Dog-man, you were right. The property is available to you and Snake for the price of eighteen hundred dollars." He had a pained look on his face and Snake wondered if the pain came from having to admit that he was trying to squeeze way too many dollars from them or from having to take far less money than he had asked.

It took less than an hour for all the paperwork to be properly written up and the group was off to Pioneer Crossing to finish the process at the bank. "Well, partner, we are now the proud owners of our second holding, twelve hundred acres of land with no cows," Dog-man laughed as they rode toward their camp. "It's late. We'll make the move tomorrow morning, eh?"

"You'll love what Louise and I learned from our get-together with Lefty Greene." Snake said.

"You can tell me all about it over some whiskey when we get to camp," Dog-man said.

THERE SEEMED to be many eyes on the three as they rode through the little village, including those of the sheriff, Tom Mallory. "You boys had some fun today. Lefty Greene won't take that without a fight. Want to tell me about it?"

"Not sure why, Sheriff, but he rode out for the Saucedo place before us this morning and was going through our kits on the horses when Louise found him. Sending him back to town in his long-johns seemed like a fair thing to do. We were in negotiations with Mendoza to buy the place. It was a busy time," Snake said.

"A lot of people got a kick out of it but you can bet Greene wasn't one of them. Watch your back, you two. You've made some enemies who don't play fair. Did you get the place?"

"Sure did. Settin' up to start ranching tomorrow morning, Sheriff. Tell your wife thank you."

The rest of the ride out to camp was quiet and slow, each letting their thoughts roam over the fact they now owned a large tract of land in the San Bernardino Valley. Dog-man was thinking how best to build a herd, Snake had his own thoughts on cattle, and Louise was worried about Lefty Greene and what the outlaw might try to do.

SNAKE SETTLED down near the fire with some fresh coffee helped along with a splash of whiskey and finally got to tell what he and Louise learned from Lefty Greene. "He is an outright thief, Dog. What was most surprising was that it was he and Rocky Lawrence who bamboozled Juan Saucedo. Lawrence worked with

Greene for some jobs and Skinny Dave Morgan for others. Now, here's the good part." He added another splash of whiskey to the cup before continuing.

"All right, Snake, you got our attention," Dog-man said.

"Well, seems he and Lawrence managed to move Saucedo's herd into the mountains north of here, but haven't sold them yet. That's right, Dog, they're probably spread all over the mountains up there by now. When we bought the ranch did it include Saucedo's brand?"

"Oh, hell yes," Dog-man sat right up at the question. "Mendoza went out of his way to include the phrase, 'any and all stray animals with the Saucedo brand should be included in this sale.' It was Mendoza's idea. He said Saucedo wasn't very good at keeping track of his herd."

"I know where we can start on keeping track of our herd. How are you at working wild cattle, Louise? Gonna learn quick if you don't already know."

"Rocky Lawrence is dead." Dog-man said. "Do you think Lefty Greene will make a move on those beeves before tomorrow morning?"

"I think he'll make a move on us before the cattle," Louise said. "I've never seen that kind of anger in a man as I saw today. He wants us, in particular me, dead."

They talked, made plans, and ate supper over the next hours. Snake laid out a rough map in the dirt on where Lefty said they had the herd. "Mendoza said there should be five hundred. Lefty said there might be three hundred. Either way, there will be several bulls and they'll be the hardest to move down out of those hills."

"Show off some fresh heifers and the bulls will come right along, Snake," Louise laughed. "Do we need help? Look for drovers or something?"

"No," Snake said. "It's best if not too many people know what we're doing until we get that herd back on their home grass."

"That little valley is one hillside north of our place?" Dog-man asked and got an affirmative nod back. "Maybe ten miles?" Another nod from Snake and Dog-man had one more question.

"Lots of standing timber?" Another nod and Dog-man grumbled. "That will make it difficult, but we may have to bring them back in small groups rather than build a large drive. It might take days. We'll break camp in the morning, get all our stuff out to the ranch and head out."

MORNING BROKE clear and chilly at their high camp. Louise had a fire, hot coffee, and fresh biscuits ready when the boys rolled out. "Gonna be a beautiful sunrise in a few minutes," she said. She had venison steaks roasting on a hot rock in the middle of the fire. "We gonna have real cookware at the ranch?"

"When was the last time you lived in a house?" Dog-man asked.

"I must have been young as young can be," she laughed. "I don't remember living in a house. How about you, Snake? When was that?"

"We had three walls a rotted out roof on the place at the mine, Dog. Remember that? The owls put up with us and dropped their form of greetings from time to time. Lived in a house in Texas until I ran away. Gonna be some interesting times coming our way."

Dog-man laughed at Louise's and Snake's answers

but didn't contribute his answer. *I ain't talkin' about living with aunt Beatrice and her fowl husband. He's the reason I ran away and I ain't talking about that shack they lived in.*

It was early afternoon before the three were able to ride off to their new spread to see about rounding up what was now their herd. They were standing in front of the cabin, looking at the hills to the north. The rolling hillside they had to ride across dipped and rose, and was covered in heavy timber. Much of the standing trees were oak and other hard woods and of course, lots of pine, spruce, and cedar.

"You say where Lefty left the herd is about ten miles?" Dog-man asked.

"By his reckoning," Snake said. "Rocky Lawrence weren't no cow man, but I think Lefty has some background. He said about three hundred head and about ten miles."

"Best bet is to gather as many as we can find and get them settled in a meadow," Dog-man said. "One of us stay with them and the other two bring small groups to the ranch. Done that a couple of times, Snake. We did that at the ranch in Colorado where we worked."

"Worked good, too, Dog. You might remember me and that pretty little girl did the same thing in Arizona Territory. Let's load the mule with a lean-to and supplies. This might take a couple of days, depending on the personal feelings of our cows," Snake laughed.

Louise took in a breath and pointed at the road. "Got some company coming. That's one scrawny horse."

"Just a kid and he's just as skinny." Dog-man said. Both men kept close to their horses and rifles.

The boy, maybe fourteen years old, riding a fourteen hand ancient horse rode slowly up to the group. A dog of many breeds was slowly wagging its long tail, giving the group a full look-over. "You are Snake?" He asked, looking at Snake. His English was fair with a heavy accent. "I am Santiago Valdez. I am here to offer my services. I clean, cut wood, mend fence, even cook. Good worker."

Snake smiled, looked at Dog-man and motioned the boy to dismount. "Señon Mendoza send you?"

"No," the boy drawled out. "Sheriff Tom said you might need my help. I've been working odd jobs for him." Snake took a step forward and the dog growled a warning.

"Easy there boy, we're friends. He put his hand out and the dog ever so carefully took a sniff, wagged its tail, and sat down at Snake's feet. "Well," Snake drawled out, "we just might want your services. You need to know, though," he said carefully, "you'll be working for us, not spying for the sheriff."

Dog-man chuckled. "You ever worked around cattle? Sheep? Hogs?"

"No, but I learn good. My horse is slow, though."

"Looks like he's lucky to still be alive," Louise said. "If he's coming with us he's got to have a better horse than that."

"We ain't got a whole lot of time to go horse trading," Snake growled. "Them cows need our attention more." He looked over at the boy. "You got extra clothes in those saddle bags?"

"One shirt, Señor Snake. That's all."

"Have to do. What do we call you? Santiago is a long name to holler out when we're moving cows."

"In Spanish, the short for Santiago is Chago. You can call me Chago."

"Good. Let's ride." Snake mounted, threw the mule's lead rope to Chago, and led the little caravan out. The boy's smile might have been seen at the top of the ridge they were ascending.

26

"THERE'S plenty of room to move small groups of cattle through this forest, Dog. We've done it too many times." Snake was leading them along a cutback trail up the hillside, climbing for the crest through the trees.

"It's gonna take some cow savvy drovers, Snake. A boy and a lion hunter ain't gonna put those critter on home range."

"I think I might know a couple, Dog. Just might know a couple."

"Sounds to me you're working on a plan. I want to hear yours and then I'll tell you mine. This kid is gonna need a horse and clothes sooner than later."

"I do have a plan, Dog. We'll work as many of the beeves as we can into some kind of meadow and then Louise and I will drive a group down to the ranch. You and Chago bring more strays down while we're gone, and then Louise and I will move more. Can do this until we have the whole herd back on home grass."

"Better plan than mine," Dog-man laughed.

They crested the hill and worked down toward a

large meadow and the closer they got the more cattle
they saw munching good grass. "I do think we're a
couple of lucky old bastards, Dog. They been waitin' for
us." Snake pointed out the brands on the heifers and
steers, spotted a couple of bulls doing battle in the trees
and pointed at them, too.

"Better keep our eyes open, Snake. Lefty could have a
night hawk out there. Don't want to ride into a gun
battle."

Snake and Dog-man rode side-by-side as did Louise
and Chago as they followed some twenty yards back.
Chago was leading the well packed mule. "I been looking
for some kind of sign, smoke, horse prints, movement,
and I don't see any," Dog-man said as they slowly moved
out of the trees and into the open spaces of the meadow.
"Looks like a stream or spring near that stand of spruce,"
he said, pointing.

The gunshot echoed back and forth across the peaks
and valleys, mixed with the cry of a wounded boy. Chago
fell from his horse, letting go of the mule's lead rope.
Snake and Dog-man were out of their saddles, rifles in
hand and Louise jumped from her horse as a second shot
rang out, striking her horse high in the neck.

Louise rolled away from the horse's flailing hooves,
had sense enough to bring her rifle, and with her free
hand snagged the mule's lead rope. She crawled the few
feet to Chago and found the boy dead. The rifle bullet hit
in the middle of the boy's chest and exploded out the
middle of his back.

"You see him?" Dog-man called out to Snake.

"In the trees to your right, Dog. I saw the puff of
smoke on his second shot. Lay a few rounds into that
mess of pines over there."

Snake moved fast through the grass, used every

bush, rock, and dip in the ground and was close to the copse of pine when a third shot rang out. "I gotcha now," Snake muttered He took a quick aim and squeezed the trigger, levered another round in and waited. *I know I hit you. Give me a sign you bastard. Don't want to kill you. Need some information from your filthy hide. Come on, yell out.*

There was no howling in pain, no cry for help, and the tension finally forced Snake to move slowly to where he thought the man fell. Snake crept alongside a felled tree and when he was just a few feet away saw Lefty Greene laid out on his back, sightless eyes staring up through the trees. "Damn it," Snake said. "Wanted you alive. Why did you shoot the boy? Were you that bad a shot? Aimed at Louise and hit the boy?"

"Sheriff ain't gonna like this, Snake. Have we started a war of some kind?" Dog-man walked up to take a look. "Did he shoot the boy on purpose or was he looking to hit Louise?"

"I just asked the same thing," Snake said, shaking his head.

They moved over to where Louise was holding Chago's body close to her. The cur-dog was whining, its head as close to the boy as it could get. "Never even had a chance to be friends with him," She said. "Who was it?" Her tears hid the building anger in the girl. Killing the boy made no sense to her and she was afraid she wouldn't be able let go of his frail body.

"It was Lefty Greene fulfilling his promise. We've got us another mess, Dog. One of us has to run into town and get the sheriff. It can't be Louise. I won't let that happen."

"I'll go," Dog-man said. "I'll bring back a horse, too. You can't ride that old nag Chago had," he said to Louise.

"Cows would laugh right out if you tried to move 'em along."

"We'll get the bodies buried and make up camp while you're gone," Snake said. "We can also see if we can make a count on how many animals are in this little basin. Be as quick as you can. There might be more of them."

"No way I can be back before tomorrow," Dog-man said.

"Watch your back," Louise cried out as Dog-man rode out.

IT WAS ten miles back to the ranch and then several more into Pioneer Crossing, and Dog-man felt the change in the air more than saw the failing light and knew the long day was finally ending. He tied off in front of the sheriff's office and waited just a moment to gather his thoughts before walking in. "Evening, Sheriff," he said.

"Dog-man. Well, this is a surprise. What brings you to town this late in the day?"

"I'm afraid it ain't good news. It's gonna take a few minutes to tell the story. You got some coffee?"

"With a taste of whiskey too," Sheriff Mallory said with a chuckle. "From the look on your face, I'm not gonna like this story."

Dog-man took his time and spelled out why they were in the little mountain meadow and what happened. "No one saw it coming, Sheriff. Snake is sure that Lefty was trying to hit Louise, not the boy. Does he have family?"

"I guess my wife and I are his only family. His father died rustling some cattle and his mother, weak and sickly, died two years ago. I was hoping working for you two would put some meat on him and it's never a bad thing to know how to work on a ranch. Mamacita isn't going to like this."

Mallory took a deep breath, poured the two of them more coffee, well laced from his flask, and sat back in his chair. "As long as the brands are right, what cattle you find are yours, bought and paid for. Watch the brands carefully. With Skinny Dave Morgan, Rocky Lawrence, and now, Lefty Greene out of the picture, there isn't a big outlaw threat in Pioneer Crossing now. Just that fool Freddie Barton and his gang."

"We were grateful for you sending Chago to us, Sheriff. Is there someone else you would recommend? We could use another hand."

"Let's go to the café and have supper. Maybe I can come up with a name. If Tony Mendoza is around let's not say anything about the cattle. Not say anything until you get them all back on their own grass." Mallory had a twinkle in eyes as they left the office.

I wonder if the sheriff is trying to tell me something. I've had second thoughts about Mendoza right from the start. Couldn't get straight answers, find out Lefty moved the herd but didn't sell it off. Was Mendoza planning to bring the herd to us and selling it? Did Lefty actually work for Mendoza? Dog-man had a million questions and no answers. *Can't come right out and ask the sheriff either, him being married to Mendoza's daughter.*

What supper conversation there was, was muted at best after Maria-Elena had her crying fit. "Maybe a brandy at the Elkhorn Saloon, eh Dog-Man?" Mallory asked.

It was a short walk on a warm night and Mallory took the time to ask if they thought they made a good deal with Mendoza.

"It appears so," Dog-man said. He wasn't going to go into any detail, wasn't going to tell about how Mendoza was trying to charge some hefty prices. "What is Mendoza like, Sheriff? You're his son-in-law, you must know how the man thinks."

"Your question already tells me how your deal played out. Tried to take you, did he? Not surprised. I don't really think his moves and actions are illegal in most of his land deals, but he does stretch the letters of the law. He's a master of intimidation. I have a suspicion that you haven't said a word to him about knowing that Greene hadn't sold the herd. Clever of you to get the phrase about stray steers in the bill of sale."

"Should we consider the man dangerous?" Dog-man asked. They stepped up on the boardwalk in front of the saloon and Sheriff Mallory stopped before going through the bat-wing doors, scratched at his day old beard, and half-way smiled.

"Tony Mendoza, dangerous?" He stood on the board-walk, pushed his hat back, and rubbed his forehead. "The man himself? No. Mendoza's people, though? That's a different question. He's able to get things done without being involved, if you know what I'm saying."

Dog-man chuckled and walked into the saloon. *That's the kind of answer I like. Pretty much what I figured, too. He's going to be trouble and the fact that the sheriff is his son-in-law makes it a little dangerous. Which side is Mallory on?* "A quick brandy or two and I'm riding back to the ranch, spend the night and find the herd in the morning. Think I could find a cow man in here?"

"They're in here but probably already working for some of the near-by outfits," Mallory said. "If I see one who might fit in with you and Snake, I'll say something. After that, it's up to you."

The Elkhorn Saloon had a hotel attached along with a restaurant and was busy. Card tables were filled, men were lined up at the long bar, and the few drinking tables scattered around were mostly filled. A man in a white shirt, black vest, and bowler hat was pounding viciously at a piano that simply couldn't be heard over the crowd.

"Seems almost like a party, Sheriff," Dog-man said. "Most of these people are not cow men or ranchers, though."

"Mostly people arriving after crossing the Mojave Desert, Dog-man. They're happy to be back in civilization. Not that many locals in here right now. They'll come in later. See the skinny kid in the red shirt?" Dog-man nodded. "Name's Francisco Alvarado. Good hand, good English, and quick temper. Be good for you, I think." Mallory nodded to the kid and made room for he and Dog-man. They settled in, one on each side of Alvarado.

"Want you to meet somebody, Cisco. This is Dog-man. He and his partner, Snake, just bought the Saucedo place and are looking to hire a good cow man. You working?"

"Lookin'," the tall, thin, dark eyed gentleman said. "Just rode in from Mormon Station. Heard all about you, Dog-man. Saucedo's place? Why you looking for hands if you ain't got cattle?" There was a lot of snide in the comment and Dog-man remembered what the sheriff said about the man having a quick temper.

"We've got cattle," Dog-man said, quietly, not offering anything else. He looked the man up and down, saw a lot of strength, saw rough, worn hands, and saw a man who could put in a full day in the saddle and still get it on after night-fall. "Looking for a man who can throw a straight loop and ride for the brand. Fifteen dollars a month and found."

"You've made some enemies in the territory," Alvarado said. "I ain't signin' on to fight your battles, just keep your cattle safe. Don't need more enemies than I've already got."

"Be at the ranch at sunrise ready to go to work," Dog-man said. He drained his brandy and nodded to the barman for another. "I'll be heading out after this one, Sheriff. Thanks for your help."

"You heading back to the ranch?" Alvarado asked and Dog-man nodded. "Everything I own is on the back of my horse. I'll ride with you."

27

ONLY THE STARS TO light the way, Dog-man and Francisco Alvarado rode back to the ranch on an almost balmy evening. Francisco was riding his horse and trailing one Dog-man bought from Mallory. He wanted two but the sheriff only had the one for sale.

"You and Snake rode into Pioneer Crossing without any cattle, Dog-man, and bought a ranch that had no cattle. How it is you told me you have cattle?"

Dog-man chuckled. "It's a long story, Francisco, and one you might enjoy." Ten minutes later the two men were laughing as they made the turn into the little valley and the home ranch.

"Oh, you pulled one on Mendoza there," Alvarado said. "He won't take kindly to that. There are three men who work for him that do his bidding regardless of consequences. You understand what I just said?"

"Loud and clear, Cisco. From the minute I met the man I was sure he was not this wonderful kind-hearted old Spaniard he claims to be. Snake and I are looking to run a ranch not get in a fight with Mendoza. Or anyone else, either," Dog-man said. "We need you as a cow-man, not as a gunman. Clear?"

Alvarado smiled. "Está bien, Dog-man. Clear as a bell."

SUNRISE FOUND Snake and Louise getting saddled after a hearty breakfast. "This poor old horse won't make the day, Snake. I feel so sorry for that boy."

"Ain't nothing more can be done for him, I'm afraid. I need you to ride your horse in a long, wide circle around these cows that are here in this valley. Don't try to herd them, just keep them contained as best you can. I'll be riding through the trees and brush, bringing groups down to you. Any problems with that?"

"I'm sure I can handle that. Think we'll have any trouble? I'm worried about how much trouble I've caused you," she said. "First with the Indians and the horses, and now with this Lefty Greene thing. Am I just a trouble maker?"

"Ha!" Snake said. "You, my wife, are the best kind of troublemaker. Me and old Dog seem to draw trouble to us, but the kind you draw isn't something to worry about. I'll spend the rest of my life with your kind of trouble." Snake felt himself redden some and had to look away as he pulled the cinch tight on Louise's old horse.

She turned him around and had her arms around his neck that fast. "Thank you," she whispered, gave him a long kiss, but wouldn't let go. She just held on tight, squeezing as hard as she could, kissed him again, and as she drew back he saw tears running down her cheeks.

"Best go find some cows, eh?" he said and helped her in the saddle. "Don't be worrying if you don't see me too often. I'll bring small groups down to the meadow as often as I can."

She watched the tall Texan ride off into the trees and brush as she rode along the edge of the meadow. The cattle were spread out along a cut-bank created by a spring and its runoff and Louise stayed well back from them as she began her wide circle.

Papa told me there would be men of different sorts, some to like, some to avoid at all cost, but he never mentioned a man like Snake. My lord I'm one lucky girl. The sun was bright and warm as Louise made her first circle of the pastured cattle. She did her best to make a count and thought she had about a hundred cows. They were moving around rather leisurely, she thought, moving from a patch of grass to the water, and back to eating.

She was half way around the herd the second time when she saw Snake driving fifteen or so steers down off the hillside. She waved and rode toward him at a walk. the old horse wasn't able to trot or lope, she was sure. As she got closer, she saw two riders coming up from the opposite direction and waved to catch Snake's attention, pointing the riders out to him.

Snake saw the two, motioned Louise to stay where she was and turned toward the riders. *Don't recognize these fellers. Damn. Wish Dog-man was here. Ain't no reason I can think of for two men to be out riding following no kind of trail.* He continued moving the cattle onto the valley floor, letting them join and mingle with those already there and turned to the men coming in.

The two rode in at a lope and pulled up some twenty feet or so from Snake. "Just what do you think you're doing with those steers, Mister?" the largest of the two yelled out. "Them's Mendoza cattle you're hazin'."

"Ain't," Snake said. "My cattle. My brand." He looked

over and saw that Louise had dismounted and was standing to the side of the old horse, that rifle of hers at the ready. The two men saw her too. "Don't believe we've met," Snake said. He let his hand hang close to the handle of his revolver and wished he had the rifle in hand instead.

"Don't matter none who we are," the big man said. "What matters is them cattle. They belong to Antonio Mendoza and we're taking them."

"As I said, them's my cattle, my brand. Make a move to take them and my wife will shoot you dead. When she's through shootin' you, I'll shoot you a couple of times too. Time to move off, gentlemen. We've got work to do."

Snake said it loud enough for Louise to hear and she brought her rifle up to her shoulder, aiming it at the big man first, and then his partner. Louise spotted two more men riding in at a trot, maybe a quarter of a mile off to Snake's left. "Got more company, Snake. Off to your left there." She never moved the rifle's sight off the big man as she talked and the big man took his eyes off her for the first time, looking for the newcomers.

"Well, will you look at that. Looks like you boys got here at the wrongest time possible," Snake laughed. "That be my other partner riding up to join us." Quick as lightning, Snake drew his revolver and pointed it at the big man. "It's time to throw your weapons onto the ground, boys. You first, big man. Nice and slow, now. Rifle, then the hand gun."

Snake and Louise watched the man slowly lift the revolver from its leather, but instead of dropping it, he whipped it up to take a shot at Snake. Louise's rifle barked first followed immediately by Snake's Colt and the man was flung from his saddle. His partner didn't move a muscle and Snake rode up to him, his gun still smoking and growled, "Drop the damn guns."

Dog-man and Francisco rode up quickly, their guns drawn as the second outlaw dropped his rifle first, and then the sidearm. "Good boy," Snake said. "Let's ride up toward them trees over that way so's we can have a little chat." He motioned the rider and Louise rode up along-side Snake, took the reins dangling from the dead man's horse. Dog-man and Cisco followed along.

"Can't leave you two alone for even a minute, can I?" Dog-man said. "Meet our new hand, Francisco Alvarado."

"Welcome," Snake said. "You been around this country for a while? Happen to know either of these fellers? Said they worked for Antonio Mendoza?"

"They do," Cisco said. "The dead one was called Walt, and this one is known as Shannahan. Known as enforcers, getting done what Mendoza needed done. They come for the cattle?"

"Indeed," Snake said. "Question now is, what do we do with this fool? We gotta get the other one buried before it gets hot."

"Did anyone make a count?" Dog-man asked and Louise told him she thought there were about a hundred on the valley floor before Snake brought the new ones in. Well," he said, slowly, as he worked out a plan. "let's bring what we have in to home grass, make Shannahan ride with us, and work on what to do with him."

"At least we got you a good horse to ride, Louise," Snake chuckled. "I think it might be best to just turn this fool loose, and you, me, and Cisco work these hills and bring the rest of our herd down. This group down here is happy with good grass and cool water."

"Best plan," Dog-man said. He looked at Shannahan

and scowled. "Your lucky day, buster. Sometimes my partner gets all riled like and just starts shooting. Coulda put three big holes in the middle of your chest. Maybe he shoulda. Well, don't be gettin' in our sights, ever, cuz you won't live to talk about it."

Louise slapped Shannahan's horse with her rifle butt and the horse galloped off. Shannahan never looked back, just sank his spurs deep and laid low over the saddle's horn. Louise stripped the saddle from her worn out pony and re-set the stirrups on the horse Walt was riding. "That old pony will be happy in this meadow. Grass and water for his old age."

THE SUN WAS DROPPING FAST when Cisco rode down into the meadow with the last fifteen steers. "Can't be any others up there," he said. Snake and Dog-man had ridden in just minutes before, got their horses ready for the night and were standing close to the fire Louise had burning.

"If that's not three hundred head of cattle out there, then I don't know how to count," she said. "Will Mendoza try to take them tonight?"

"I doubt it," Snake said. "He's played his hand and lost. Any move now would bring in the sheriff and I doubt if he wants that. I'll ride first night-hawk, Cisco, you relieve me, and we'll move them down to the ranch at first light. We can make ten miles in a day, I think. Maybe," he said.

"Mendoza won't make a play for the cattle," Alvarado said. "What he's most known for is hurting people, not killing them. He can't hurt you by trying to take the cattle, because the story is too well known, but he will try to hurt you. Some have found their homes burned to the ground, others have found their children hurt or abused, some have found loved ones dead or injured to the point of being crippled for life."

"Nasty man," Snake mused. He looked at Louise and found her looking right back at him. Were they thinking the same thoughts? Would Mendoza hurt Snake? Or hurt Louise? Or hurt both in order to hurt Dog-man?

"You said the man has children hurt?" Snake didn't drawl out the question, he fired it out. Children to Snake were all angels, to be loved, hugged, cherished. He remembered the man in Arizona Territory to hit his child, and anger roiled his blood.

"Easy, Snake. This isn't the time to get riled." Dog-man saw it coming, saw hard times for Señor Mendoza if what Cisco said were true.

"Let's get a good supper down and sleep sound. It's gonna be busy tomorrow," Snake said, trying to break the gloom that had settled in. "I'm pretty sure we brought some nice juicy venison steaks along and I've got a jug of good whiskey buried in my kit somewhere." Dog-man smiled knowing that Snake himself saw the danger signs.

28

CISCO HAD the fire burning hot and got the crew up well before dawn. "Not a piece of trouble, Snake. Cattle are calm, well fed and watered, ready for a nice ten-mile walk." It was a beautiful morning, calm, warm, and skies filled with a light haze blowing up from the deep valley to the west. The only thoughts were of hot coffee, hot biscuits, and an easy drive to home grass.

Snake chuckled to himself. *Nice easy drive through standing timber, pines, oak, manzanita, rocks, steep grades, and always the possibility of being ambushed by a nasty old Spanish Grandee. Yup, nice and easy drive.*

Within minutes they found the lead animal, there's always at least one who moves out smartly, and cattle love to play follow the leader. They put Louise on her new horse to ride point, Cisco rode drag, and Snake and Dog-man rode the flanks as they moved slowly through the timber, open meadows, and rocky gulches toward home grass.

Louise hadn't said anything the night before but riding alone, all the thoughts returned. *I've killed two men*

now, men I've never met, can't say I hated, but took their lives.
In both cases if I hadn't pulled the trigger, Snake would be
dead, so, in his way of thinking, I was justified in shooting
them. But what about my way of thinking? Papa's way of
thinking? What would Papa say?

The thoughts were with her through the rest of the
morning until she finally told herself to set them aside
until she could talk to Snake. As planned, they didn't
stop at mid-day for something to eat, just kept the cattle
moving downhill, slow and steady. It was mid-afternoon
when they were flagged down by Sheriff Tom Mallory.
Snake motioned for Dog-man to join him, hollered at
Cisco and Louise to keep the herd moving.

"Come to get a lesson on driving cattle, Sheriff?"
Snake asked riding up to the big man. "Got about three
hundred of them. Had some trouble yesterday, though."

"That's why I'm here," Mallory said. He wasn't
wearing his natural smile and gave the impression that
he didn't want to be there. Some men wear their
emotions spread all over their face while others keep
them locked in solid granite. Sheriff Mallory's face was
grim most of the time, but when he did let a smile out, it
could be seen for miles. Snake thought it was locked in
granite.

"A man filed a complaint against Louise, Snake. We
need to have a nice long, quiet talk about that."

"We're less than three miles from the ranch, Sheriff.
You ride on down with us and we can talk in the quiet of
a warm kitchen, drinking fresh coffee and eating fresh
biscuits." Snake didn't sound as light and airy as his
words were. He had a hard look on his face, saying, do it
this way or not at all.

"You got a way about you that I like," Mallory said. "I
won't ride drag, though." This time there was a chuckle

and the man had his smile back. "Even my wife is upset with her father this time. Why don't you and I ride point, Snake, and we can talk some."

Three miles at a quiet walk through some of the most gorgeous country in southern California may have had an influence on the outcome of the talk between the sheriff and Snake but by the time they walked the herd back onto their own pastures, the idea of a complaint against Louise didn't exist.

Sitting around the heavy, rough hewn oak kitchen table with a pot of coffee boiling on the iron stove and a jug of good whiskey being passed about, made for a comfortable end to a long day in the saddle.

"So," Sheriff Mallory said, "the three of you, Dog-man, Cisco, and Snake agree that Walt made the first move to shoot you, Snake and Louise killed him. I'll expect that in writing before I head back to town. That should give you, Louise, more than enough time to bake a pan full of biscuits, eh?"

That broke the tension of the moment and the jug and coffee pot made a round of the table. "From Lion Killer to Camp Cook. That's the way it's gonna be?" She was laughing knowing full well that Snake was a far better cook than she was. "Biscuits it is, then."

I've been working with my father for so long, free as any bird you've seen, and here I am, married, part owner of a ranch, and still wearing my buckskins. I ain't giving them up. I ain't. She had half a smile, half a frown as she mixed up a bowl of dough. *I'm just as free as Snake, and he's the only man I'll ever be with.*

"I'll bring the statements in with me this evening and I think it might be best if the three of you ride into town tomorrow morning when I present these to the justice of the peace."

"We'll be there. Cisco, you ride on the herd, look for any injuries or sick ones that might need attention. Keep your eyes open for problems," Dog-man said.

That night, Snake and Louise were in their lean-to near the barn and Louise told Snake about her doubts. "Papa always said killing another human was simply wrong, but if I hadn't, yesterday or last week, you would be dead. I don't know right from wrong anymore." She wanted to cry and found she couldn't. "Damn it, Snake, I can't even cry anymore." She flung her arms around him and hung on tight.

"Trying to settle things based on somebody's ideas of wrong and right isn't always the best way, dear girl," Snake said. "Sometimes reason and logic have to come into play, sometimes deep feelings are the point. I'd take on Sitting Bull himself to protect you. You just did the same thing. Don't worry about justification, think love, honor, even duty, to protect a loved one."

Louise sat quiet, letting those words flow through her, and found that she really could still cry. "Well, look at this," Snake said, "Lion Killer is a cry-baby." The wrestling match turned into a love-making match in just seconds.

———

DOG-MAN LED the group into town at eight o'clock, and they went into Malloy's office. "Got time for coffee before court?" Dog-man asked.

"No, actually, we don't. Judge gamble set a hearing for nine instead of ten and didn't tell me until moments ago. I thought your statements would be enough but they weren't. I think he wants to see Louise again. We better get over there."

The courthouse was directly across the main street from the sheriff's office and when the group arrived they found Justice of the Peace, Hiram Betterman drumming his fingers on the bench top. The large clock showed it was two minutes before nine.

"Take your seats, please," Betterman said, "and we'll get this show underway." Snake looked around as he found a seat, saw Antonio Mendoza and another man talking, but could not find the man called Shannahan in the courtroom.

"The complaint is that you, Louise Peabody aimed your rifle at Mr. Shannahan with intent to kill. How do you plead?"

"Before she pleads, your honor, I have statements from everyone present that contradict the complaint."

"That's fine, Sheriff, but I want to hear the plea before we continue. Mrs. Peabody?"

Dog-man's head swiveled about. He was looking for somebody called Mrs. Peabody. He caught the slightest grin from Louise.

"My father, Raven Hawk, along with being a preacher, was schooled in law, your honor," Louise said. Snake looked at her, amazed at her poise, her open faced dialogue with the judge, and no tears.

"I believe the person making the complaint needs to be present. I don't believe Mr. Shannahan is in the courtroom. I can't confront the complainer," she said.

"Is Mr. Shannahan present?" Judge Betterman called out. "Come now, is Mr. Shannahan present?" The irascible old judge, his white beard shaking in anger, glared around the courtroom.

"I'm speaking for the poor and frightened man," Mendoza said, striding toward the bench. "He's not fit to be here, your honor."

"Most unusual," Betterman said. "Mrs. Peabody?"

"Indeed," Louise said. She looked at Mendoza who stood, a stern look frozen in place across his almost regal face. "Does Mr. Shannahan work for you, Mr. Mendoza? Or is he a relative?"

"No, just an old friend who needs help. I believe in helping old friends."

"May I interrupt, your honor, since these proceedings haven't actually begun?" Snake stood and asked. "Mrs. Peabody is my wife, as you know." Dog-man almost broke out in a laugh but caught himself. He saw Louise give him another grin.

"Most unusual but I have no objection. What do you have to offer?"

"Mr. Shannahan told my wife and I that he was working for Mr. Mendoza when he and a man named Walt attempted to take our cattle. The cattle were all carrying my brand. Mr. Mendoza had no claim to them in any way."

Judge Betterman sat back in his large, hand-carved chair and coughed, softly. "Mendoza, can you explain yourself? Remember this is a court of law, even if no one has been sworn in, the threat of perjury exists." Judge Betterman sighed but wasn't about to let this get away from him. He was generally an easy man to get along with until you try to take advantage of his good humor. Men have faced ten days on bread and water for thinking they could.

Mendoza was in a pickle. He had Lefty Greene rustle the cattle for him, and they were supposed to have been sold. When he found out they were loose in the hills and that he had signed papers saying stray cattle with Saucedo's brand belonged to Snake and Dog-man, he immediately sent Walt and Shannahan to gather and sell that herd.

Snake watched the man squirm, saw sweat gather on his brow and, along with everyone in the courtroom, waited for his answer. "I'm only here to help an old friend," Mendoza started to give his answer.

"Does Mr. Shannahan work for you? Is he in your employ?" Judge Betterman's voice had risen a note or two and Mendoza glared at him. Betterman backed down from no one, and his glare back carried the weight of the courtroom. Deathly silence was the current order of the day.

Mendoza's glare was moved from the judge to Louise, then to Snake and Dog-man. He did not answer the question, just stood, glaring at everyone in turn.

Snake's mind was quick. *Is the judge in Mendoza's employ? That cagey old Spaniard might just pull this off if he is. Gotta think quick, old man.* Snake was startled when the gavel came down with sincere authority and Betterman continued to glare right back at Mendoza.

Betterman coughed again, tapped the gavel good and hard, again, and told Mendoza to sit down. He looked about the courtroom and asked, quietly, "Is Mr. Shannahan in the courtroom?" There was no answer and he told Louise to stand up.

"Mrs. Peabody, there are no charges against you. You are free to go. I'll not hear any more about this issue. This court is adjourned." The man stood up, pulled his robes off, and looked at the sheriff.

"Tom, if you are any kind of politician, you will lead us to the Elkhorn Saloon and stand for the first round. I will stand for the second, and Snake, since you are married to this charming young legal eagle, you will stand for the third."

Thunderous laughter, groans of complaint from Mendoza, and cheering from the gallery led the group down Main Street to the Elkhorn. They even let Louise stand at the bar with the men, even though she only had root beer. It was a long and boisterous ride back to the ranch several hours later.

No one heard Antonio Mendoza tell the man who was sitting next to him that he would see that woman dead, that herd destroyed, and the ranch burned to the ground.

29

It was a long and crooked trail back to the ranch with loud singing from Snake and Dog-man and continued urging-on by Louise. "That arrogant old Spaniard ain't gonna let this go by," Dog-man said more than once.

"I ain't worried. I'm married to Lion Killer," Snake would laugh, and Louise would whack their horses to keep 'em moving. It was nearing sunset when they rode up to the main house. "I gotta build us a house, Louise. We can't live in that lean-to forever, you know. Better start tomorrow, eh?"

It was Cisco who prepared their meal and got them calmed down enough to eat it. It was late in the evening that he sent Snake and Louise off to the lean-to, told Dog-man he'd check on the herd before bedding down himself, and a long day came to an end. *Those are wild buckaroos,* Cisco chuckled to himself. *I wonder if ranch life will be good for them. Louise ain't gonna calm 'em down. She's one of 'em.*

The breakfast table conversations centered on what each person thought about how Mendoza would extract his revenge. "He's a cruel man," Cisco said. "He's been out-foxed and he'll never let that stand. Fire is his first weapon of choice followed by threats and intimidation. He won't attempt intimidation in this case."

Dog-man laughed but also questioned the idea. "He understands his strengths and he knows he's been bested. No, Cisco's right, intimidation will have teeth if he tries. It won't be loose talk, it'll be real violence with a threat attached."

Snake drank his coffee, ate an extra helping of flapjacks covered in fried eggs, and listened to all the comments without offering one of his own. He and Louise had already had their say before coming up to the house. "I'm cutting timber for our new house," he said. "Cisco, we need to know how many good bulls we have, we need pregnancy checks on our heifers, and we need a real count of marketable steers. What are your plans, Dog?"

"I'll just sit in that old rocker out on the porch and watch the day go by. Might watch for visitors if I think about it. There is one thing, though, that's been bothering me." Dog-man got a sly smile, poured a cup of coffee, and looked at Louise. "Just who is Mr. Peabody if you are Mrs. Peabody?"

Snake jumped to his feet. "Gotta get started if we're gonna get anything done today." Louise chuckled at the reaction and added to the fun by giving a crooked answer. "Mr. Peabody is your partner, most often called Snake." She let it go at that, didn't offer any more and Snake stood by the door ready to run if she did.

"There is more to the name, I suppose?" Dog-man asked. His eyes were blazing with anticipation. For years neither man had let the other know their full and legal names and Dog-man was sure that he was about to find out Snake's.

"I would imagine," Louise said. She had a wonderful smile on her face as she moved to Snake's side, took his arm, and walked him out the door. "Time to build a house, Mr. Snake." She had a strong hold on his arm fearing the man would run at any moment. "I never gave him your whole name, Alonzo Cornelius. You're safe for a while."

"He don't need to know things like that," is all Snake said. "Gotta get us a house built, girl." They were both laughing by the time they got back to the lean-to.

TOM MALLORY WAS HAVING coffee and a sweet roll with his wife in her café when Antonio Mendoza arrived. There was a stiff wind blowing in from the north promising the arrival of a storm before the end of the day. "You've done a fine job embarrassing me, Mallory. Come election time it won't be forgotten. You won't just lose the election, Sheriff, you'll be crushed."

"That's no way to talk, Father." Maria-Elena stood up with Tom and scowled at her father. "Tom is an outstanding sheriff and you know it. The way you treat people is what's wrong. Some of the stories I've heard make me ashamed that you're my father."

The slap could have been heard as far as Mormon station and Mallory took one step forward and punched the venerable old Spaniard hard, driving him back. He crashed into the door, shattering the glass that was so hard to obtain on the frontier. Mendoza bounced off the door and was met by a second fist that shattered the man's nose. He fell to the floor, moaning in pain, writhing in his battle to get his feet under him.

Mallory was about to punch him again when a large man burst through the broken door, saw Mendoza on the floor and went for his side-arm. Mallory grabbed a café chair and swung it as hard as he could, smashing it into pieces across the man's head. The sheriff drew his weapon and it followed the path of the chair knocking the assailant unconscious.

"Burt Holloway," Mallory murmured. "Should have known." Mallory thought of the list of names he had left at the office. "Didn't even have his name on that list. Are you all right, Maria?" She nodded through her tears that she was fine.

Tom Mallory, his pistol still in his hand, towered over the cowering Antonio Mendoza. "You ever raise a hand to my wife again and I'll kill you, old man. Get out of this café, take your bleeding baggage with you." He jerked Mendoza to his feet, grabbed the still dizzy Holloway, and shoved the two out the door.

Maria-Elena was sitting at a table sobbing and Mallory sat next to her, his arm around her shoulder. "I swear to you, he will never touch you again."

"I'm afraid he's started a war, Tom. He wants to be the big man in San Bernardino County. You and the judge are the big men." Her sobbing had ended, the sting on her cheek was fading, and anger was rising. "He's a mean old man, Tom. I'm worried for us."

"He has more than me and the judge to worry about, Maria. Now, Snake, Dog-man, and Louise have more standing than your father. He won't let that last. Raven Hawk's daughter made a fool of the man in front of a lot of people. I'll get someone to fix that door but the chair is a gonner," he chuckled.

She was laughing and crying at the same time and went into the kitchen returning with a broom. "He has some terrible men who work for him, Tom. Be careful. I know he's had people murdered for less than what you did."

Mallory was sure his wife was right and went back to the office to fill out that list of people he might need to keep an eye on. The list carried the names of men who had spent time in the cells in the back of the office.

Mendoza liked to appear as this old-line Spanish grandee, the Alcaldo, while in reality he ran a gang of outlaws who regularly sold stolen livestock, acquired property from those not willing to sell, and bribing some of the businessmen to pay for protection from outlaws who destroy property and steal merchandise. Threats of physical abuse, threats of danger to family, including children, and threats of death were the tools of the trade.

Because of Maria-Elena I've been hands-off the old man but not after this morning. He had those thoughts but he was also aware that despite being sure of the old man's criminal behavior he simply didn't have the evidence necessary to arrest the man. It was the open handed slap that changed his attitude. No man has the right to slap a woman, daughter or not.

Pete Sanches, Freddie Barton, and Shannahan had their names at the top of the list, which now contained Holloway's. Mallory figured Mendoza would surely have words with Shannahan after that courtroom episode and his life is probably in danger.

He walked over to Leonard Ames' farm and ranch emporium to hire someone to fix the door at the café and ran smack into Snake and Louise. "What a nice surprise. What brings you to town on a windy and chilly morning?"

"Gotta build a house, Sheriff. Louise wants a dress. Don't know why. She's mighty fine looking in those buckskins."

"Let's see if old Leonard has some coffee brewing on that stove of his. Got something to talk about," the sheriff said.

"You gentlemen have your talk, I'm going to find a dress. Something fit for a rancher's wife." She worked her way through plows, harness, saddles, men's trousers and shirts, and finally came to where women's clothes were displayed. There was more to it than wanting to look like a rancher's wife. It had to do with the fact it wouldn't be long before she wouldn't fit in her buckskins. Louise was almost positive that she was carrying Snake's baby.

30

"You've got something on your mind besides coffee," Snake said as they found chairs near the pot-belly stove. "Your knuckles are bleeding and you've got a grim look on your face. Does that have something to do with it?"

"Everything to do with it," Mallory growled and spent the next several minutes telling Snake of the café episode. Snake was sure the more the man talked the angrier he got. "I'm gonna take out Shannahan first and then the Barton gang. All of them work directly for Mendoza."

"I ain't spent a great deal of time in towns and cities, Sheriff," Snake said, "But one thing I've learned, if there is a man who believes he can get away with illegal activity, it usually means he has some kind of political backing. It was obvious that Judge Betterman isn't backing Mendoza. Does he have someone in the county commission, or even at the state level behind him?"

"California isn't like many of the other states and territories, Snake. Sometimes it's difficult to remember that it was under Spanish rule and then Mexican rule long before it became a part of the United States. Mendoza's strength comes from those who still yearn for the Spanish and Mexican ways. He still believes his Spanish background is all he needs for political strength. There are those with political strength who feel the same way. I plan to change that."

"From what I've seen, Sheriff, you need a lot of help. The man's a land broker who sells what he has stolen and has hired guns doing the dirty work. Are there people in this area who will be on your side, work with or for you?"

"That's why we're talking, Snake," the sheriff said, just the slightest hint of a smile across his rugged face. His eyes were piercing as he glared at Snake. "I need real help, tough, angry, sometimes mean help. I'm the elected sheriff of this wonderful county and I'm authorized to hire up to three deputies. Right now, I have one who acts more as the night jailer than a gang-busting deputy."

Snake took in a deep breath, and knew what was coming. "No, Sheriff. No. Me and old Dog just bought us a ranch, I just got myself married off." He reached for his coffee, wagged his head back and forth, scowled, and said no several more times.

"It wouldn't be a full time job, Snake. All I need is someone I can trust, someone I know will back my plays, someone who values the rule of law." Mallory sat back in his chair and watched Snake mull everything over and over. Didn't say a word, sipped his coffee, even stuck a log in the stove.

If Antonio Mendoza, the land broker, the man with the hard sell, knew just what a salesman Tom Mallory was, he wouldn't even need hired guns. Snake sat quiet, slowly shaking his head back and forth. "Dammit, Sheriff," Snake said. "Half a dozen lawmen in New Mexico

Territory called me an outlaw as soon as they saw me and you want to pin a damn badge on me. Ain't right for a man to know that much about me."

"You won't have to wear a badge, Snake. I want to know that if I need help, can I call on you and Dog-man to come a-running?" He sat back in his chair and gave Snake a long look, shaking his head. "Now that I think about it, you do have the swagger of an outlaw, a hired gun, maybe."

Snake laughed and took a long drink of hot coffee. "You left Lion Killer out, Sheriff. Mendoza has already threatened her, and she will back your plays right along with us. She's saved my hide more than once."

Leonard Ames walked up to the stove, stirred the coals about and added a log. "Mighty intense conversation going on back here." He looked at Snake. "You the one they call Snake? Glad to know you. I'm Len Ames. Own this wreck of a store. Done old Big Al some good, didn't you? Big Al's coming to town next week, he says. Needs some stuff."

Snake stood up and shook the man's hand. "Pleased to make your acquaintance, Ames. Gonna build a house and need to buy what's needed. Me and Louise made a list to get us started." He handed the list to Ames. "Let Big Al know where we are. He's a good man."

"And you, Sheriff? What are you building?"

"A new door, Len, and somebody to build it. Wrecked the door at the café this morning."

Ames looked at him, the question burning in his eyes, but the look on the sheriff's face told the shop keeper to keep his mouth shut. "Got a man knows how to build doors. I'll send him over."

Louise walked up holding two dresses and some of

the underthings she would need to wear them. "Ain't they pretty?" She said. "I like green."

Snake shook his head but had a smile on his face. "We'll be back with the wagon to pick the building stuff up, Ames. You think there's something we missed on that list, add it and the cost of these dresses." He looked at Sheriff Mallory. "Why don't you drop by later this afternoon, Sheriff. Might even put you to work."

Ames wrapped the dresses in paper and tied the bundle so it could ride behind Louise's saddle for the ride back to the ranch. "I want to ride back with you when you come in with the wagon, Snake. We ain't got much for food out there, 'ceptin meat of course. Cisco said we need to have what he called a kitchen garden, too. He said every ranch should have one."

"Yup," Snake drawled out. "We always had one growin' up. Ma was good with growin' things."

"I'm gonna have to learn all about things like that. I'm a hunter, Snake. There's a whole bunch about livin' in one place that I don't know nothing about."

Snake had to laugh. "Me too, little darlin'. Me too."

They rode out of town on a breezy and almost chilly afternoon. "Just heard that Big Al is coming to town next week. It'll be good to see him again. As long as he isn't bringing us more problems." Snake said.

"What was so important that the sheriff wanted to talk to you about? Hope it wasn't a threat against us or something," Louise said. "Must be difficult for him to be married to Mendoza's daughter."

"That's part of what he talked about. Mendoza came to the café and slapped her, which of course got Mallory pretty much riled. He whipped the old man. Wants us to be able to back him up when things get nasty around the valley." Snake didn't go into any more detail and Louise took it as something a friend might ask.

Snake pulled up short when they topped a rise and looked down on their new ranch. "Whew. Will you look at that? Cattle on our grass, Louise. Never thought I'd see that. I was ten years old the last time I saw cattle that belonged to the family on land that belonged to the family. Oh, my," he said a couple of times. Nostalgia was not one of Snake's serious thought patterns and this caught him by surprise. "We actually do own that, Louise. You, me, and Dog own all that land and all them critters running around down there."

"I ain't never looked at property I owned or animals of any kind. This is all so new and exciting." Louise said.

Snake drew in his breath fast. "There's a man on a horse in that stand of pines over there, Louise." He nodded without pointing at a stand of pine maybe four hundred yards away. "Get off your horse and keep the horse between you and him." He stepped down from his and led the two of them off the main road and into a jumble of rocks. "We'll just watch for a few minutes," he said. "I'm sure he must have seen us."

"Do you think he was going to ambush us?" She asked. Snake looked over at her and was amazed at not seeing any fear or anxiety on her face.

"No," he said. "He's too far away for an ambush. He's watching the ranch for some reason. Look. He has a spy glass." The man was standing, leaning against a tree for solid support and peering through a long glass at the ranch.

"Stay here, honey. I'm gonna sneak up on that feller," Snake said.

"Oh, no," she said. "We are going to sneak up on that feller. He's on that rounded ridge and we can come up from behind, nice and quiet. Follow that line of rocks that almost lead right to him."

Snake looked at what she was describing. *She is a good hunter. That line would put us below and behind him and he seems mighty intent on watching the ranch not payin' much attention to anything else.*

"All right, Lion Killer, Let's be as quiet as the little critters." Snake led off with Louise five or so yards behind and got behind the line of rocks that marched up and across the side of the hill. The grass was green but there were also large patches of busted up rocks that they had to negotiate. Louise was wearing her moccasins and was able to be far more quiet than Snake in his big heavy boots.

"Let me lead, Snake. I'll find the quiet route," she whispered. "You sound like a buffalo charging through here."

I'm gonna learn something everyday from this girl. She brought them to within twenty yard of the man and gave the lead back to Snake. He crept slowly, rock to rock, tree to tree, with Louise standing behind a tree, her rifle aimed at the intruder's back. When Snake was just ten yards from the man he spoke. "See something exciting, do you?"

Snake's jaw dropped when the man jumped back and turned around. "Why, will you look at that? It's Mr. Shannahan, not frightened to appear in public. Drop the long glass and ease that side-arm out and drop it. Louise," he called back, "shoot the bastard if he makes one wrong move." Snake's rifle was cocked and aimed at Shannahan's belly and the man did as he was told.

"I ain't done nothing against the law," Shannahan said. "You ain't got right to aim a rifle at me."

"Drop the side-arm or die, Mister Shannahan. Ain't

got time to play games. Now!" Snake took several steps forward, the rifle always aimed at Shannahan's belly. "Gonna spread your belly all over this mountain in a minute, fool."

Shannahan saw Louise step out from behind a tree, her rifle aimed at his head and slowly undid his cartridge belt, let it fall to the ground, and stood rock still. "Ain't go no call for this," he said again.

"We let you go last time, fool. Time now for a little chat," Snake said. "You got to the count of one to tell me who sent you and why. You ready?" Snake took a breath getting ready to say, "One," and Shannahan was visibly shaking. "You just ain't the outlaw type, are you? All right, then. Who?"

"Mr. Mendoza wants me to keep him informed is all. I ain't doing nothing illegal. You ain't got no right to do what you're doin'."

The fist came from down at knee level, straight up from bended knees to standing tall, and smashed into Shannahan's jaw, right close to the chin, lifting the man three feet or more into the air and driving him back five full yards, dumping him in a scattering of rocks and brush.

Louise picked the man's gun belt up and slung it over her shoulder before walking up to where Snake was standing over the unconscious Shannahan. "Ain't never seen that done, Snake. Impressive. If we're gonna get the wagon and get back to town for the supplies, we'd best keep moving."

Snake laughed, grabbed her and gave her a hug and kiss. "Gonna be a fun life, little girl. Yes, sir, gonna be fun. Go on back and get the horses. I've got a little job to do here."

She looked at him with questions but headed back for

the horses. Snake took Shannahan's boots and pants off, emptied his pockets on the inert body, brought the outlaw's horse over and tied it off, and walked up, carrying boots and pants, to meet Louise.

"This is the second time you've sent someone to town without his pants, Snake. Gonna be a legend someday," she laughed.

"He's gonna be sore all over, angry as a wet cat, and laughed at too," Snake said. "Mendoza will take out his anger and hurt on the man as well. We won't be running into Mr. Shannahan again, but we've made a serious enemy of Mendoza. Him we need to worry about."

31

CISCO AND SNAKE took the wagon into town for the building supplies and food, Dog-man cut wood for fires and staked out some prime lodge-pole pine for Snake's house, and Louise took the time to learn how to get dressed in her new things. *I can't remember the last time I had a dress on. Lordy but this ain't fun, either.* Half an hour later she had the dresses folded and put away, was back in her buckskins getting a cook fire started in the cabin.

I ain't cut out for girl stuff. She gave that a second thought and chuckled. *Says the pregnant little girl. I've got to tell Snake but I sure don't know how I'm gonna do it. We ain't talked about children at all except that we both want some. Mama was like me or it's the other way around so I ain't been brought up as a little girl. Don't matter none. Snake likes me.*

Dog-man came in, wringing wet with sweat and poured some coffee. "You and Snake were laughing when you rode in. What was so funny?"

"Found old Mr. Shannahan spying on the ranch and sent him back to town without his trousers," she laughed. "Snake's gonna get a reputation soon if he keeps it up." She took that time to bring him up to date about the sheriff's fight with Mendoza and the fact that Big Al Barrington would be visiting next week.

"I'm glad we bought this place, Louise, but I hope these problems with Mendoza don't turn into some kind of long-time feud. What would Shannahan tell Mendoza even. That we have someone working for us? That the cattle are eating well? Don't make much sense."

"It would if he was putting together our schedule, to know when a good time to attack would be. He's a sneaky, shoot-'em-in-the-back type of person," Louise said.

Dog-man dropped a load of firewood next to the stove and went out to get some more. *She's right about that. That's a hunter talking. Know your prey and we're his prey. I gotta talk with Snake about turning this thing around. That we go after Mendoza instead of him coming after us.*

———

"THANK YOU, LEN," Snake said. "That's a load for sure. You sure that if we cut logs for the walls and roof, that this load will finish off the cabin?"

"You'll have an outstanding cabin, Snake. Outstanding. That lumber is straight and dry, and my son-in-law Billy Carver made every single one of those iron nails. He ain't too bright but he sure can make nails." Leonard Ames looked again at the bank draught Snake gave him, smiled, and waved as the two drove off for home.

"All of this might keep me out of trouble for a while, eh?" Snake was in a good mood, had laughed loud telling Cisco about sending Shannahan into town without his pants, and was busy talking about what he would build.

"There's a good stand of lodge-pole pines less than a mile from where you want to build, Snake," Cisco said. "We can cut them to length and the mule can drag them in. I'm glad Ames added that good cross-cut saw to the load. Makes the job much easier than using an ax."

Both men spun around hearing horses coming up fast from behind. The three riders raced past Snake and Cisco, pulled their horses up short, spun around and faced the two. Snake pulled the team to a stop and had his revolver out and cocked. He saw Francisco pull his shotgun from under the wagon seat and was about to holler out at the three.

"We ain't here to fight you," one of the three said. All five horses were dancing about but the three men did not have weapons in hand. They were close enough that Snake could see hate in their eyes. "Just want a friendly little visit," the big one said. "Señor Mendoza has declared that you are not welcome in his valley."

"His valley?" Snake laughed. When he laughed the man's eyes narrowed down, anger and hate were obvious. Nobody laughed at a Mendoza man. Snake could see the man wanted to go for his side-arm but could plainly see Snake already had his in hand. Snake threw some salt on the wound by wagging the big pistol back and forth and smiling wide in his contempt.

"You're a fool, Freddie Barton," Francisco said. "You, too, Holloway. Mendoza is pulling your strings and you're gonna get yourself killed while he drinks fine tequila." Francisco Alvarado leveled the shotgun at the big Holloway and sneered, "Gonna die hard and soon."

"Move aside, gentlemen. And tell your puppet master that Spanish land grants don't exist anymore. Move aside or we'll move you aside." Snake gave the reins a good snap and the team stepped out smartly. Cisco's shotgun menaced the two on his side as they passed through and Snake's revolver kept the third at bay. "Don't make a mistake here, boys," Snake yelled out. "You've still got your pants."

Snake got the team in a solid trot and Cisco sat sideways in the seat, watching the three men, making sure no one would get shot in the back. "Well done, Boss," Cisco said. "I was sure one of them would go for his gun. Mendoza must have lost his mind pulling something like this in broad daylight."

"Which tells me you and me better start riding night hawk for the next few nights. Gonna be tough to get that house built and then stay up all night nursing the herd, but Mendoza might just try anything." He let his mind take in everything that just took place. "That big feller, Holloway, was with Mendoza when he slapped the sheriff's wife. You called the other one Barton. He of the Barton gang?"

"That's him. Holloway and another man whose name I can't recall are the gang. Mendoza has a mean and ugly temper," Cisco said. "What you said, about him slapping Maria-Elena right in front of her husband, proves that. Forget the fact the husband is also the sheriff, just doing it shows he is not right in the head."

Cisco got contemplative for a moment or two. "A man raised as Mendoza was, his ancestors Spanish gentry, noblemen and ladies, holding large land grants from the crown, has a sense of being better than others. This change to the American way of individual worthyness is almost a slap in his face. He's fighting a losing battle and it's personal. He'll strike out at those he perceives as enemies."

"We need to be on our guard around the clock, I think," Snake said. The rest of the five mile ride was quiet, each man working to think what Mendoza might do next. Would he try to run the cows off? Burn the cabin down? Or just murder the bunch of them?

Me and Dog been on the road for a long time. Maybe this isn't the right time to settle down. Damn me but I do love that girl, I do enjoy looking out and seeing the herd, the green grass, these mountains. No, dammit, I ain't gonna let no damn Spanish Grandee run me off. Ain't.

SUPPER WAS quiet as Snake dominated the conversation, telling what went on with Sheriff Mallory. About Big Al coming to visit, and about the three men telling him that he wasn't welcome in Mendoza's valley. "Sheriff wants to know if we would back his play when he tries to clean up the outlaws. Kinda went out on a thin limb and said we would. Hell, we're already involved up to our sunburned necks, might as well get a little deeper."

"You done right," Dog-man said. "Don't like being told to leave by someone what don't own what he's talking about. We've been through that, Snake. In El Paso, in Las Cruces, at that little ranch somewhere in Arizona. No, sir, we bought this place fair and square and we're keeping it."

Snake smiled, nodded gently, and stabbed his fork in a piece of tender beef. "Eatin' off our own brand, Dog. Think we'd ever do that?"

Louise looked back and forth at the two long-time partners and smiled. *I got me a husband, gonna have us a baby, and we got the finest partner, too. I just wish Pa was here, sittin' at this table, enjoying what we have.*

"That Spanish bastard's gonna do something stupid," Snake said. "I'll ride first watch, Cisco, and you relieve me. I don't want to have to be in a defensive situation for much longer. Tom Mallory is right. He's gonna chase hard on these fools and we'll run 'em out of what's now our valley."

"Speaking of that," Dog-man said. "I've got some fine lodge pole staked out in the hills just north of us. Be easy to drag 'em in."

"We'll start in the morning," Snake said.

32

Tom Mallory rode in early in the morning, accompanied by a man neither Snake nor Dog-man recognized. "Good morning to you," the sheriff said, stepping down from his saddle. "This here is Wayne Nichols. Rode into town a couple of years ago from somewhere in Texas. He's been telling us he's the best darn drover ever born."

"He ain't," Snake said. "I am." Even Wayne Nichols joined the laughter. "Howdy, Wayne Nichols. We got coffee brewin'. Come on in." Snake looked at the sheriff and wagged his head some before saying, "Got stopped comin' home last night by Holloway and Barton. Sent by Mendoza."

"I heard." Mallory wasn't laughing. "Also the Shannahan affair. You might be pushin', Snake." The scowl slowly turned to a wry smile, which took the tension out of the situation. "Nichols here is looking to hire out. You got room for another?"

"You got any attachments to Mendoza?" Dog-man

asked straight out and saw Mallory almost choke on his coffee.

"Only hate," Wayne Nichols said. His eyes were narrowed, his mouth turned down, and Dog-man saw his jaw muscles bind up tight. "Burned me and my wife out, killed our cow and chickens, and at some point you'll see the scars across my back welted up by a rawhide quirt."

"You're married?" Snake asked. "We ain't got a bunkhouse yet, more or less quarters for a married hand. Gonna build a house for me and Louise, then a bunkhouse." He looked at Dog-man, then Louise, then the sheriff. "Damn."

"Yup, married. Jeannie got a busted arm, and the bastard hit her in the face with his rifle butt, breaking her nose." Louise took in a breath, stood up and wrapped her arms around Nichols, hugging the tall Texan tight. He was squirming to get away, but Louise was gonna have her say in the matter first.

"Oh, my God. That's horrible," she said. She released her hold on the man and turned to Snake. "We got to do something, Snake. We gotta."

Snake knew Louise could show emotion but this was more than he had seen before and wondered what brought it on. "Want you on our crew, Nichols, but got no place to put your wife up." He got up from the table, put his hand on Louise's shoulder, and looked deep into her worried eyes.

She's almost demanding that we take this feller in but where would we put him and his wife? Cain't shove Dog-man out of the house, gotta get ours built. Even Louise was surprised by her abrupt show of emotion, but when she thought about it, it had a lot to do with being pregnant, which of course is why Snake was surprised by the show. He didn't know.

"We can't ask you and your wife to just make camp," Snake said. It was almost a question. He remembered that Saucedo had the outlaws working for him sleep in the barn. *Wouldn't do that. All right for a traveler, but not a hand and his wife.*

"Me and Jeannie have an old wagon that we been living in since getting burned out. Put big hoops up and it's covered from the weather. We could live in that and help build a house, too. I'm a fine carpenter. Sheriff Mallory will verify that."

Dog-man was raking it all in, hadn't said a word. He saw a long tall Texan who desperately wanted a job. The man had all the right stuff. Youth, muscles, and desire. "Is that true, Sheriff?" Dog-man asked

"I've known Wayne since he arrived in the valley," Mallory said. "He's a hard worker, Jeannie is a fine woman, and your ranch will be the better for him being here."

"Settling down in one spot, Dog, has a lot more problems than following the trail out of town." Snake was chuckling, looking around the group for help. Dog-am just looked at him, Louise was begging with her eyes, Cisco was busy stoking the fire, and Nichols found a chair and plunked himself down.

Snake kept looking around at the group. *Why is it my decision. Why not Dog's? Why not Louise's? Man's got all the right answers, looks to be a good hand and if he and his wife are willing to live out of a wagon for a while, I'm in favor of signin' him on. What a change this is, from following trails that lead from here to somewhere else to running a big old ranch. Kind of like when me and Dog found that mine. Sure enjoyed those days.*

The long tall Texan took a deep breath and looked Nichols in the eye. "Bring the wagon out, set it in the trees back yonder. Breakfast at five, supper at six. Cisco is ranch foreman," Snake said. "Me, Louise, and Dog own the place." He got it all out in one breath, took a long look at Dog-man and got a smile and nod back. "Good. Well that's settled."

Nichols shook his hand, Mallory shook his hand, and Snake just looked at Louise and smiled. "Let's go look at those lodge pole pines, Cisco. Thank you Sheriff."

Louise walked Wayne and the sheriff out. "Is there anything you and your wife need? Gettin' burned out ain't much good for personal belongings."

"The sheriff pretty much got us put together," the big Texan said. "I guess, from what Snake said that we'll be eating with you?"

"The way it should be on a ranch," Louise said. She liked saying that, liked the idea of owning a ranch but was constantly worried that she didn't know the first thing about living on a ranch. Her father, the traveling preacher who sold finished pelts and buckskins killed by his daughter, had never even had a place to call home.

She stood in the grass and watched Nichols and the sheriff ride off. *What a horrible thing. Lost everything. Horrible. Señor Mendoza will pay dearly for that.* She would not have been amazed to find out that those same thoughts were in Snake's head as he and Cisco rode off to find some logs for their new home. Louise's thoughts were harsh and she wasn't sure she could back them up. *That Spanish gentleman won't never burn us out. Won't never.* Her fists were doubled up as she strode back to the cabin.

"NICE AND TALL AND STRAIGHT," Snake said as he and Cisco rode into a large grove of trees. "Take 'em down close to the ground, strip those branches for firewood, and drag 'em back down to the ranch. Up on the hillside like this will make the dragging easier on the mule."

"See you changed your mind on cutting them to size up here. Best to do that on-site," Cisco said. "So, I'm the foreman, eh?" His smile told Snake that he made the right decision. "Good. Nichols is a good worker and a good carpenter. I've seen some of his work. The three of us will have your house built in nothing flat."

They unstrapped the cross-cut saw from the mule and tied the mule and the horses off in some good grass, far from where they would fell the trees. The mule's harness was connected to a single tree with chains attached that would grab hold of the logs. "That old mule has had a lot of things attached or loaded, but these logs will be a first for her," Snake said.

"Best bet is to lead her," Cisco said. "One of those chains break loose it could come flying right at you."

Snake caught that right away. What Cisco implied was that Snake would be driving the mule down to the ranch and walking her back up. "Good thinking," Snake said. "We'll take turns running them logs down." Snake caught the grin from Alvarado and turned to hide his. He enjoyed little games like this.

Within minutes the two men were stripped to the waist and the long, multi-toothed cross-cut saw was singing, one man on each end, pulling one way, pushing the other. They had three long, straight, pines on the ground within a couple of hours and took a break.

"Whoowee," Snake belted out, taking a long drink of water. He handed the canteen to Cisco. "Get those limbs trimmed off and that will be a heavy load for that mule.

"I think we need to bring the team and wagon for our next load. Mule can drag the trees and we'll haul the branches in the wagon. That way we can haul all these branches down, too. Make for some fine fire wood. We'll get an early start tomorrow. All them visitors this morning put us way behind."

"One more change, Snake." Cisco wiped the sweat from his face and took another drink of that sweet water. "How about you and me cut the trees down and Dog-man and Wayne do the trimming and hauling? Sure get this done faster."

"Best idea yet," Snake said. "By the time we get these trimmed out and lashed for dragging, we'll be lucky to be back before sunset."

SNAKE BROUGHT up the idea of all four men working to bring the timber down to the ranch and Louise took in a quick breath, wagging her head. "No, no, Snake. You can't run off and leave me and Mrs. Nichols alone down here. She's already been whupped on. Got a broken nose and all. I'll fight whatever Mendoza throws at us but I doubt if she can."

It was only a few seconds of quiet but seemed like an hour before anyone said anything. "She's right," Dog-man said. "One man's got to stay down here. Got to be out and be seen by anyone venturing in."

"If it weren't for Mendoza, my plan would work fine, but you're right, got to have protection down here," Snake said. "Draggin' those three logs in was too much and we've got more branches cut than will fit in that wagon. We'll limit the draggin' to two logs, which will probably fill the wagon with branches as well."

"What a damn shame that little boy got killed," Louise said. "We could sure use another like him. Maybe I'll ask Jeannie Nichols if there are any other boys in town that need a place to live and learn about life on a ranch."

"There are some, but they've already picked up some bad habits like thieving and armed robbery," Cisco said.

"If we can drag four trees a day down off that grove, we'll have more than enough logs for a nice sized home in just a short time," Snake said. "You need to stay down here, Dog-man. You'll be in more danger than us."

Dog-man laughed and gave a long look at Louise. "I don't know if I should worry more about Lion Killer or Mendoza," he said.

"You might be safe from me, Dog-man," Louise laughed, "but there will be two women down here. Don't you forget that."

33

WAYNE NICHOLS DROVE A TEAM IN, not far from first light, helped Jeannie off the wagon and had the wagon parked, mostly level. Jeannie helped with the team, getting them unhitched and stripped of harness. The two walked to the main house hand in hand. "Morning," he said. "Want y'awl to meet the missus. This is Jeannie."

Jeannie Nichols was just about as young as Louise, stood almost but not quite five feet tall and was heavy. Very heavy. Her Indian blood was also evident but it was the bandage across what had been a sharp nose that had everyone's attention. She tried, but couldn't hide the fact that she was ashamed of it, too.

Wayne Nichols stood well over six feet tall and didn't weigh one sixty on his best day. Jeannie didn't make the five foot mark and weighed about the same. They were a sight and their feelings for each other overpowered the visual impact. Her eyes shone when she looked at him, and he had his arm around her the whole time. Snake smiled, looked over at Louise, and found her looking right back at him.

With a combination of bright, already warm sunrise, the quiet of the moment had a flavor all its own. Mournful cries from the herd were mixed with sunrise birdsong and the crackling of a hot fire in the cookstove, all adding up to a peaceful morning on a mountain side ranch.

"She ain't got all her English down right yet, and I ain't got good at Paiute talk neither," Wayne said. He looked at Louise and saw her almost staring at Jeannie.

"I'm really good with my buckskins and lion skins, but that's the most beautiful dress I've ever seen." Louise was dressed in her buckskins and sidled up to Jeannie. They compared the stitching, beading, and fringe work on each other's clothing, and both smiled. Jeannie pointed out some fine work by Louise and Louise did the same back.

"Looks like the women folk are gonna get along just fine," Snake said. "Let's get to work, gentlemen."

"Just as we talked, Snake," Dog-man said. "Three shots, wait several seconds and three more and come-a-runnin'. That goes both ways. I don't think Mendoza will hit in broad daylight but we'd best be ready, just in case." The stand of timber was about five miles distant so gunshots should be heard. "Louise has her rifle and I have my guns."

"Jeannie is a fine shot and has a shotgun and rifle," Nichols said. "She drew a picture of Mendoza on a large piece of wrapping paper from the store and uses it for a target. She's fearsome when she's got her blood up," he chuckled. Snake remembered how Louise saved his bacon twice, being a fine shot.

Nichols drove the wagon and Snake led the harnessed mule up the well worn trail to the stand of lodge pole pine. They planned to fill the wagon with cut branches for firewood and drag logs for Snake's house.

"Best bet is to drop four trees before we start the long process of getting them off the hill," Snake said. "Two men on the saw and the third man trimmin' branches, and we'll be a working force."

"As soon as that wagon's full of branches, run it down and unload it, Wayne," Cisco said. "Me and Snake will run the saw."

DOG-MAN SADDLED his horse and rode out to the meadows where several hundred head of cattle milled about and chewed grass, checking for indications of visitors, making sure there were no hurt or ill cattle. He was getting it straight in his head that he and Snake have driven stakes deep in this San Bernardino country. Hillsides were covered in a thick carpet of grass, timber stood tall and strong, and the water seemed to be plentiful.

Just a few miles that-a-way and we'd be in the Mojave Desert. Boiling sun, limited water, and almost no grass. More than once I was ready to shoot old Benjamin Franklyn Cruikshank, but that bastard knew what he was talking about with his underground river. It's these mountains where the Mojave River begins. Whoever heard of rivers running through deserts?

His mind drifted back to when he and Snake had found that old mine, deep in Mexico. "Some of the best times we've had," he mumbled. *I think tomorrow I'm going to leave Cisco down here with the herd and me and Snake will run that cross-cut saw. Like when we were driving our steel drills in that hard-rock mine. Sweatin' and cussin', bustin' our own knuckles with our own hammers.* He found himself chuckling right out with more than one steer giving him sideways glances.

He could almost see the crushed gravel moving down their rocker boxes and the little stream of gold that was left behind. *Hardest thing we've had to do, giving up that old mine.* He sat straight up in the saddle, looked out across the backs of his cattle and hollered out. "You're our gold, you flea bit old critters. Make beef, now. Don't be slow about it."

His laughter was cut off by something bright and shiny glittering at him from a stand of trees on the hillside that the main trail runs across. *This is when there should be two of us out here.* He turned his horse as casually as he could and rode at a walk back toward the house. He was still some ways out when he saw Louise riding out toward him, just as casually.

"Spotted some men moving in the trees out near the road, Dog-man. Thought it best to let you know."

"Didn't see them but did see something glinting in the sun. How many you suppose Mendoza sent?"

"I think I counted four at least. I took it on myself to send Jeannie out to tell the men. That girl grabbed her rifle and led her horse up through the trees before mounting. Hopefully she wasn't seen by our visitors."

"Let's you and me take the long way around the herd, seeming to be making a count or something, and work our way toward those fools." *I don't think I've ever been in a position like this,* Dog-man pondered. *I'm being protected by two women wearing buckskins. I was left down here to keep them safe and instead, they're working to keep me safe.*

"Something else," Louise said as they moved through a bunch of steers. "Jeannie's family is in the group of Paiutes led by Asshole. Good Inyun is her uncle. She hasn't seen either one for more than a year so didn't know about our relationship with them."

"That's almost amazing," Dog-man said. "You must have had quite a conversation, not knowing the language."

"Hand-talk, Dog-man. She wants to send a message to the tribe about where we are. I think it's a good idea."

"I do too. We've got movement up there," he said. "Don't point, just look in the direction my horse is moving. See that glint, there?"

"Yup. Three men on horseback, standing in the shadows. I'm sure I saw four earlier." Louise slowly eased her rifle across the front of the saddle and saw Dog-man do the same. "You watch those three and I'll see if I can spot that fourth one."

As they rode Louise cast her eyes in just about every direction, seemingly looking at the cattle but searching for the missing man. She kept thinking about everything they had heard about Antonio Mendoza and his tactics.

We heard 'burn 'em out' more than anything else. Physical intimidation like what they did to Wayne and Jeannie, but even then, they burned 'em, out. "We gotta get back to the house," she said quickly. "That fourth man is gonna burn it down."

Dog-man didn't hesitate, pulled his horse around fast and sank his spurs. Louise was with him, step for step. "Hyah, hyah," he howled, leaning far out over the neck of his racing pony. Louise took a quick look into the trees and saw the three men come racing down the hill toward them.

"They're coming," she yelled, spurring her horse, howling at it for more speed. They were running at break-neck speed, cattle almost getting stampeded, making for the house. "Smoke," Louise yelled.

Dog-man saw the fourth man race up to the cabin and heave a burning torch onto the roof. At a full gallop he was not about to try and shoot him, instead just kept racing in as fast as the horse could run. Louise though, pulled up to a stop, leveled that Winchester of hers, and knocked the man right out of his saddle.

Dog-man ran his horse as close to the cabin as he could get, stopped him, stood up on top of the saddle and climbed onto the roof. He ran up the shake shingles to the torch and threw it back into the yard, stomping out what little fire had started.

Bullets were tearing up the roof as Dog-man jumped off and rolled across the yard, ending up behind a rock near the entry-way path. He pulled his revolver as he jumped. Louise turned her horse to face the three coming in and fired off two shots, hitting one of the men. She knew she was in a pickle and spurred the horse toward some rocks, scattering more cattle.

As she jumped from the moving horse she felt the bullet hit, and the force of it tumbled her to the ground. Burning, searing pain, like a red hot poker from a stove, raced up and down her back as she crawled behind the rock. The two men saw that she was hit and turned their horses toward that rock she hid behind.

She had her rifle, she still had her revolver and her knife, but she also knew that bullet did a lot of damage and she was bleeding hard. *Don't got time to stop the bleeding and fight them boys. Can't do both but gotta.* She ripped her neck kerchief off, fired two round at the fast approaching riders, and tried to stuff the rag into her back. The buckskin shirt was tight fitting, blood was running thick, and Louise felt dizzy, couldn't think, wanted to lay her head down and sleep. "Snake," she whimpered, laying her head down.

Heavy gunfire didn't wake her up.

"GUNSHOT," Wayne Nichols yelled out.

"Just one," Cisco said. "Not three."

"Don't matter," Snake said. "Let's go." Nichols had the wagon and team closest and the two men grabbed their rifles and jumped on their horses. Nichols had the team running down hill, Cisco and Snake racing along behind when they spotted Jeannie racing toward them.

"Men come," She said. Nichols didn't stop, just kept those two horses at a fast run. Jeannie turned her horse and ran along behind Snake and Cisco. Snake passed the wagon as did Cisco and the five mile run was furious.

Snake heard more gunfire and tried to get more speed. "Come on, boy, give it all. give it," he howled, kicking the ribs hard. The five miles seemed like twelve or more as more and more gunfire could be heard. Finally he broke out of the trees, saw two men racing toward a rock, firing their revolvers.

Snake spotted Louise's horse Throwing a fit near that rock and turned to face the oncoming men. He had his Colt in hand and laid out across the horses neck, kicking constantly, and started firing as the riders closed fast. "Wrong, boys" he said and pulled the horse to a stop, grabbed the rifle and fired four quick shots, that lever working faster than he'd ever tried. Both men were flung from their mounts and Snake spurred his horse into a run for that rock.

"Louise," he cried, jumping from the saddle and running to her fallen body. "Louise, no, no." He gathered her up in his arms and heard her moan, ever so softly. He felt the warm, sticky blood on her back and turned her over on her stomach. "No," he said again, grabbed that rag, used his knife to rip the buckskin away, found the wound and stuffed the rag in it.

Cisco rode toward the house where Dog-man was stomping out a small grass fire from the torch and Wayne drove the wagon to where Snake was sitting with Louise. "Gotta get her to a doctor, Wayne. Shot bad."

They threw branches aside to make room for Louise in the bed of the wagon and Wayne drove off for town. Snake jumped on his horse, caught up, and led the way. The wagon bounced across the open meadow and they rode onto the main road to town. Wayne had the horses at a full run all the way to town and brought the sweat caked team to a stop in front of Doc Steppenfield's office.

Wayne jumped down from the high seat and raced for the office door while Snake picked Louise up and carried her in. "Shot bad, Doc," is all Snake could say. Steppenfiled showed them where to put her, motioned for his nurse to get the filthy men out of the surgery, and started cleaning the wound.

Snake didn't want to leave her but knew he had to. "Take the wagon back, Wayne, and tell them I'll be staying here until I know Louise is all right. Dog-man is going to need all the help you can give him." He turned to the nurse. "I'll either be at the Sheriff's office or the Elkhorn Saloon. That's my wife in there and I want her back."

"Doctor is very good at what he does. You're the one called Snake?" Snake nodded with a question in his eyes. "Tom Mallory is my brother. He says you are a good man. We'll take the best care of your wife."

"Thank you." Snake walked his horse down the street

and tied him off in front of Sheriff Mallory's office. "I saw you racing in," the sheriff said. "What happened?"

It was half an hour later the two men walked to the Elkhorn Saloon for a needed drink. "This has gone as far as I'm going to let it go," Mallory said. "We'll have a couple of drinks and them I'm going to round up the whole bunch of those bastards. I want you with me, Snake. This is dead or alive time for Mendoza and company."

Mallory had been fighting the wrong fight and he knew it. Being married to Mendoza's daughter was the problem. He was afraid that bringing the Spanish Don in on serious charges would have a negative affect on his marriage. That was wrong thinking if the man wanted to continue as a lawman. He knew it, most of the town knew it, and after the dust-up at the café, there was no reason not to arrest or kill the gentleman.

Mallory's thoughts were almost pitiful at this moment. If he'd done his job Louise would not be fighting for her life, Snake and Dog-man would not be fighting to protect their ranch and herd. If he'd done his job, Wayne Nichols' wife would not have a broken nose and they would not be living in a buckboard wagon. "I've neglected my office, Snake. That part is now over. We get the man and all who work for him."

It takes a big man to come out like that, Snake thought, looking into the sheriff's eyes. *You damn right I'll help, Mallory. That's my wife bleeding all over the doctor's office. I'll get Mendoza with or without you.*

"Don't know who those varmints were out there, Sheriff and don't know even how many might still be alive." The two men strode up to the long bar and Mallory looked the saloon over, hoping to find a Mendoza man or two in there.

"That's Barton over by the piano, Snake. Why don't you say hello to him." Mallory had a wicked smile on his face. "Maybe remind him of last night."

"Yup," Snake said. He was carrying his rifle and walked across the saloon floor, making a straight line for Freddie Barton. Men moved aside after one look at Snake's face. His eyes were narrowed to slits, his jaw muscles working hard and some said they could smell death. Barton was busy making eyes at a dancehall girl and didn't see Snake coming.

"Remember me, Barton?" Snake said. When the outlaw turned he was met with the butt end of the rifle square in his mouth. Blood and teeth were splattered, and foul language could be heard over the din of the saloon. Barton made a move for his sidearm and Snake whipped the rifle around and slashed Barton across the side of his head with the barrel end, bringing the curtain down on the play.

Mallory helped get Barton to his feet and they half dragged the bloody gang leader across the busy street to the jail. "Still haven't had that drink," Snake laughed. "Maybe that's best."

Mallory sat down and pulled a flask from his desk. "We'll do it this way."

It was Doctor Steppenfield who interrupted the drinks this time. "I don't have good news, Snake," he said coming into the office.

34

"No," Snake said, over and over. He slumped into a chair and held his head, rocking back and forth. "No," he moaned.

"The bullet just did too much damage. I'm afraid she will not be able to have another child, either."

"What?" Snake bolted to his feet. "We've just gotten married. What are you talking about?" His eyes were wide with questions. He looked at the sheriff, at the doctor, at the floor. and back to the doctor.

It took Steppenfield just a moment to realize that he didn't do a good job of explaining the situation. "Louise's wound was terrible, Snake, but she's going to pull through. I don't know if she knew, yet, and I'm sure she hadn't told you, but she was pregnant. She's alive, Snake, but she won't be able to get pregnant again."

Snake stood absolutely still, staring with almost blank eyes at the doctor. "Pregnant? We were going to have a baby? She's all right?" The questions poured out as Snake looked at the doctor, the sheriff, back to the doctor. "How bad is she hurt? Oh, God, Louise, don't leave me. Don't never leave me."

"She's hurt bad, Snake. I won't try to make this to be less, but she's going to live. She'll need a lot of good care and it will take some time for her to be back to normal. It was the damage done internally that will keep her from having another baby."

Snake slumped back down in the old cane chair, shaking his head back and forth, smiling for a moment, glowering for another. "I ain't gonna be somebody's Pa? We ain't gonna have a passel of yappiin kids? That's what we've talked about."

The longer he sat there the angrier he got. Sheriff Mallory and Doctor Steppenfield both saw the change slowly come over the long Texan. Snake got to his feet. "I want to see her," he said. His voice was soft but his eyes were blazing. "I want her to know how much I love her, and then, Sheriff, you need to tell me where I will find Antonio Mendoza."

"She's sleeping, Snake. It's the best thing for her right now. She'll be awake and alert in the morning. She wants to see you, too," the doctor said. "She called out your name several times during the operation. Let her sleep and come over in the morning."

Snake wanted to go right that minute but he'd been around enough doctors to know that what they said is usually the way things went. Doctors don't get pushed around very often. "Morning it'll be," Snake murmured. "When can I bring her home?"

Home. I've not been able to say that since I was a little boy. Home. Has a nice ring to it. Bring my wife home. Wife. What a wonderful word. This old trekker ain't going on the long trail again. Never again as long as I have a wife and home.

He remembered the words he said to April so long

ago. *I told her for sure I'd get itchy feet, develop a great need to travel. Not this time. No, I won't be runnin' off, won't get wandering legs. Home with Louise and hundreds of head of fat cattle.*

"It'll be several days before I feel she'll be ready for that wagon ride home, Snake. I'll see you in the morning," Steppenfield said. He shook hands with Snake, nodded to the sheriff, and slipped out the door.

"She's gonna be fine, Sheriff, but I can tell you right now, Señor Mendoza ain't gonna be. Where should I look for that animal first?"

"I'd like to have at least one more man with us, Snake. Let's you and me ride out to the ranch and see if Wayne Nichols wants to join us. You two have priors in this chase."

"YOU'RE DAMN right I want to ride with you." Nichols was pacing along the corral fence, his fists knotted, his face as angry as a man's face can get. Nichols and his wife Jeannie, Dog-man, and Fransisco Alvarado were spread out along the fence line. Sheriff Mallory and Snake had ridden in late in the evening, found out that one of the four who attacked the ranch was still alive but the others were dead and buried.

"These men were hired to burn the place down and kill whoever was around. You folks fighting back wasn't in the plan," Mallory chuckled. "That wounded man talkative?" Mallory asked. They had moved back inside the cabin and Jeannie made roast beef sandwiches for them since they missed supper.

"Says Mendoza offered them twenty dollars each and employment," Dog-man said. "His name is Whistler,

Jimmy-John Whistler. Been riding for a large outfit on the Cajon Pass."

"I know the name," Mallory said. "Slimy bastard. Where you got him?"

"Tied to a post in the barn," Dog-man said. He looked at Snake, saw the hurt, saw the anger, didn't know if he should let his partner anywhere near the outlaw. "He was unconscious when we left him, a couple of hours ago."

Dog-man took a long look at Snake. "What did the doctor say about bringing Louise home?"

"Said it would be a few days and she would need lots of care."

"I take care," Jeannie said. "Good care. My friend. Maybe go see."

"No," Snake said. "These men need you here. I'll bring her home just as soon as they let me. Right now, I want to see this Jimmy-John fool."

The whole bunch of them made the walk from the cabin to the barn and Dog-man lit a lamp. Jimmy-John Whistler wasn't this big tough outlaw Snake expected to see, but was just a skinny kid. "This little kid has a reputation, Sheriff?"

"Knifes 'em or shoots 'em in the back, Snake. Late at night he sneaks into homes, kills whoever's there, and walks off with what8iever they owned. He looks like he's fourteen at best, but he's actually somewhere around twenty-five. Uses that little boy act and look to get in the door."

Snake bent down and shook the boy-man getting some groans. He whacked him with an open hand across the side of his head and he snapped awake, almost growling at the slap. Sheriff Mallory knelt down too, and got in Whistler's face. "Where would we find Mendoza?

You're dyin', Jimmy-John so you don't have to worry about that old fool finding out. Where?"

Snake smiled at the comment. The man was beat up pretty bad, gun-shot too, but far from dying, far from bleeding to death. Mallory looked over at Snake and gave him a quirky smile.

Whistler tried to move, found his arms tied around a post behind him and had a questioning frown on his face. "Who …?"

"I'm Sheriff Mallory, Whistler. You've been shot and you're bleeding to death. You were sent to this ranch to burn it out and I need to find Antonio Mendoza. Where is he?"

"Hurts," Whistler groaned. "Hurts bad," he whimpered.

"That's your game, Whistler," Mallory said. "Play the hurt little boy, but not this time. Where will I find Mendoza?"

"Old mission," Whistler said and passed out.

Mallory stood up and motioned for Fransisco Alvarado to join him. "He said old mission. What or where is that?" He couldn't imagine an old mission in the area. He'd been county sheriff for a number of years and there weren't any missions in the area.

"The old Mendoza land grant headquarters is north of here, about fifteen miles, and the headquarters had its own chapel. Mendoza's ranch headquarters are called Old Mission Ranch but only by the old Spaniards. It's fortified by Mexican and American outlaws. They run Mexican rustled cattle north and rustled American cattle south. Horses by the hundreds, too."

"I need to raid the Old Mission Ranch, eh Cisco? How many men does Mendoza have there?"

Cisco thought for several moments before answering.

"I've never been there, Sheriff, but probably twenty five at the least. Not all are outlaws. Some Mexican charros, some American cowboys, and some outlaws."

Mallory looked over to Snake and Dog-man, then back to Alvarado. "How many of those would stand up for Mendoza if we rode in with guns?"

"He pays them, Sheriff. I'd guess all of them."

"Take a big posse to bust into a fort like that. Well, I'm heading back to town. Bring this fool into the jail in the morning, Snake, and we'll do some planning."

"I TOLD you I was coming to see you," Big Al Barrington said with a hearty laugh. He stepped down from the wagon he was driving and wrapped his huge arms around Snake. "You and Dog-man bought yourselfs a ranch, eh? What'r you doing in town?"

"Got lots to talk about, Big Al. Antonio Mendoza tried to burn us out and I brought the surviving outlaw to the sheriff. Lots to talk about and some cold beer to wash it down with."

"Let me drop the wagon off so Leonard Ames can fill it up. Cold beer will taste good after all that desert dust. I'll meet you at the Elkhorn Saloon."

It was late in the morning and the Elkhorn was mostly empty. The late night hangers-on had tripped home and the early birds, looking for that pick-me-up weren't out and about yet. "Seen stages running through town regular," Snake said. "No more troubles?"

"No more than usual. Utes have been peaceful and friendly, regular desert outlaws been thinned out some, and the weather, well, you know all about that. Heard some bad stories, though. Ain't been in town an hour and heard that you lost Louise." Big Al bent his head some saying that. "I'm so sorry. I really liked that girl. Had some stuff in her, didn't she? The kind of stuff that makes for a good person."

Snake smiled, looking at how sad Al was. "No, Big Al, I didn't lose Louise. She was shot bad, but is recuperating as we speak. She's about as tough an old gal as I've ever wanted at my side. We got married, Big Al. Can you imagine that?"

"Married. Well now, that calls for a celebration. Roast a steer, sing some songs. Good for you, Snake. How did Louise get hurt bad?"

Snake spent the next half hour along with two tankards of beer telling Big Al about Antonio Mendoza and company. "That's nasty," Big Al Barrington said. "So Mendoza sees himself as a Spanish Grandee, holding a land grant from the king of Spain? Loony in la cabeza," he laughed. "That went out of style some time ago."

Barrington sat back in his chair and drummed his fingers on the table, drank a long draught of cold beer and smiled. "You and a couple of beat up old cowboys are gonna raid the fool's castle? Well, how about if we made this a real raid. I've got an idea."

Snake called for another round of beer and looked at his friend from Mormon Station. "I could use a couple of good ideas. Dog-man doesn't think we could make a dent in Mendoza's defenses, and I tend to agree. The sheriff has his doubts as well. The thing is, I have a great need here to end Mendoza's life."

Snake's eye's told Big Al all he needed to know. Snake was going to see to it that Mendoza never ruined another person's life. "I've got a home, Al. A wife. Never had a home since I was a boy. Man is responsible for killing what was going to be my baby, hurt my wife real bad, and needs to pay for it."

"Five men against a fortress holding twenty five? What if you had fifty or so seriously bad men on your side?"

"As long as they weren't outlaws I'd like that," Snake said. "Wouldn't be fifty men in this town willing to go up against the Spaniard. He keeps a lot of them on his payroll. No, I need a real plan, Al, not a wild hope."

"You're the one told me that your hand is married into Good Inyan's family," Big Al said. He was quiet, sipped a beer, and smiled like a cagey old fox.

"Well, just damn my rotten old hide," Snake laughed. "Just smack me across the side of this old head." He chuckled some more and then sobered right up. "Don't think the sheriff would go along with us startin' an injun uprising, Al. Great idea but it ain't gonna happen. Next thing the army would be involved. Damn good idea."

"I think if I was you, Snake old man, I'd surely bring it up to him. The most he could say would be no. I've known Mallory for a long time and he's been known to bend the law some when he felt it necessary."

35

"ABSOLUTELY NOT!" They could hear Mallory's thunderous response at the end of the block. "You want me to start an Injun war? My God, Snake." Mallory had jumped to his feet at the offer and paced around the small office, kicked a leg of his desk, growled at the pot-belly stove, and swore a ten second sermon at the wall.

Snake looked at Big Al as if to say, I told you so, and reached for the coffee pot. "Can't think of a better plan. You got a better plan, Sheriff?"

"I will have. I won't allow yours, though. Won't." His pacing slowed down and he plopped down in his chair. Stern, angry eyes peered across the desk at Snake and Big Al, and Mallory reached in that bottom drawer and produced a full flask. "I ain't gonna try to explain a Paiute war to the county commissioners, Snake."

"Jeannie is kin, Sheriff, and Louise might as well be. Both women brutalized by Mendoza's men." Big Al made a fine argument but the sheriff wasn't buying.

"No!" He took another long drink out of the flask and handed it to Snake. "I'll go to the judge and get an arrest order. Mendoza isn't going to stay away from his office for long. Too much money involved. We don't need no Injun war. Damn." Mallory had a hard time calming down, took another swipe at the flask and glared at Snake.

"Doc is back in Whistler's cell and we might get a little more information when he comes out. I talked with Maria-Elena last night about Mendoza's ranch, the Old Mission, and she said it's just an old Spanish building that once was a home and now is a chapel. She's only been there once, years ago. It ain't a fortress. After I get a court order to arrest the man and if he don't come to town soon after, then we'll ride out and see what happens."

Mallory looked at Big Al Barrington. "Not another word about bringing the whole damn Paiute nation in. I won't have it."

Doctor Steppenfield came out from the cell area. "Snake, glad you're here. Louise asked for you this morning. Why don't you come over with me. She's doing fine but needs to know that you're all right, too. You got yourself quite a woman, there, old man."

Big Al said he needed to gather up his wagon and get back to the station. "You're welcome here anytime, Barrington," Mallory said, "but don't you be bringing a bunch of wild Paiutes with you."

The three left the office, left Mallory to sit at the desk with his flask and frown. "Next visit will be at the ranch, Snake. Say hello to Louise for me." Big Al shook his head. "I still like my idea best."

SNAKE FOUND Louise stretched out on her side, having a hard time getting comfortable. "Snake," she almost yelled it out. "I'm so glad you're here. Take me home, Snake." He smiled and sat carefully on the edge of the bed, rustling his hand through her dark red hair. "We lost our baby, Snake. I never had a chance to even tell you."

"Having you is the only thing that counts. Doc says you should stay here one more day. That ride home in the back of the wagon would be rough as all get out. Only been two days and they got a good start on the walls of our home."

"I was just a little girl the last time I had a home," she said. "Ain't never really wanted one until I met you." Snake saw the tears well up in her eyes and she reached out to take his hand. "Won't be able to bring you any babies, Snake, like I promised."

"I got you," he said. He wanted to gather her up but that wound wasn't going to let that happen. "I got you, you got me, and we got a home. That's a tall bunch of stuff we got," he chuckled. She wiped her nose and laughed back at him.

"You talk funny sometimes, but you're right and I love it. Sheriff stopped in this morning and got a statement from me. He said you're gonna arrest Mendoza, that it was his men who attacked. Sure would like to put a bullet in that man."

Snake looked at her sad face and realized that what she said was a considerable change from what had been.

This is the girl who cried after shooting two men. She must hurt something awful. Mallory ain't gonna arrest Mendoza, not if I'm in the posse. I'm gonna kill that man long and slow. This is twice now that I've lost the chance to have a family. With April and those two little scallywags and now with Louise. Dog is right, I do want a family. Bad.

Louise was angry from being shot. The bullet did more than damage to her body. The hurt came from losing the baby. She was looking at Snake and let her mind drift off some. It really was just a few months ago that she met Snake and everything she ever thought about life changed. From being a hunter, working with her father, as free as any wild bird could be, to finding love, desire, and being with child, to today. Wounded in body and heart.

"I wanted us to have a lot of children, Snake. I'm so sorry."

"You got nothing to be sorry for or about," Snake growled. "You're my wife, Louise. Always will be. Sure, I wanted children, and, you know, we might still have some." She looked up at him, big questions in her eyes. "Take in a stray or two and teach 'em the ways of the world as known by Snake and Lion Killer."

They were laughing loud when the doctor walked in. "Some kind of party going on in here?" Steppenfield wasn't the type to offer smiles often, but he was smiling, even his eyes were. "I like it when my patients respond to treatment as you have. If you walk around some today, show me you can manage to get around despite the wound, then you can go home tomorrow."

"I'll run a mile if that's what you want," Louise said. Her smile was wide and bright, her eyes sparkling with anticipation. "Go home and count cows with my husband, that's all I want. Did you know he's building us a home? He is and we're gonna live there a long time."

Filled with exuberance, thrilled at the thought of going home, Louise also knew that she hurt with every movement she made. The rifle bullet did considerable damage to internal organs, some of which had to be removed, and muscles, tendons, and sutures hurt. She was not going to let either of these men know it.

"Skedaddle, Snake. I've got to check these wounds. You can pick her up in the morning. Bring something she can lie down on that will absorb some of the shock from the rough road home."

They hugged and kissed and Snake left the office to find the team and wagon he came in on for the ride back to the ranch. Thoughts of bringing Louise home, thoughts of ending Mendoza's colored career, and thoughts of building their home filled his shaggy old head. "I still think Big Al had the right answer as far as Mendoza is considered," he mumbled, getting the team on the road. "Sure as hell the army would mess up our plans." Pictures of he and Dog-man leading a Paiute war party lit up his ride home.

MORNING BLOSSOMED in reds and golds, light breezes forewarned of winds later in the day, and Jeannie was laying blankets in the back of the wagon in anticipation of Louise coming home. "I ride here with Louise," she said to anyone venturing near the wagon. "She my friend and I take good care."

Snake was at the site of his new home, inspecting the work that had been done. He could plainly see where the bedroom would be, the kitchen, and the great room. Rocks were being brought in for a wonderful fireplace and logs were cut to length and notched, waiting to be fitted into place.

"Dog, this is wonderful," he said. "You boys find out you don't need me? Maybe I'll just take a few more days off."

"Big change for us, Snake." Dog-man didn't join in Snake's mirth but got mighty serious. "Don't like to talk about some things, but I was sincerely afraid our partnership was going to end."

"I know." Snake looked into Dog-man's eyes, could almost read what his long time friend was thinking. "Would have been horrible. I had thoughts of being together with April, but it wasn't April, it was those two kids and I knew I would run off at some point. This is different, Dog. Don't rightly know how to explain myself."

"Then don't," Dog-man said. "They ain't no question in my mind that you and Louise belong together. I'm just sad, broke up, cuz of you two losin' the baby. You got the makin's of a fine father."

"Me and Louise talked about takin' in a stray or two," Snake chuckled. "Big Al was in town when I took that outlaw in. Pugnacious old man wants to bring Good Inyan and Asshole in to charge Mendoza's fort. Mallory went crazy when we brought it up."

Dog-man guffawed loud and long at the comment and said more than once that it was a great idea. "We are gonna go after that man, Snake. Maybe not with Paiute back-up, but we are going after that man." The two walked back to the main house, joshing each other about starting an Indian war.

"Learned something from Alvarado while you were gone," Dog-man said. "He was raised somewhere around a town called Santa Barbara by what he calls Californios. These were Mexican Vaqueros, the horse trainers, and Mexican Charros, the cowboys. I think, along with our cattle business, my dear friend, we are going into the horse breeding and training business."

"That's why he rides the way he does. He's a work of

art sitting in that saddle of his," Snake said. "The Spaniards brought all their deep knowledge of horsemanship with them, Dog. To be a part of that would get my blood boiling. Let's do it."

"He wants us to hire two Mexican charros. The three of them and the two of us can manage the cattle and horses." Dog-man said. "Gotta get rid of Mendoza first, though."

"Where are we gonna find a couple of Mexican cowboys, Dog?"

"Don't have to," Dog-man said. "Cisco said he sent a letter out inviting two old friends to come here."

"Gives us six guns to go after Mendoza," Snake murmured. "I'm bringing Louise home later today, so that actually gives us seven guns. That old Grandee won't know what hit him. Sheriff said he's going to get an arrest warrant from Judge Betterman and wants to first try to arrest the man before using force."

"Might just as well plan on using force, then," Dog-man laughed. "I'll ride in with you. We can leave Francisco and Nichols here although I really don't think there'll be any more trouble. Between you and Louise, you've killed off most of his gang."

36

LOUISE WAS ON HER FEET, dressed in her now sewn-up buckskins, waiting with some impatience when Snake drove the wagon up to Steppenfield's. Jeannie jumped down and rushed to Louise's side. "Look good," she said, and held her hand as they walked to the back of the wagon. Snake had a short step ladder propped up and ready. Dog-man had a wide smile on his face as he jumped from his saddle.

"By golly we're gonna have us a real home-coming," he said. "Snake, just think of something. For the last couple of years, with a mis-step or two, it's just been us roaming all over and now we gots us a ranch with critters, we gots ourselfs employees, and by damn, you gots yourself a wife. Sumbitch if we ain't the rich cusses."

"He's trying to make himself talk like you, Snake," Louise laughed.

"Done a poor job of it, too," Doctor Steppenfield laughed. "You take good care of this charming lady, Snake. Don't want her back except for a friendly visit."

It was almost a mess as everyone tried to help get

Louise in the wagon. "Enough," Snake finally said. "I'm the husband, I'll get my own wife settled." He helped her up the three steps and into the wagon, and turned her over to Jeannie. "Now, Dog, you ride behind the wagon. Don't want my wife breathing in all your dust."

Snake snapped the reins and the little cavalcade moved off for the ranch. Sheriff Mallory waved them down as they came up on his office. "Just got word that Mendoza heard about my arrest warrant and sent word that he will not be coming to town. When can your boys be ready to ride, Snake?"

Snake looked over at Dog-man, looked down at Louise and knew she couldn't for some time. "Me and the boys can ride in two days, Sheriff. Louise won't be joining us, though. Not this time."

"Two days it is, then," Mallory said. "Meet right here, early."

THE ONLY TALK around the long table that evening was how best to take out Mendoza, whether to simply shoot him, maybe lynch him, or let Mallory actually arrest the fool. "Whatever we choose, it's got to hurt and he's got to know why he's hurting," Snake said. This was as personal an attack as any could be. Snake's wife attacked and shot, his baby, not born, lost forever, and the threat of losing his ranch and herd in the process drove Snake's rage.

"He's got you riled, Snake. Be careful." Dog-man had seen this many times. "You get riled and people get hurt. Let's make sure it's the right people."

"We got two women here got whupped on bad because of Señor Mendoza," Snake said, his voice as quiet as Dog-man had ever heard it. When Snake got riled, people got hurt bad, but when Snake got quiet like this, people died. Dog-man couldn't hide the smile as Snake kept up his tirade.

"Tom Mallory wants us to help him arrest the man, has a legal court order to do that, but don't any of you get between me and the cigar smoking señor because if you do, you'll get yourself shot. If I can help it, our Spanish Grandee will not get arrested."

"We really don't know what we're riding into," Dog-man said. "Ain't none of us has ever seen this Mission of his, only heard what Mendoza's daughter told Mallory, so we'll have to let the sheriff lead us in." Dog-man got a little smile cooking and continued. "Ain't none of us wearing a badge, ain't none of us being paid by the sheriff to do this, so once we're there, I think our real leader will be Snake. Agreed?"

Every man at the table said a loud yes. Wayne Nichols looked over at Jeannie and smiled, giving her a thumbs up and Snake reached out and took Louise's hand. Francisco Alvarado and Dog-man sat and smiled. "Sure wish I could ride with you boys but I guess you're right. Sure as all get out I'd start bleeding or something." Louise said. She was out from the doctor's little hospital for less than a day and knew she could not ride a horse without breaking open that terrible wound.

"Mallory wants us to leave out in two days," Snake said. "If word gets out that we're coming, that Spanish fool might just try something. Attack us here, way-lay us on our way to attack him, or something just as stupid. We need to keep close watch on the place, the herd, everything."

"I'll ride out on the herd now," Cisco said. "You take second watch, Wayne."

"When are these charros of yours arriving, Cisco?" Snake asked.

"Have three men coming, Snake. Also you and Dog-man bought five mares and a stud, and coming along for the ride. Spanish Andalusians. Two of the mares are pregnant." He got an almost angelic look across his rugged Mexican face.

"You've never ridden a fine horse until you've sat an Andalusian, my friend." Cisco looked up at the ceiling and smiled, thinking of the last time he sat on one of those grand horses then got back to the business at hand. "Don't have a date, just know they left the coast two days ago. It won't be a fast ride driving that small cavvy."

Cisco rose and left out to ride night hawk and the party broke up. Louise tried to help clear the table and Jeannie shooed her off. "I clean. You sleep." Louise nodded and smiled. grabbed Snake's arm, and they took a slow walk to their lean-to.

"Living in this lean-to is about to end," Snake said. He looked around at the pine poles, the canvas, fire pit, and their buffalo robes spread out on their sleeping pads. "I'm not really sure I want to give this up." They laughed and Louise slumped down on the robes. "I was just a boy the last time I actually lived in a house," Snake said. "All closed in by walls and ceilings and floors." He settled down next to her.

Louise laughed and whacked him across his broad shoulders. "You getting second thoughts, big boy? Don't remember cooking on a real stove, myself. Might want to keep doing our cooking over a camp-fire."

"Gonna be a lot of fun learning how to be all growed up, civilized, not looking for a tree for relief."

She whacked him again but was laughing hard, hard enough she worried about breaking that wound open.

She looked out into the deep twilight at the herd. "Think he'll try again before you get him?" Louise sounded frightened.

"He's a strange man," Snake said. "Arrogant, proud, and now, belittled by his own son-in-law, the sheriff. He has a great hate for you after you embarrassed him in court. He just might."

————————

LOUISE AND JEANNIE stood on the porch of the cabin and watched the men ride off just as the sun broke free from the eastern ridge of mountains. "Don't you leave me, Snake," she said to the big Texan just moments before. She was holding him in a desperate grip. "You come home to me."

"That's all I'll be thinking of," he said. She knew better but let it go. He'll be thinking of teaching a hard-earned lesson to one arrogant Spanish gentleman, were her thoughts. Snake led Dog-man, Cisco, and Nichols at a strong trot up to the main road and on into Pioneer Crossing. Sheriff Tom Mallory was standing at the open door to his office, waiting for them.

"Where's your posse?" Snake called out.

"You're looking at it," Mallory said with a frown. "Men here are afraid of Mendoza and what he has always promised would be his retaliation for anyone going up against him. It's just the five of us." He snarled the words out.

"Let it be known," the sheriff continued. "I want to arrest the man and bring him to trial but at the same time, you have the authority to respond if he resists."

"That include those who ride for him?" Cisco wanted some of Mendoza's hide, too. Mallory chuckled his answer and Wayne Nichols gave out with howl, speaking for Jeannie's broken nose and their burned out home.

"Let's ride," Snake said. "You know the way, Sheriff." Snake thought they were looking at a five to ten mile ride from the little that had been talked about. "How far?"

"Northeast about twelve miles or so," Mallory said.

"Hell, that's almost back down in the desert," Dog-man said. "He calls it a ranch? What's he growing, lizards?" They were laughing loud as they rode out of town. There were a few eyes watching, many with hope almost buried in them. Mendoza and his arrogant and despotic ways had not been good for the community and those five men represented many hidden hopes. One set of eyes belonged to Maria-Elena. "Vaya con Dios, my love," she whispered.

Mallory left the main emigrant trail and followed a slightly used wagon track across the high ridge, down through a jumble of rocks and cactus, braved a wide and still muddy ditch before riding up another steeply sloped mountain side. From the looks of what passed for a road, it hadn't been used by a buggy or wagon in some time.

"Access to this Mission Ranch must be cross-country," Snake said. "Ain't been much traffic along what we're following. You know of another way in, Sheriff?"

Mallory shook his head. "It's just over this ridge," the sheriff said. "Down in a little valley, maybe two miles from where we are."

"You don't suppose we've been spotted, do you?" Snake wasn't interested in the answer, he already knew it. He and Dog-man had traded hand signals when they saw two riders move off from the ridge fifteen minutes before. "What's the real lay of the land, Sheriff? We need to know a hell of a lot more than what you've told us so far."

"Let's hold up and talk about that," Dog-man said. "If this trail leads over that ridge and down to the ranch, we're riding into an ambush. Me and Snake already saw two men ride off to tell Mendoza we were coming."

Mallory had a surprised look on his face as did Wayne Nichols. Cisco on the other hand just smiled. They rode off the trail a few yards and dismounted, gathered in a circle, and squatted in the dirt. Mallory took up a twig of brush, cleaned a spot to draw on, and talked as he drew what they would be looking at from the ridge top.

"That's all fine, Sheriff, but what you said still has us crossing that ridge on the main trail." Snake was getting frustrated. He had better thoughts of Tom Mallory but learned all at once that this was a town lawman who rarely left the security of streets and buildings. "We need another way in. Cross country and through great fields of big rocks, tall brush, and deep arroyos."

Dog-man chuckled at the way Snake put it but knew the man was right. He had been in many battles, side-by-side with this tall Texan and knew the man could almost see the battle before it got started. "Snake's right, boys. They're waitin' for us on the other side of that ridge."

"I've hunted this country just never knew that broken down old mission was supposed to be a ranch," Wayne Nichols said. "I can lead us in without us being seen. If they're setting up an ambush, they surely would have a look-out."

"They would," Snake said, "and he would need to be silenced before we make a move. Wish Good Inyan was here right now. I'll go get the look-out. Make some coffee while I'm gone, something for the fool to watch."

37

"Dog, you and Wayne separate and gather some firewood," Snake said. When they moved out to gather, he gave the impression that he, too was gathering then ducked into the arroyo they were alongside of, and sprinted down the wet middle until he was far away from the posse. *Hope I'm right and that look-out is watching those two gather wood, thinking I'm doing the same.* The ridge-top pass they would have ridden through was to his north and the arroyo had its beginnings there.

Snake moved to the east side of the gulch and took a quick glance over the edge, spotted some heavy brush close by and climbed out, to duck behind the spiny branches. Using brush, rocks, depressions in the desert floor, he moved slow and quiet and made his way up to the ridge. He eased out from behind a large rock fall and he spotted a big man with a rifle trying to get a cigarette put together.

Damn fool. Thought all us boys were getting some fire wood and forgot to count. Are you alone? Snake worked off to the man's left side and moved as close as he dared.

The man appeared to be a cowboy, was thin, wore his black hair long, and had a wild, bushy beard. He was far more interested in his smoke than he was with the men down below. *You just tied yourself to the wrong brand, mister.*

The man had his back to a large outcrop, the road over the top of ridge on the other side, and Snake wasn't going to have an easy time of it, getting close enough to do harm. Snake was less than twenty feet away, nestled under a bush and behind some rocks, well hidden but it was open ground from those rocks to the lookout.

Shootin' him ain't in the program. Tell everyone at the ranch what's goin' on.

Snake got himself primed for an attack, picked up a rock and tossed it onto the road. The big cowhand jumped to his feet and reached for his sidearm. Snake's rifle crushed his skull before the man's fingers touched the gun butt. He pulled the body away from the rock and roadway, stuffed it under a bush, and worked his way back down to the posse. *Got a nice pistol and rifle out of the deal,* Snake mused stuffing the Remmie into his belt.

"Time to find the señor," he said, slipping his rifle into its scabbard and tying off the new one. He and the rest were in the saddle following Wayne Nichols across the ridge, but half a mile south of where the road crossed. When they were on the other side, so they weren't silhouetted, Nichols stopped and pointed at what almost looked like ruins. "Mission Ranch," he said, shaking his head.

Snake and Dog-man took in the view. "Ain't what I'd call a Grandee's palace," Snake said. There were three buildings, the main house, a barn, and what was prob- ably a small storage shed, all very old and desert worn. Blasting hot air, great thunder storms, and continual wind had done its duty on the wood. Snake pointed out a long depression to the south of the main ranch and Dog-man pointed at what looked like a trail, probably that old road, leading up to the main house.

"We can circle down into the little valley and ride right up to the house," Snake said. "They'll be watching the road, not that gully."

"Near as I can tell, there ain't but a couple of cowhands moving about," Cisco said. "Seem to be doing regular ranch chores. Can't see nothing else moving." There were a few horses in a corral, two saddled horses in front of the house, probably belonged to the look-outs, and some scrawny heifers grazing nearby.

"Probably in the house and barn waiting for us," Mallory said. "Ain't no doubt he knows we're coming."

Snake was looking some south, then east, back south, and finally started talking. "We get in that shallow valley, Cisco, you move out and around so you are east of the main house. I'm coming with you but will continue on to be able to come in from the north. Dog-man, you lead Mallory and Nichols on up as close to the house as you can get. Give me and Cisco enough time to get in place, then call out for Mendoza to give it up."

"And you'll take over from there?" Dog-man chuckled.

"Yup," is all Snake said. Mallory, the sheriff, didn't say a word. It was obvious to Snake that the man was out of his comfort zone. He might have been a good town lawman but he didn't know his butt from beans out in the wilds.

"Let's move south and get in that depression." Tom Mallory simply followed along, letting Dog-man lead, accepting that Snake was running things. Snake never gave it a second thought. Of course he was running things.

IT WAS ALMOST an hour later that Dog-man had Sheriff Mallory positioned behind a small outcrop, less than thirty yards from the main house. Wayne Nichols was off to his left side and Dog-man on his right. He nodded to the sheriff who cupped his hands and yelled out.

"This is Sheriff Mallory. Antonio Mendoza, you are surrounded. I have a warrant for your arrest. Come out un-armed and no one gets hurt. Come out now, Mendoza."

He was answered by a volley of gunfire emanating from three windows in the front of the house. Dog-man motioned not to return fire, instead yelling out. "You're surrounded, Mendoza. Give it up."

"You're wrong," Mendoza yelled back. "You're on private property. I demand you leave at once. If you don't we will kill you and your families. Surrounded? Bah." He motioned for two men to check the back windows.

As if on cue, Snake waved to Cisco to put two rounds into the house after which he did the same.

"That answer your questions, Mendoza?" Sheriff Mallory hollered. "Give it up, Antonio or we're coming in. This is your last chance."

Dog-man could hear men running through the house, going room to room, looking out the windows, trying to locate the shooters. "How much time you willing to give him, Sheriff? Won't be able to hold Snake back for much longer."

Mallory answered by yelling at the house. "We're

coming, Mendoza. Throw down your weapons and come out of the house with your hands empty and in plain sight." He was answered by three quick shots from the center window. Dog-man and Wayne Nichols each put two rifle shots back, and heard one man yell out, hurt.

Snake took the shots as a green light for he and Cisco, and motioned for the man to take a few shots into the house, giving him cover to move much closer. The house was not adobe, but desert dry old wood, and the place was surrounded by dry grass and brush. Snake raced up and got within ten yards of the north side, he too fired three quick shots into an open window.

He spotted some dry and brittle straw piled along one wall and crawled as close to it as he could get, There was the slightest breeze at his back as he twisted some of the straw into a bundle. He then made another, lit one and threw it through the open window, firing three shots from his sidearm, then lit the second bundle and threw it onto the pile of straw. It lit up like a Roman candle and he could see smoke billowing out the window as well.

Snake crawled back to his first spot behind a desert tree and waited for the alarm to spread. He didn't need to wait long, just long enough to reload his pistol and rifle. He could see figures through the smoke and fired into the open window at them. More than one man was hit inside the burning room.

Mallory spotted the smoke first, heard the panic from inside the house, and yelled again at Mendoza. "You can roast or you can surrender, Mendoza. It's your choice. Come out with empty hands held out in front of you and you will live."

Loud voices could be heard inside the building.

"They're fighting amongst themselves," Dog-man said. "Some know they're looking at prison while others are just cowboys, charros. they want out."

"Somebody's coming," Nichols said pointing at the front door. The wood was ancient, dried to a crisp, and burned fast and hot. Flames were already boiling through the roof, the north wall was sending hot embers hundreds of feet up, and a few men were trying to get through the open door.

"Don't shoot unless they do," Mallory yelled. The first two held their hands high up and raced across the empty space toward Dog-man. He motioned for them to get down, which they did. Two more emerged through the smoke, firing their pistols and Nichols and Mallory shot them dead.

"How many are you going to kill, Mendoza? Come out, now. the house is completely on fire. Drop your weapons and come out."

One of the outlaws, flattened in the dirt near Dog-man yelled, "He's mad, crazy with power. He won't come out."

Another man came racing out the door, and before he cleared the porch was shot by someone inside the cabin. "There is only he and little Pedro in there, now," the man said.

"Little Pedro? Who is little Pedro?" Dog-man asked.

"A little boy who does all the chores around the house. Maybe eight years old."

"You hear that, Mallory? Mendoza has a little boy trapped in there with him." Despite all the noise of the burning building, Snake heard what Dog-man yelled and howled his response. Dog-man chuckled. "He's riled now, boys. this is almost over."

"You filthy scum," and Snake was on the run, dove

head first through the flames at the open window, hit the floor and rolled twice before trying to get his feet under him. He dropped immediately back to the floor and crabbed his way from the smoke filled room into the large great room. It was filling fast with smoke and the heat was intense..

Mendoza was plastered against the front wall, holding the boy close to him. He had his pistol held against the boy's head. "Come one more inch and the boy dies," Mendoza said. "Tell those men to pull out, leaving me a horse. Do it or the boy dies."

Snake could see a wildness in the man's eyes that hadn't been there in previous meetings. The big pistol was cocked, and Mendoza was shaking in anger and fear. That gun could go off at any second and the fire was already gnawing at the inside walls of the room. "Best pull out, Dog-man," Snake yelled out. "Man's holding the boy at gun-point and we're alone in here. Leave Mendoza a horse and go on back to town."

Dog-man knew Snake would never say or do anything like that, motioned for Wayne Nichols to move to him. "Gotta be quiet and listen to me. Gather our horses, get on one, and trail them out at a gallop. Circle around to where you can't be seen from the house and hold up. Stay with the horses. Got it?"

Nichols saw the plan, plain as day, smiled and nodded. He crawled away and moved to the horses. Mallory was too far away to have heard and Dog-man hoped like all hell the man would not foul it up. "All right, Mendoza, We're leaving. Let the boy live," Dog-man called out. He used his hands to tell Mallory not to move. "Snake, when we're gone, you'll have to make your own way back."

Snake chuckled at the comment and he, Mendoza,

and the frightened Pedro heard horses gallop off. "There you go, Señor. The door's already open. Leave the boy with me. No need to hurt him." Snake stood facing Mendoza, his pistol in one hand, his rifle in the other, and Mendoza moved slowly from the wall to the open door.

"Do not follow me out, Snake. I'll leave the boy when I get on my horse. follow me out and I will kill him immediately. You have not seen the last of me. I will see you dead and soon." He had his arm around the boy's neck and moved for the door keeping the boy between them. He backed out, backed down the walkway to where a horse was tied to a rail, and began to untie him.

Pedro felt the arm around his neck loosen, dove to the ground and crawled as fast as he could away. Snake had the rifle up, one shot fired, and saw Mendoza try for his pistol even while falling backward. Snake put a second round through the man's right eye and raced for the boy, grabbing him and holding him tight.

"It's over, boy. It's over. Calm down, cry your eyes out, and hold on tight. It's over." He walked the boy away from the grisly scene, back away from the intense heat of the burning building, and waited for Dog-man who was walking up with the prisoners. Nichols heard the shots and rode up with his horse.

It's over. Snake said it to himself over and over, carrying the little boy. "You got a mama? A papa?"

"No, they died in a bad fire. I live here and work for Señor Mendoza. He's not nice."

"He surely ain't a nice man," Snake chuckled. He also figured that the bad fire that killed the boy's family was probably started by the cigar smoking señor. "You like cows and a big ranch?"

It was too late to try and retrieve the bodies inside

the house, but they did have those outside strapped onto what horses were available. "I'll take the bodies and these two into town," Mallory said. "I know you boys want to get back to the ranch. I'll need written statement from each of you. I wanted Mendoza alive but you didn't have any choice. Thank God the boy is okay."

"He needs a family, Sheriff. I'm taking him home with us," Snake said. Mallory just nodded. He was quite willing to let Snake make the decision. Legal formalities would follow along their natural course. He waved and watched as Dog-man led the ranch crew off for home.

38

"LOOK WHAT I FOUND," Snake yelled as the bunch of them rode up to the main house in a cloud of dust. He was amazed when Louise and three large Mexicans walked out the door. "What the hell?"

"Hola!" Francisco Alvarado jumped from his sliding horse into the arms of the three, all of them pounding backs and talking loud and long. "Snake, Dog-man, my charros, Jose, 'Tonio, and Juanito."

Snake handed little Pedro down to Louise and clambered off his sweat stained horse. He gathered her in his arms, careful of the wounds, and kissed her. "It's over, Lion-killer. Mendoza is no more and we have a son. Meet Pedro."

She held the smiling boy in her arms, felt Snake's strong arms around her shoulders, and burst into tears. *I've never felt like this, ever. My God. I have a husband and we have a son? We have a ranch?* "Snake," her voice was shaky, her eyes were filled with tears, her nose was running, and she was laughing and crying at the same time. "Welcome home."

Wayne Nichols and Jeannie walked off to their wagon and Dog-man took control of all the horses. Cisco called to Snake. "Time to see what else we have on this ranch," and started for the new horse corrals off behind the barn. Three large, mostly gray mares, one very pregnant, came right up to the fence.

"Andalusian," Cisco said, almost as a proud father would. The stallion was in a separate pen and was almost as excited as all the humans surrounding him were. "The start of your cavvy, Snake."

It was several hours before things returned to peace and quiet on the place and Louise and Snake were resting in their lean-to before supper. "This is really happening, isn't it?" Snake said, so soft that Louise wasn't sure she heard it. "I'm a married man, my partner and I own a fair sized ranch, and I have a little scamp for a son. Louise, you may have to pinch me often to make me believe all this."

She did and he yelped, grabbed her and held her close, kissing and squeezing until she winced from the pain to her back. "It's getting better but it still hurts some," she said. "That big stud gonna be your horse?"

"Well, don't it stand to reason that the man with the prettiest wife should ride the finest horse? Man with the fattest calves needs to ride the finest stud. I think it's written, somewhere," he said. They were laid out across the buffalo robes and he looked down into her face, a serious look on his.

"I had to bring the boy, Louise. Mendoza was going to kill him. Little Pedro says he's eight years old but he's so skinny, hasn't been treated well at all. Says his folks died in a fire and Mendoza made the boy into a slave at that run-down mission of his. You and me have been lost wanderers and now we have a lost little boy to ride with us."

"You've got a heart as big as the whole world, Snake," she said. "I'm glad you brought the boy. I've got a mind that he won't be the last. You say you deserve that fine looking stud, and I say, a woman of my superb qualities deserves a man like you."

Supper was a little late that night.

IF YOU LIKED THIS, YOU MAY ENJOY JACK SLATER: GUNS OF MOUND VALLEY

JACK SLATER BOOK 5

Thrilling action from page to page, from the valley floor to the granite spires of the Ruby Mountains.

A vicious gang of killers moves into Elko County, Nevada and stages a robbery following the Fall Stock Sales killing several and nabbing thousands. Disappointed by the sheriff's slow response, Jack Slater, whose herd was at the sale, takes matters into his own hands and leads a posse of ranch buckaroos in chase.

The gang is led by Pa Appleton, a couple of prison friends, and his son and daughter, each with numerous killings under their belt... and each harboring doubts about Pa as their leader.

A more inept gang would be hard to find, yet Pa's gang continues to evade capture, killing people at every chance as they're chased through Mound Valley and into the rugged wilds of the Ruby Mountains.

Personalities play a large part in this western novel as extreme danger brings out the best and the worst in those taking part. Despite heroic efforts by the good guys, it seems the bad guys are going to win this time.

AVAILABLE NOW

ABOUT THE AUTHOR

Reno, Nevada novelist, **Johnny Gunn,** is retired from a long career in journalism. He has worked in print, broadcast, and Internet, including a stint as publisher and editor of the Virginia City Legend. These days, Gunn spends most of his time writing novel length fiction, concentrating on the western genre. Or, you can find him down by the Truckee River with a fly rod in hand.

"It's been a wonderful life. I was born in Santa Cruz, California, on the north shore of fabled Monterey Bay. When I was fourteen, that would have been 1953, we moved to Guam and I went through my high school years living in a tropical paradise. I learned to scuba dive from a WWII Navy Frogman, learned to fly from a WWII combat pilot (by dad), but I knew how to fish long before I moved to Guam.

"I spent time on the Island of Truk, which during WWII was a huge Japanese naval base, and dived in the lagoon. Massive U.S. air strikes sunk thousands of tons of Japanese naval craft, and it was more than exciting to dive on those wrecks. In the Palau Islands, near Koror, I also dived on Japanese aircraft that had been shot down into the lagoons.